**Also available from Emma Salah
and Carina Press**

Dirty Plays

T0014750

DIRTY TACTICS

—

Emma Salah

carina
press

carina
press®

Recycling programs
for this product may
not exist in your area.

ISBN-13: 978-1-335-48424-6

Dirty Tactics

Carina Press
22 Adelaide St. West, 41st Floor
Toronto, Ontario M5H 4E3, Canada
www.CarinaPress.com

Printed in U.S.A.

To my siblings for believing that I can actually write romances—hope it doesn't make you blush too much!

Dear Readers,

I have taken liberties with city names and football and hockey teams since I don't want any die-hard fans to feel they have to defend the honor of their teams. Instead, you may invest in my fake teams to your heart's content.

Prologue

Reagan Thomas was fifteen and she was mad. So mad, she kicked a big, fat boulder and instantly regretted it.

"Ow, ow." She hissed, hopping up and down on one foot. She tried to keep her voice down, because if her father knew she had snuck out past curfew and was standing in the Muckberry Field, instead of being tucked up in her bedroom—at 9:30 pm!—there would be hell to pay. It didn't matter that it was dark outside and that they had school the next day, because everybody who was anybody, including all her friends, was at Hill's ice cream parlor having fun.

Except me, she thought bitterly. Here she was in the middle of an empty field like a loser, while all her friends forgot about her. They were all probably chatting and laughing. She could just see Jen and Mickey whispering to each other, making eyes at Jason and his crowd. Not that she really wanted to go to Hill's and boy-watch when she could be at home. *But that's not the point!*

With her foot still throbbing, Reagan slid to the ground, shoulders hunched, her back against the boulder. It wasn't fair. All her brothers could go anywhere they wanted and stay up as late as they wished. Why was she the only one who wasn't allowed? Hell, Aidan was only a couple of years older than her and he had never been told to go to his room like a naughty child and to stop asking questions about things that weren't important.

When *she'd* asked to go to Hill's, her father had reacted like she had asked "what is sex?" and not just "can I hang out with my friends?"—not that she needed him to explain what sex was. Why was she the only one who had to be taken everywhere like she couldn't be trusted to walk down the street?

Reagan pulled at some of the grass beneath her Converse-clad feet, her frustration getting the better of her.

CRUNCH.

Reagan lifted her head and saw a silhouette moving towards her. She scrambled to her knees and considered leaving. If she got caught alone outside and her dad heard about it, she wouldn't see anything but the inside of her room until she was twenty-one. She squinted her eyes, trying to make out who it was, and almost had a heart attack when she saw who was coming.

Zachariah Quinn.

What's he doing here? Oh god. Oh god. Chill, Reagan, it's all good. Heart pounding, she waited for him to get closer. He was almost on top of her before he noticed her, huddled against the boulder. He came to a standstill.

"Ree." His blue eyes were filled with surprise as he stared at her.

He leaned over her, all six feet and three inches of him. He was one of the tallest boys she had ever met (other than her brothers and her father) and definitely one of the prettiest.

Licking her lips, she asked, "What are you doing here?"

His mouth curved in amusement. "I could ask you the same thing."

"I asked you first."

He shrugged as he slid down to sit beside her, his long legs stretching out.

"It seemed like a nice night for a walk."

Reagan had a feeling he wasn't telling her the whole truth, but she'd known Zac since she was four years old and Aidan and Zac became best friends. She knew he wouldn't talk about something until he was good and ready to.

"And what about you? I thought you would be with the usual suspects at Hill's."

Reagan frowned. "Usual suspects?"

"Miss Giggles and Miss Gigglier." He grinned at her, his cheeks creasing and showcasing those dimples of his on either side.

She tried not to laugh, because that was horrible. Except it described Jen and Mickey perfectly. The girls couldn't stop giggling for longer than a few seconds to even have a decent conversation with a guy. She had a lot of fun with her girls when it was only them, but when they added boys to the mix, they became really stupid. Sometimes she gave up even trying to hold a conversation with them when one of their crushes was in their vicinity. And that included Zac.

Reagan peeked a glance at him from the corner of her eye. He was really pretty. His dirty blond hair was overgrown, falling into his eyes messily. His square jaw and long nose made him look more like the man he was becoming, rather than a boy. And his body... She'd accidentally (okay, it wasn't an accident!) seen him changing clothes at her house one day after coming over from hockey practice. She had stopped dead in the middle of the hallway and stared. Maybe even drooled a little. Her cheeks grew hot just thinking about it.

"That's just mean," she said, bringing her knees back to her chest.

"But true."

Zac's shoulder brushed hers and she felt the slight pressure all the way down to her curled toes. It was a comforting warmth that did nothing more than just... be there. And even if it was only in a small way, she felt connected to him.

"Anyway," she said, clearing her throat. "My dad said I couldn't go. Said I was too young to be out this late."

"Do you even want to go?"

"Yes!"

He raised his eyebrow. "Really?"

"Okay, maybe I'd prefer to be at home playing *War of the Worlds* or the new *Future Fantasy* game," she said, begrudgingly. "But I do want to hang out with my friends."

"So, you snuck out anyway?" he asked her, tapping her Converse with his index finger. "Naughty, naughty, Ree."

Reagan pressed her ankle against his thick thigh, her knees so close to her chest she felt the heat of his body.

"Not to Hill's! So, I consider that a compromise."

"I don't think your dad will see it that way."

Yeah, she didn't see her dad thinking the same way either, but she was sick of always doing what she was told. For what? Her dad never let up. Zac faced her, his finger continuing to tap away on her shoe. They were sitting so close, but Reagan didn't want to shift back. Her chest squeezed tight, not like she couldn't breathe, but as if suddenly she was aware of every heartbeat.

"Zac, can I ask you a question?"

He nudged her shoulder with his. "You can ask me anything you want. You know that."

She placed her hand on her knee, picking at the denim.

"Do you think Dad hates me?" she whispered.

He looked at her, eyes narrowed.

"Never mind." She shook her head quickly. "I don't know why I asked that."

But Zachariah wasn't going to let her off that easy. He tilted her chin up and stared into her dark brown eyes as if he was searching for something. She was help-less to pull away from him. His hands against her dark skin fascinated her; the golden sun to her night sky.

"Why would you ask that?" he finally said.

She tried to shrug, but didn't let go, his fingers tight-ening.

"Don't try to bullshit me, Ree. I know you."

"Fine," she grumbled. "Sometimes... I see him when he doesn't think I'm looking and he just looks at me funny. Like he's not really seeing me. But seeing Mom."

Reagan's voice dropped down to a whisper as tears filled her eyes. "I think he hates me because I look like Mom and I killed her. Oh god, Zac, it's my fault that she's not here. It's my fault."

"Stop it." He shook her. "Ree, it wasn't your fault. You were just a baby and it was your mom's choice. Not yours."

"Her choice cost us everything."

"Not everything," he told Reagan. "Her choice gave us you. Without your mom, you wouldn't be here and your dad knows that. Stop torturing yourself this way, okay?"

The hand holding Reagan's chin reached up and palmed her cheek. "I mean it, Reagan. Your mom wouldn't want you hating yourself; there are better ways to honor her."

She had no memories of the woman who had given birth to Reagan. Her dad found it too painful to talk about Mom, even Reagan's older brothers couldn't mention their mother without their faces twisting in pain. So, she stopped asking altogether, but there was still so much she wanted to know about Mom. What she did know was her mother had been a beautiful and wonderful person and she had given up her life to allow Reagan to live. She wouldn't dishonor that. She would try harder to not act out, to make things as easy as possible for Dad.

"You're right."

"Damn right, I'm right."

She laughed through the tears. He grinned back. She opened her mouth to continue the playful banter, when she noticed the dark purple smudge beneath his eye.

"What happened to your cheek?" Frowning, she reached out and touched the bruise.

He jerked back, letting go. Reagan's hand fell uselessly to her side.

"It was him, wasn't it?"

Everyone knew what was happening at the Quinns'. They could see the bruises and cuts plain and simple on Mrs. Quinn's face when she came into the supermarket, pushing her trolley all hunched forward and moving like a ninety-year-old instead of the thirty-four-year-old woman she was.

He sighed. "Just let it go."

No, she would not. His living situation was shit. It was the reason why Zac spent so much time at her house and not his own. And there was nothing that she could do since his dad wasn't just his abusive father, but Sheriff Quinn as well.

"Does it hurt?" she asked quietly. "I could get you something for it."

He shook his head. "Nah. I've suffered worse on the ice."

"Yeah, but that was your choice."

"Ree."

They were facing each other now. She let go of her knee.

"I don't like knowing you're hurt," she admitted, the back of her neck and cheeks feeling hot. Today, she counted herself lucky that her cacao skin didn't reveal her true feelings.

"It's not going to be forever. One more year and I'm off to college," Zac said.

Like Aidan, Zac was in his senior year and already had a scholarship for college to play hockey. Soon, they would both be gone, like her other brothers who were all at college already. She was going to be the only one left. Alone with her father. Oh god, what were they going to talk about at mealtimes, especially when she wasn't allowed to have dinner in her room? *I can do it. I can do it.* Maybe if she chanted it to herself a few times a day, it'd become the truth?

Zac's hand touched her knee. The warmth seeped into her through her jeans. His blue eyes stared into hers.

"I can see your mind plotting all the ways you're going to escape. Just be careful of the ladder, you don't want to have to explain to people why you wince every time you sit down again," he teased.

Reagan groaned, hanging her head down, so her black, curly hair fell and hid her face.

A couple of months ago, she had tried to sneak out of her friend's house by using the ladder in their back garden. Except she had slipped and fallen. Luckily, there had been a bush to break her fall, but unluckily she fell into a needle bush. It had hurt like hell taking those things out of her ass and thighs. And to top off her embarrassment, Aidan and Zac had to drive her home. They had laughed their asses off. *The idiots.*

"Can you please just forget that ever happened?" she asked him.

"Mm, let me think about it." He rubbed his chin. "Nope. Sorry, no can do."

Zac laughed. It was so beautiful that Reagan couldn't help but stare at him. Her breath hitched. For all that he had been through, Zac never lost his sense of humor. She adored that about him. Still staring at him, she noticed the instant he stopped chuckling. His eyes grew dark. Her heart began to beat faster, her breath coming out in little pants. They were so close.

She shifted her face a slight inch. And when he leaned in to brush his mouth against hers, she stilled.

He pulled away, just enough for them to breathe.

"What are you doing?" she whispered.

"Kissing you," he murmured. "Kiss me back."

He kissed her again.

His lips were soft and pressed against hers all so delicately, as if he was afraid she would back away. No chance of that. She was hooked on one taste. Her hands slid up to his shoulders, kissing him back, having no idea what she was doing. She had never been kissed. Every one of her friends had said it was awkward at first, but there was nothing awkward about Zac. The moment his mouth touched hers, everything about it felt right. Reagan's eyes flickered shut as she pressed deeper into him. His hand tentatively came up and touched the back of her head, his fingers warm on her neck. But it wasn't until Zac ran his tongue across her lips and she opened up for him that something new happened to her.

She fell in love with him, with Zachariah Quinn.

Chapter One

Ten years later

"Do you think beautiful people have better sex than ugly people?" her best friend, Leticia "Letty" Garcia, asked.

They were sitting at the bar, completely alone, trying to get drunk on champagne.

"Why would you think that?" Reagan replied, amused.

She was used to Letty and her random thoughts of the day, but Lord some of the things that came out of her mouth honestly boggled her mind.

Letty shrugged. "Movies. Advertisements. Every romance novel. They're all filled with seduction, with teasing touches, little kisses and lovemaking."

Reagan's eyebrows raised at the disgust she heard in her voice. "And you don't want romance, seduction or lovemaking?"

"I want to be fucked," Letty said bluntly.

Reagan almost choked on her champagne. "What?"

"You know, I don't want to have sex under the covers with the lights turned off in bed. I want to be pressed roughly against the wall, have him push up my dress, rip off my panties, unzip himself and just—"

"Okay, okay." Reagan held up a hand. She shifted uneasily in her chair, trying to erase the images running rampant in her mind. "I think I get the picture."

Letty grinned before popping a peanut in her mouth.

"Then, go for it. What are you waiting for?" Reagan encouraged.

Being half Hispanic, half Caucasian, Letty had big wide brown eyes with long eyelashes Reagan would kill to have and beautiful golden skin that looked amazing paired with her sleek white dress and siren-red lips. Letty was much bolder in life than Reagan. She was gorgeous, funny as fuck and so talented with watercolors that whenever Reagan stepped foot in Letty's apartment she couldn't help but stare in awe at all the canvas she kept haphazardly behind her sofa. Letty was never afraid to send back food when the waiter messed up the order or to tell a man at the bar he was cute. Her best friend sighed. "You saw the men at this party. Would you fuck any of them?"

Reagan laughed. "Yeah, but you know how picky I am."

"I'm picky too."

"Since when? Have you told your vajayjay this? And don't roll your eyes at me, girl. You and I both know you can snap your fingers and get whomever you want."

"But that's the problem." Letty set down her champagne. "It's too easy. I want the chase."

They might be best friends, but here was where they were very different. And, it wasn't just their personalities. Reagan was nowhere near bold, brazen and beautiful. If it wasn't for Letty, she would have come dressed to this event in her *Future Fantasy* T-shirt and her blue Converses.

Letty was a ten without even trying. Reagan, on the other hand, struggled to be a passable eight on her best day. Not that she thought she was ugly. No, she knew she was pretty. Her black skin was the color of Ethiopian coffee beans—or was it cacao? She never could remember what food people described her skin as—and was just as smooth. She had long legs that went on for miles. Reagan's thick black hair had mostly grown back from when she cut it a few years ago. It now reached down her shoulders. All natural, thank you very much.

Reagan just wasn't…girly. The side effect of having grown up in a household of only men. Her mother had died giving birth to her. She never had anyone to help her with picking dresses, trying on makeup and navigating the world of boys.

Instead, she had her older brother Malcolm explaining to her on her twelfth birthday about all the changes happening in and to her body. To be fair, he had told her in a very straight, calm manner. It had been Dean, Malcolm's identical twin, who had stood behind him and mimed some crude gestures and who had told her that one day she would wake up with double D sized breasts. She was still waiting for them, but in the meantime she made do. Not too big, not too small and they looked amazing in the little black dress she was wearing. A classic, as Letty had stated when she pushed and bullied her into it.

All in all, growing up with four brothers, she wasn't surprised she was more into video games, beer and sports. It was why she chose to become a sports agent. She had no regrets, but being a tomboy did make it hard to have a love life.

"I don't want the chase," Reagan said, softly. "I

don't want grand gestures. Or flowers. I just want to be wanted."

"You are. And you will be by someone who'll love you unconditionally…and fuck you against walls too." Letty gave her a salacious smile while fluttering her eyelashes.

"Aww, true love," she teased.

"And at least we won't die alone. We'll always have each other, great hair and Netflix."

"True dat."

They clinked glasses.

"Okay, enough of being antisocial," Letty said.

"We're not being antisocial. We're just sitting at the bar, trying to get drunk when there is a whole party going on behind us filled with celebrities…" Letty stared at her until realization dawned. "Yeah, we're being antisocial."

"Exactly. Besides, enough time *must've* gone by for the arrival of some hot, mouth-watering, sexy celebrities." With that last remark, Letty downed her champagne and stood up. "Let's go. Mama needs to get laid."

Reagan sighed. Did they have to? She had already spent an hour in there. Wasn't that enough?

Letty leaned over, her mouth close to her ear. "Think of this as work. We go in and see if we can schmooze some more new clients. Hey, you never know, we might even steal some of Brittany's clients, wouldn't that just bite her ass?"

Brittany was, for lack of a better word, their archenemy. Blonde and stacked, Brittany was anything but typical; she was ruthless and smart. Both Reagan and Letty worked for Mitchells, one of the best PR agencies in the country. Working for their competitors, Brittany had the underhanded talent of stealing clients from them. Reagan hated tearing down other women, but she didn't consider Brittany a woman. More like a hoofed devil sent to make their lives a living hell. *Burn, bitch, burn.*

"I'm more concerned about Daniel though," Reagan said, ruefully. "He's probably in there, right now, getting a hundred more clients just to spite me."

As junior agents, Reagan worked with athletes in Mitchells' sports department, while Letty looked after models and actors in the entertainment section of the firm. Above them were the senior agents who, as the crème de la crème, held the most exclusive clients on their list, and then each department's executive managing director.

To say that Daniel, a senior sports agent, was pissed at her would be an understatement. All because he felt that her newest client should belong to him. *Over my dead body.*

"Even with a hundred new clients, he still wouldn't beat you. Do not let that conniving bastard see you sweat." Letty paused. "Actually no one should ever see anyone sweat."

"I'm pretty sure I've broken that rule, once or maybe a million times. But I hear ya."

The day couldn't come soon enough when Reagan looked around and there was more representation and diversity working alongside her. As two of the few females working at the agency and the only people of color, Reagan and Letty had bonded over their mutual dislike of Daniel during a coffee run when they had started working at the agency three years ago. How fucked up was that? If she went up in flames, Daniel probably still wouldn't piss on her.

Reagan stood up. "Let's go."

Arms linked, they rejoined the party.

The party was in full swing.

They were in the ballroom of the luxurious Heart Hotel. It was highly renowned tech CEO Steven Costa's annual party, exclusive and hard to get into. The party, not the man. Reagan was pretty sure he was on his fifth wife. As Mitchell was one of Steven's closest friends, every year all his top PRs got invited. Reagan felt the thrill of success rush through her as she looked around. She was damn good at her job and this invite proved that.

The ballroom was large with a diamond chandelier dripping from the ceiling. On the stage, Andy Types, a rising composer, was playing a soothing melody on a grand piano. People stood around, mingling, talking or sitting at the back as discreet staff wandered around with appetizers and champagne.

"Look!" Letty whispered, fingernails digging into her arms.

"What am I supposed to be looking at?"

With a little flick of her chin, Letty pointed to the south corner where a group of ridiculously good-looking, tall men stood laughing.

"Why didn't you tell me he was coming?" Letty asked.

"He always comes," Reagan said absently as the man in question finally noticed them staring. Aidan broke off immediately from his group and came striding over. Tall, dark and handsome, he was taller than Reagan by a good few inches. He kept his black, curly hair short and wore a black Armani suit that looked good against his mahogany skin. His brown eyes were a little darker than hers. Women watched him with thinly disguised lust in their eyes as he made his way through the crowd.

"You mean to tell me that you could have gotten us into this party last year, but you chose not to say anything?"

Reagan frowned. "I am not using my brother for things like this. Besides, they'd all just hold it over my head until the end of days."

"Fine," Letty grumbled, just as Aidan reached them.

"Reagan," he said.

He enveloped her in a hug and she hugged him back. God, she missed him. It had been two weeks since she had seen him last, but they usually never went that long before seeing each other. Aidan was her closest brother in age and friendship. At just two years older, Reagan had practically worshipped him growing up. And now she couldn't be prouder. He was an ice hockey player for The Comets. She knew it must be hard being one of the few black people in the NHL, but Aidan never complained. Not even in the infamous interview where he was asked if he got preferential treatment because of his skin color and if that was why he was traded to The Comets. Aidan had coolly replied back, "Look at my stats and you'll see my color has absolutely nothing to do with how I skate." He proved himself every day as one of the best defensemen in the league and all his hard work had paid off. As the current winners of the Stanley Cup, he and his whole team were currently hot shit.

"Hey, big brother," she said in greeting. "You said

nothing about coming today. I thought you were still in Vancouver."

"You know I come to Steven's party every year. You're the one who never said you were coming."

Oops, good point.

"Sorry. I forgot?"

He sighed. "You're lucky you're the baby of the family."

Aidan shifted and looked down at her best friend. "Hey, Letty, you good?"

"Yeah." She smiled. "What? No hug for me?"

Reagan turned her head in shock. "But you said hugs are reserved for holidays or only as a prelude to f—"

And immediately stopped talking when Letty gave her a death glare. *I guess she's being friendly or...* Reagan watched as Aidan hugged Letty. With her added advantage of heels, Letty wrapped her arms around Aidan's neck while he lightly touched the base of her back, hands dangerously close to her ass. Letty pulled away.

"Mmm, yeah, maybe this hugging thing still isn't for me. I'll see you guys later. I'm going to go mingle." With one last wicked smile, she sashayed away, drawing attention as she went.

Aidan turned to Reagan.

"What the fuck was that?" he said through clenched teeth.

Reagan held her hands up. "Don't ask me. I'm in the dark too. Maybe it was some weird experiment to see if hugging should exist outside of sex?"

"Don't say that."

"What? Sex?" Reagan grinned.

"Yes." Now he sounded like he was grinding his teeth.

"You know, not only can I say it, but I've also had it. Shocking, isn't it?" Sometimes it was fun having brothers just so she could mess with them. She particularly liked when they got that twitch under their eyes whenever she talked about her love life. The same twitch Aidan had right about now.

"Stop being such a brat, Reagan. Aren't we too old for this shit?"

She pretended to think about it for a moment. "Nope. Besides, I'm twenty-five, not twenty-seven. Still years away from being old."

"Hah."

A server offered them a glass of champagne, which they both happily accepted. *Keep on with the bubblies.*

"How've you been, brat?" Aidan asked.

"Good." She smiled. "Business is good. I'm here, aren't I?"

"I can see that. I heard you landed Trent Newman as a new client."

Ah yes, Trent Newman. A rookie who just got signed by the New York Giants. The player everyone would be watching this year. And he had signed with her! She thought it would have taken months of ass-kissing, but, with some clients, it just clicked. It helped that Trent hadn't reached that level of douchery that usually came with fame. Yet. He was still in the "I'm-so-surprised-it's-happening-to-me" stage and he was sweet with it. She really hoped he kept that sweetness, but she'd been around sports players all her life and it meant she wasn't going to be holding her breath.

"Yeah, I'm pretty excited actually. Trent is one of those rare players who doesn't think with his ego or think he's hot shit and that everyone should bow down to him."

"I hope you are not suggesting that I am anything like that." Aidan shook his head.

She laughed. "I wouldn't dare. I still have nightmares from the prank of '09."

Her brother's eyes wandered over her shoulder and she watched as his mouth curved into a smile.

"Zac's here," he said, simply.

Casually, she turned and looked. Her heart stopped, and then began to pound, exactly as it had that night in Muckberry Field when she was fifteen years old. Reagan had already come to terms with the fact that no matter how long she lived, or how much time passed, the sight of Zachariah Quinn would always affect every part of her being.

What is it about him? She lifted her champagne to her mouth to help with her suddenly parched throat. Was it the way the light gray suit molded to his lean, athletic body? His thin hips and broad shoulders? His full lips that stretched easily into a smile to flash his delicious dimples? She hadn't tasted those lips in months. Not since that evening at Aidan's house when they had suddenly found themselves alone in the living room, on the sofa. One teasing smile and casual flirting remark later, she somehow ended up with her hand curled around his nape, kissing him like there was no tomorrow.

She remembered how he'd brushed his hands up her blouse, to touch skin, making her gasp desperately into said mouth. How she had rocked into him and felt him harden against her and a groan vibrate his chest. They had sprung apart like two teenagers caught necking when they heard the front door open and close. By the time her brothers had walked in, Reagan and Zac looked like nothing had happened at all.

Whatever it was about Zac that attracted her, it definitely wasn't the cool and beautiful blonde clinging to his side. Reagan's eyes narrowed, a Victoria's Secret underwear model, if she wasn't mistaken.

Fixing a smile on her face, she turned back to her brother. "I guess you want to go and check in with your BFF, no?"

"And abandon you to every desperate guy in the room?" Aidan raised an eyebrow. "Not a chance, sis."

She let out a puff of breath. "I can take care of myself, you know—Hey, what do you mean desperate? Do you think the only guy I can get is a desperate guy?"

"Frankly, I don't want to know how you get *any* guy. Desperate or otherwise."

"Brothers are just great for a girl's ego."

"Hey." His mouth lifted into a half smile that had fooled millions of girls around the world to look past his abrasive, rough and tumble personality to only see his handsomely roguish good looks. "You're not exactly good on our egos either. You've always given as good as you got."

No compliment could have pleased her more.

"Go." She nudged him. "I'll be fine by myself, mingling with all these hotshots. Go and be a hotshot."

He gave her an absent-minded kiss on her cheek and walked away. As soon as he left, the smile slipped off her face and, because she could already feel the familiar tingles of hurt, she clung to the anger of seeing Zac and his "girlfriend," instead.

Reagan rubbed the spot on her chest where her traitorous heart lived.

Even angry, she couldn't tear her eyes away from him. Where he stood laughing with their host, Steven, one hand curled around the cool blonde's waist. They moved away from Steven just as Aidan came to join Zac's side. The two exchanged their customary handshake and back slap. She watched as Zac introduced Aidan to his date for the evening.

It was really petty of her, she knew, but Reagan really wished the blonde suddenly got an attack of acne… between her thighs. No, no, not acne! Maybe she had some kind of disease—not a life-threatening one, because Reagan wasn't that evil—and the disease would make her lose all her hair, teeth and so sad, too bad, it deflated her obviously fake breasts. Yep. That she could live with.

"Oh god." Reagan half gasped and half swallowed a mouthful of her drink, just as Aidan pointed a finger to where she stood. Zac's eyes followed Aidan's finger and those gorgeous blue eyes met hers. *Shit, shit*, she thought as he watched her for a second, the champagne in her stomach turning to lead.

Reagan didn't know why she did it, but she whirled around. Okay, she knew why she did it. She was a big fat chicken, that's why. Panicked, she spotted one of the waiters for the night and dropped her half-drunk champagne onto his tray, nearly toppling the whole thing. *I can't speak to him. Not now.* Not when all her emotion was so close to the surface, she might take one look at him and blurt out the truth.

Without thinking, she left the room in the opposite direction of the open bar. Even though there was a rope blocking people from entering this side of the hotel, Reagan pushed it aside and rushed down the hallway. There were three doors in front of her. She took the door to her left and stepped inside.

The room was lit by a chandelier and there were racks and racks of coats. What kind of hotels had a chandelier in a coatroom? Maybe there was a sale at Chandeliers-R-Us? *It's okay.* Everything was going to be okay. She fanned her face, trying to control the blood rushing up to her cheeks. *What the hell is wrong with you, Reagan? You would think you would be over a ten-year crush by now.* She needed to get herself together and until she did that she was staying in this closet. She and these mink coats were about to get very acquainted with each other.

Chapter Two

Arms outstretched, palms against the wall, Reagan took in a shuddering breath. She stood deep in the coatroom, behind the third and fourth rack. The room smelled of fur and musk. The light was on, but it was still a bit dark in her little corner. The wall was painted what the owner probably thought was a soothing yellow, but looked like someone had thrown up on it. Whoever decided on this particular shade as an official color deserved to be shot. It was not helping her calm down. *I knew I should have worn a looser dress*. But nope, vanity had won out in the end. She wasn't very curvy, but the little black dress made her small hips look fuller than they were, before it came down to right above her knees. Well, none of that mattered now, because all it did was keep her looking cute while she had trouble breathing through the tight contraption.

Why did Zac affect her so? Why couldn't she just ignore him? If she was being honest, she found herself drawn to him even before the day they kissed for the first time. Except now, she wasn't content with secret accidental kisses and moments of longing. *But what can I do?* Zac—and all her brothers—had made it perfectly clear that a relationship between them was definitely not in the cards. So, what was she supposed to do? To keep ignoring her feelings seemed like the best possible option. Suppressing them wasn't exactly helping with her breathing though.

Creak. The door opened and Reagan didn't bother looking up. It was probably just the person who looked after the coats—the coat manager?—and here's to hoping they didn't come this far in. But, with heavy and determined footsteps, whoever it was walked deeper into the room, not stopping until they reached where she stood.

Reagan stiffened as she lifted her head. He was close enough that she could feel his heat against her back, smell his aftershave with definite hints of sandalwood, and know exactly who it was standing behind her.

Why was this happening to her? Coming to Steven's party was important for her career, but now she just wished she had stayed under her covers while binging on Oreo cookies and playing *Future Fantasy.*

"Hey," Zac said.

"What are you doing here?" she whispered to the puke-yellow wall.

Take deep breaths. And whatever you do, don't turn around.

"I saw you come in here. I wanted to make sure you were okay." A second later, he asked, *"Are* you okay?"

"I just...need a minute."

When she didn't hear the door opening and him leaving, she sighed.

"What do you want, Zac?"

She felt him come closer.

"I want to know, is it going to be like this every time we're in the same room?" His voice was smooth and she loved the sound of it. Even when she didn't want to answer the question that he just asked with said voice.

"Like what?"

He huffed out a breath. "Like you leaving as if the hounds of hell are on your heels. Like you can't stand the sight of me?"

I must not give in.

"It's not you that I can't stand to see," she said through gritted teeth.

"Then who—*Ah.*"

Oh great! I've said too much.

"Brandy is really something," he said, in a casual voice that was anything but casual.

"I don't care what she is."

"She's gorgeous."

She refused to turn around.

"Talented."

The jerk.

"Wealthy."

She was going to kill him slowly.

"Incredibly smart. Harvard graduate."

That did it.

Voice trembling, she couldn't help but ask, "Then why if she is so gorgeous, talented, incredibly smart, are you in here with little old me?"

"You're jealous."

She spun around so quickly, her elbow slammed into his gut. "I am not."

"Yes, you are." He grunted, rubbing his stomach.

Reagan stepped closer. "Say that again, Zac, and so help you I will—"

He stepped even closer and in a dangerously low voice whispered, "You'll what?"

"I will…" She swallowed.

Although her black stilettos gave her a much needed four inches, Reagan still only reached Zac's jaw. A jaw that was clean-shaven and exposed his thick lower lip. It didn't help that he was devastating in his gray suit, his arms crossed over his impressive chest. And he was watching her with those blue eyes of his that couldn't seem to decide whether they were angry with her or if they wanted to fuck her. She definitely knew which one she was up for.

Chapter Three

Zac stared down at Reagan. His best friend's little sister had always been short, even now when she wasn't so little anymore. She was small and the black dress she was wearing just emphasized that. His eyes strayed to her bare shoulders, down to her breasts, to her hips and her beautiful long legs. She might be small, but she fit damn near perfect under his hands and he remembered having those legs around his waist. The way she had shifted restlessly beneath him or above him. Not that he was going to touch her.

Zac mentally groaned. Following her in here had been the dumbest idea ever, and Zac had done a lot of dumb shit in his life. He hadn't known that she was going to be at Steven's party. Not until Aidan had pointed at her standing on the opposite side of the room, sipping on her champagne. In the instant their eyes met, he knew that they had to speak. They had barely talked for the last couple of months since they had ended up making out at Aidan's house. But they couldn't keep avoiding each other with only the bare contact of a few texts here and there. It was impossible anyway since her family was his family, so while they were in front of each other, they needed to talk this out.

Reagan's wild and curly black hair brushed her bare shoulders. Her brown eyes were wide and took up almost half her face. It was easy to see what she was feeling, because she let everyone see it. And right now, her eyes flickered down to his lips and back up to his, so fast he almost thought he had imagined it. But there was no imagining the quickening of her breath, her chest slightly touching his. He had memorized every inch of her gorgeous skin and saw a tinge of red spill across her hue of brown and black. She was blushing.

He wanted to take a bite right there where her pulse beat strong. Would she moan, gasp, or let out a husky cry? He had been dying to find out for months now. Years, if he was really being honest with himself.

He took a small step forward, crowding her closer to the wall, because he couldn't be this close to her without wanting to be closer.

"You'll what, Reagan?" he asked again.

"What…" She licked her lips, the dazed look still in her eyes. "What were we talking about?"

If he wasn't so fucking turned on right now, Zac might have been amused. But he was. All the blood seemed to be leaving his head and going straight to his cock, which was rushing to attention under his suit pants.

"We were talking about you being jealous," he reminded her.

"Oh." Reagan's shoulders rounded inwards. "I am not jealous. I just… I don't know what you want from me, Zac."

Fuck, he barely knew what he wanted from her either. Her hard nipples grazed his chest. She wasn't wearing a bra, only some padding under that dress of hers.

His cock was semi-hard and if he moved just a few more inches, he knew she would be able to feel it. He fought to keep control. *Think about hockey,* he told himself. He began to list every type of penalty in his head.

"I want to talk to you about what happened a couple of months ago," he finally said when he could look her in the eyes without thinking about fucking her.

"You mean when we…"

Zac nodded and then he told her the truth.

"We can't do that again, Ree. We were lucky that your brothers hadn't walked in a second earlier. Not to mention that it's wrong. I consider you to be not just one of my closest friends, but my family. You know that. I don't want to do anything that will break our family and I'm sure you don't either."

She turned her face, her hair sliding over her cheek.

He itched to touch her cheeks and force her to face him. He curled his hands into fists at his sides instead. *What do I know about relationships anyway?* All he knew was that he didn't want one and he wasn't built for one either. The only relationship he'd ever seen was his parents', and, yeah, they were the opposite of happy.

"You seem to forget that every time we're near each other something happens," she whispered.

"From now on, nothing more will."

"Is it so bad if something does?" She glanced at him. "Is it so bad that it keeps on happening?"

Images of blood, puke and shattered glass flitted through his mind. For a second, he was deaf to any-thing but the echo of remembered screams. Screams in his childhood. Some of them his and some of them not. His hand tightened, nails digging into his skin.

Yes, it would be bad. Very bad. He wasn't good for

her. And she deserved better than him. Aidan would lose his fucking mind if he even had a hint of the things him and Reagan had already done. Not to mention the other Thomas siblings. They weren't rational when it came to their baby sister and why would they be? Reagan deserved more.

"We can't do this," he said again.

"Then, what do you suggest we do?" she asked.

"Staying away from each other isn't possible. We've already seen that," he said ruefully.

"Like you could," she said, so low he almost didn't hear her.

His eyes narrowed.

"What?"

She didn't repeat it. Just stared him down. The same obstinate look that all the Thomas siblings shared. He loved that stubbornness of hers, but it made it so damn hard to push her away when she just wouldn't leave.

"Say it again," Zac dared.

"It's the truth, isn't it?" She stuck out her chin.

No, it wasn't. Fuck, maybe it was. *I hate this.* Zac resisted the urge to run his hands through his hair. *I hate how I turn into this indecisive mess when I'm around her or even worse, always making the wrong fucking decision.* Look at him right now. He had followed her into the coatroom to clear the air between them, but also because it had been weeks since he had last seen her. And he found that too long to bear.

She must have read something on his face, because Reagan being Reagan couldn't help but keep pushing him. She'd been pushing him since she was fifteen years old, after all.

"You can't stay away from me. You say one thing but do another," she taunted him softly.

"Neither can you," he shot back, suddenly furious. "Or did you forget who kissed who?"

"You really want to play the kissing game, Zac? Because you're the one who started this all."

He took full responsibility, but everything that had come after? That was on both of them. Yeah, he'd kissed her that night at Muckberry Field, but he hadn't meant to. It was just that Ree had made him forget all the pain waiting for him at the Quinn household. With his hands on her cheeks and his lips on hers, Zac felt like, for the first time, he was breathing free and clean. Kissing Reagan was like kissing sunshine. Just being around her, her spirit and quick comebacks, snapped his common sense. Or maybe his sanity, but definitely the promise he'd made to himself. *You had one core rule: don't get into this position with Reagan.* And yet, here he was.

Her bottom lip was moist from having sucked it into her mouth and releasing it. He could practically smell the damp heat of her pussy and he definitely knew she was wet between those silky thighs of hers. But it was the way she was staring at him that got to him. All that lust.

"And you're the one who eye-fucks me whenever we're in the same room together," he whispered.

She gasped. "I don't."

He released a short, tortured laugh. "Oh yeah, you do. You should look at yourself in the mirror, Ree. Then you'll see what I mean about eye-fucking."

"And what about you? Even while your Barbie doll— sorry, I mean girlfriend—is out there, all you can think about," she said, while stepping even closer to him, "is fucking me."

Hearing the word *fuck* coming out of Reagan's mouth pushed him right over the edge. His arms snaked around her back and brought them flush together. Her hands flew to the center of his chest.

"What are you doing?" She swallowed nervously.

His hands trailed up the small of her back, her spine, to her neck, as he took his sweet time touching every inch of her skin that was bared to him. He tilted her head back to align their mouths perfectly. Only a whisper of breath separated them. "Why would I imagine having you under me, having my hands filled with your breasts and me inside of you? Why imagine when I can take?"

And so, he took.

Reagan shuddered in his arms, clinging to him.

They took a single step backwards until her back hit the wall. She opened her mouth. His mouth plundered hers. *God, the taste of her.* Her fingers curled and tightened around the material of his shirt. He was drowning in her, but it also felt like the first time he could breathe in weeks. Her taste was all-consuming. A little bit of the champagne she was drinking earlier, but all of Reagan's stubbornness and sweetness. His tongue tangled with hers. The kiss was dark and pleasure licked down and set fire to his body. *I'm not going anywhere, not now that I can finally touch her.*

He pressed his erection against her stomach. She shifted restlessly in his arms, but not restlessly enough. He wanted her rubbing against him like a cat in heat as desperate for him as he was for her.

He pulled his mouth away from her. *More, give*

me more, Ree. Panting, she watched him. His fingers rubbed the pretty, pretty skin of her neck, leaving goose bumps in his wake. She licked her plump lips, pressing them together, as if she wanted to hold on to the taste of him. *She kills me.* His eyes tracked her movements, his cock throbbing and aching to fill her. As much as he wanted to spend all night kissing her, he was dying to touch more of her and he knew exactly where he wanted to start. There'd been one fantasy, out of the thousands he'd had of Reagan, he couldn't stop thinking about. That played nonstop on a loop in his mind. *Fuck it, I'm going to hell anyways.*

Zac spun her around. She tried to turn, but he pressed against her. His front to her back. Her hands were trapped between the wall and her stomach. She turned her head and he saw the curve of her cheekbones, heard the soft gasps from her mouth. He kept his right hand on the nape of her neck, holding her still while he allowed his gaze to wander down her back to the ass currently nestled in his lap.

"Fuck, Ree. This dress." Zac groaned.

"What are you doing?" she asked again.

He pressed more of himself against every delicious inch of her, until he surrounded her. His hair touched her shoulder as he bent his head down to hers.

"Don't move." His breath hot and heavy in her ear. "If you move, I'll spank you."

Fuck, I hope you move. He wanted nothing more than to get his hands on her. How would she take it? Would she cry out?

He bit her ear and her eyes fluttered almost closed.

His lips moved down to her neck, lingering over her pulse. He licked her, tasting a hint of his favorite flavor, cinnamon, and he couldn't get enough. Better, she tasted like perfection. *I can't believe this is finally happening and that it's* Ree *I'm getting to touch.*

"Do you know what you do to me?" he whispered, his voice thick.

"What? What do I do?"

"Drive me crazy."

He pressed his erection deeper into her, imagining his suit pants and her dress gone. She rocked her hips back and he groaned, the sound vibrating through both their bodies. Fuck, yes. Zac's hands circled her waist. She trembled.

"What did I say about moving?"

No matter how much he loved how she was rocking into him, a promise was a promise. He lifted his hand and brought it down on her ass. Hard. "Zac!" she yelled, trying to shift. Away from him? Towards him? He had no idea, but he grinned knowing it couldn't have hurt. He'd hazard a guess to say she liked it. By the way Reagan was rubbing her thighs together, she more than liked it.

"I said I'll spank you if you move. So, keep moving, Ree, and I'll keep spanking you."

Reagan froze, her breath coming out in quick pants as did his. *Yeah, driving me fucking crazy.*

"Good," he purred.

He rubbed her ass to soothe her, becoming hypnotized by the motion. And even though she felt so good beneath his touch, there was one thing that could make this all better. Skin on skin.

His hands roamed her stomach and then further up, until he palmed her breasts. Kissing her nape softly, he moved lower to explore the dark circular birthmark beneath her right shoulder blade with his tongue. He'd never seen it before and it made him wonder just how many other secrets he could uncover. He smelled more hints of her spicy body wash, but tasted nothing but the sweetness of her. With his teeth, he caught her zipper and pulled it halfway down her back. The dress split open to reveal luscious skin.

"I want to worship you." He swallowed in anticipation. "Spend hours touching you, licking you, sucking you."

"Yes, anything you want."

"Anything?" He pressed a gentle kiss to her spine as he peeled the fabric at the front, freeing her breasts. "You have no idea what all the things I want to do to you, *with* you, are."

He rubbed her nipples between his coarse fingers, felt them stiffen even further.

"Zac. Please, I need more." She moaned.

And he wasn't able to—didn't want to—say no. Zac reached for Reagan's dress and pulled it up her thighs until it was bunched up around her waist. When he saw the black sheer lace panties, his damn suit suddenly felt even tighter, especially around his cock.

"Is this what you always wear under your clothes?" He shook his head. "Fuck, don't tell me. I don't want to know."

He really didn't want to know, because if the answer was yes, what the hell was he supposed to do then? How would he ever be able to be around her again without wanting her naked?

"I only wear them for special occasions. Why? Do you like them?" He looked up and saw the smile on her face, her curls around her cheeks.

Game-loving, geeky, adorkable, that was Reagan. Lace panties, cheeky sexual remarks, it was just another side of her but one that he only got to see so rarely. It fascinated him. Zac didn't reply with words. Instead, he pushed her panties roughly to the side and slipped a finger inside of her.

"Zac," she breathed.

"So wet," he murmured, bringing his thumb up to rub her clit.

Reagan cried out, her hips moving up and down, seeking relief. He knew what she wanted, but if she wanted to tease him, it was only fair he teased her right back.

"I told you, Ree," he whispered into her ear. "If you want something from me, ask."

"Harder," she said.

"Can you be a little more specific?"

He added another digit into her pussy, groaning as his cock jerked in his pants when she immediately tightened around him.

"I want you, Zac. Please."

The pleasure of seeing her unravel, her face craning to watch him, her thighs trembling as he brought her closer and closer to her peak. *Enough, I can't take any more.*

Mad for her, Zac didn't hear the rip of her panties. He unzipped himself and pulled out his cock.

"Hurry. Hurry," she begged.

He had enough sense to find the condom he had in his suit pocket and sheathe himself with jerky movements. He hadn't been this desperate even when he was a teenager. But he was so gone for her, he couldn't do any more foreplay. Zac needed to be inside of her.

All he felt was the moment he brought his cock to her

pussy and eased himself into her. He let out a throaty groan. She whimpered. Fuck. Her heat scalded him. Inch by inch, she took him in. But she was so tight, he had to pull out and then push his way back in. The wet heat of her making it easier. Again and again, until finally his cock was fully seated inside of her.

He touched her chin and turned her face. Her mouth met his. His tongue thrusting into her mouth. Her pussy tightened around him. Fuck, fuck. This was going to end quickly. But, by the way she was moaning nonstop into his mouth and the wetness coating his cock, she was going to climax just as fast as him. He squeezed her hip as he thrust into her harder. Her body jerked.

"Zac. Zac," she panted into his mouth.

He lurched inside of her, her pussy rippling around his cock. Oh yeah, she was going to come.

"Come, Ree. Come all over me." He brought her down faster.

He kissed her deeper to stifle her scream as she did exactly what he asked her to do. She came. Not bothering with finesse, he fucked her until the pressure built and he felt that familiar stirring in his balls. And then he came. Harder than he had ever come before. She was still coming around him. Their voices echoing in the coatroom. He was blind and deaf as he kept thrusting even as he finished coming.

Their mouths pulled apart and he dropped his head onto her shoulder. Together they collapsed against the wall. *Holy fuck. That was amazing.* The best sex of his life. And he'd just had it with his best friend's little sister.

Chapter Four

We've never had sex before. That was Reagan's first thought when she could think again. She blinked. And then blinked again. The yellow wall did not disappear. Then again, they had never gone this long without seeing each other, without some kind of physical contact between them. *I feel like I've been waiting for this moment forever.* As if every moment between them had been leading up to here. And now that it had finally happened, all she could think about was how right it felt.

Zac breathed hard against her neck. She shuddered.

"Are you okay?" he murmured, words muffled.

She couldn't speak so she just nodded. She felt surrounded by him. His hand still around her hip and the other on her throat, lightly caressing her skin.

"Are you sure?"

More nodding. Oh yeah, she was okay. Damn near perfect in fact. The only thing that would have made this better is if they had been pressed skin to skin.

"I am going to let you go. Just give me a minute."

Reagan was in no rush to have him let go of her. She was going to have to peel herself off the wall anyway.

She cleared her throat. "Take all the time you need. No hurry."

Zac began to kiss her shoulder again. She sighed quietly in pleasure. His mouth moved across her collarbone, up her neck and then finally he turned her face to kiss her softly on the mouth.

He pulled away, letting go of her wrists so she could bring down her arms. She felt the loss of his heat immediately. She rubbed her arms as she heard him move around behind her. And then she looked down and felt the sting of embarrassment when she realized she was half-naked. She groaned in her mind. Dress raised up over her hips. Dress pulled down to expose her breasts. *How classy of me to have sex without even taking off my clothes*. She ran a shaking hand over her face, realizing: *I've just been fucked exactly as Letty described*.

With a few quick tugs, she righted her clothes and then quickly turned around. Zac's blue eyes met hers. He stood in front of her, looking for all the world exactly like the way he had before. His suit and hair weren't even ruffled. But she could still feel Zac's fingers digging into her thighs, the clenching of her pussy and the remnants of the aftershocks of her orgasm.

"Maybe we should rejoin the party," Zac suggested.

The party. His date. Her brother.

"Oh." She groaned. "Did we really just have sex with all those people out there?"

His lips curved into a half smile. "Yeah. Yeah, we did."

"You don't seem all that bothered," she said, curious. She thought he'd be freaking out.

He shrugged. "I am honestly not that surprised. Are you?"

Shocked, a little weirded out, yes. Surprised, no. They had been moving towards this moment since the first time they had kissed. They probably would have had sex three months ago if her brothers hadn't nearly walked in on them.

"Come on, we should go. People have probably already noticed us missing."

"You're right." She nodded.

And then he said the words she had been dreading.

"You should leave first," he said, straightening his jacket. "I'll come out five minutes later."

This was the way she expected him to react. Reagan snorted as she walked by him, pushing through the racks of coats to the door. She nearly tripped in her haste to get away, but caught herself before she went down. *God, I'm such an idiot.* Her neck was hot as she refused to look at him as he followed her.

"Don't worry, Zac. I'll make sure no one suspects you actually lowered yourself to be seen with me."

"Hey." He touched her arm just before she opened the door.

"I didn't mean it like that," he said quietly, letting go and taking a step back. "You know I didn't mean it like that, Ree."

"No, Zac. I don't know what you mean. I never know what you mean and you know why? Because you never fucking tell me anything." She swallowed.

Just one more man in her life who couldn't or wouldn't talk to her. She'd spent her entire life trying to guess what her father was feeling, an impossible feat she'd yet to accomplish. *And Zac is just as hard to reach.* She felt laid open, bare to him, and he was still pretending everything between them hadn't just changed completely, standing there with all this space between them.

"Stop. Don't you see that I'm trying not to hurt you,

Ree? What we did—I shouldn't have touched you. I don't… Your brothers…"

"I get it, but guess what, Zac? You hurt me anyway."

"Ree."

She heard the regret in his voice and it honestly killed her that what felt so right to her was nothing but wrong to him. He fell silent behind her and Reagan didn't wait any longer for him to come up with an answer. She left quickly, trying to stop her tears from falling.

Chapter Five

Reagan was crazy. She *knew* she was crazy. She had spent all night reliving every single delicious moment with Zac. And then spent all morning with her head under her pillow reliving every embarrassing moment that had come after. She had completely blown Zac's comment out of proportion. She knew that they couldn't have walked out of that closest hand in hand, announcing to the world they were a couple when her brother and his date had been in the audience.

Reagan groaned, slamming the pillow repeatedly over her head. She was glad she was wearing her silk head scarf or her hair would be a ball of fuzz. Not that it would stop her from trying to knock a few brain cells into her head. Or would she lose more? *You know what, it doesn't matter.* She was a wreck. She was still in bed even though the clock told her it was well past one o'clock on Sunday. If it was up to her she wouldn't ever get up.

Her phone rang.

She didn't want to answer it, but she knew who was calling. Without looking, she reached out for it, tipping her Black Panther alarm clock in the process. It crashed to the ground, glass splintering everywhere on her wooden floor. She winced as she crawled out of her safe cocoon and answered the phone. It was going to be a bitch to replace it, since Callum had given it to her last month with the express instruction of not breaking it. For some reason, clocks did not last long in her house.

"Hey, Dad."

"Baby girl." Lincoln's voice rumbled through loud and clear. "How are you doing?"

Well, I can't tell you this but, since the last time we talked, which was yesterday morning, I fucked Zac, who's basically your surrogate son. I guess you know now that I definitely don't think of him as a brother.

"I'm fine," she said.

"Good. Good. You coming to dinner next week?"

"Have I missed a single one?"

"You're being careful, right?"

He always said the same thing every day without fail. Just once Reagan wanted her dad not to call out of obligation. *Would it kill him to ask me about my work or my latest addiction to* Pokémon Go? She'd take him asking about anything not related to being a woman alone in the city as if she was the very first to do so, especially since she wasn't even the first in this family. Mom had done it. *It would have been so nice to be able to talk to her about it.*

"Dad—"

"The city can be a dangerous place. Keep your doors locked. Don't ever forget your phone," he warned.

She sighed. "I know, Dad. I promise I'm being safe. What brought this on?"

"Dean sent me an article on the latest crime rate. Apparently, your neighborhood is pretty dangerous."

She ground her teeth. *I'm going to kill Dean. Kill him dead.*

"I promise, Dad, everything is fine. I know how to take care of myself. You made sure of that."

"If you need anything, baby girl. Call me, okay?"

"Sure thing, Dad." The dial tone clicked in her ear.

She had no idea how to make him see that she wasn't a little girl. But he worried about her and what else could she do but grin and bear it?

She was about to throw her phone onto her bedside table when it rang in her grasp. Groaning, she dived her head back under her pillow as she answered.

"What?"

"Reagan?" Letty's voice asked. "Is that you? Girl, why do you sound like you've contracted some nasty venereal disease."

Reagan sat up, depositing the pillow onto the floor. "No, no, I'm fine. I was just…doing something."

"Okay. As long as I didn't interrupt you while you were stroking the bean. Anyway, what happened to you last night?"

"Eww, I was not 'stroking the bean' in the middle of the afternoon."

"There is no time restriction when it comes to sex. And stop trying to distract me by acting like a prudish virgin. What. Happened. Last. Night?"

Reagan wondered how much she should really tell her best friend. "I don't know. I don't think it's a good idea for me to tell you."

"Ooh," Letty said. "Now you have to tell me. You can't say something like that and not tell me. Besides, you left me to get a ride by myself."

"I told Aidan to drive you home if you needed it."

"And for that I will be forever grateful," Letty purred. "Still doesn't change the fact that you left your wing bitch, your BFF, behind."

"Letty, this thing with my brother..." Reagan hesitated. "Is this just some harmless flirting or is there something more I need to know?"

"Relax. It is nothing more than me yanking his chain. Could you really see someone like *him* going for someone like *me*?"

Reagan sat up straighter. "What the hell does that mean?"

Letty sighed. "Look, forget I said anything—Hey! Nice try. You tried to do it again. Tell me what happened to you last night."

Well, shit. Reagan leaned back against her headboard, stretching out her legs before her. She thought she was in the clear. *Oh, what the hell.*

She took a deep breath.

"I had sex with Zac last night."

Silence met her words. It stretched on for so long Reagan checked that the call was still in progress. And then she thought maybe Letty had passed out from shock.

"Letty? Are you still there?"

"How?" she finally croaked out. "Where? When? How?"

"In the coatroom at the back of the hotel. Sometime around 10:00 pm, I think. We did it up against the wall. And why? I guess because we've both been fighting this sexual tension between us for a really long time."

"I know you guys have been fighting since that kiss when you were teens, but this feels like it literally came out of nowhere, unless I'm missing something..."

"Um, maybe."

"Are you telling me you've been holding back on me, Reagan? How many times?"

"Once. Okay, shit, maybe twice."

"Twice! What the hell?"

"I know, I know!" Reagan groaned.

"We'll come back to this betrayal of our friendship later, but you can start making it up to me by telling me everything. And I mean everything."

"What do you want me to say? We've kissed a few times. I guess the worst was last year when I just broke up with Brody and Zac just broke up with that girl Jessica, remember?"

"Yeah, I remember."

"We ran into each other at the grocery store one night and somehow we both ended up in his car making out."

She remembered that night vividly. Remembered how it all began with a stupid bag of fruits.

"Bananas? Really?" Reagan wrinkled her nose.

He threw a bag of the loose fruits into his basket. "Just because you have an aversion to them, doesn't mean we all do. And what do you have against bananas anyway?"

They strolled down the fruit aisle, side by side. Zac was wearing his usual black jeans, tight blue shirt that was hidden beneath his gray hoodie and a black cap pulled low over his face. He referred to it as his "inconspicuous" look, hiding from all his fans and puck bunnies, but he still looked fucking gorgeous.

Reagan held up her hand and ticked it off.

"Firstly, they're yellow—a bright, in your face, offensive yellow. Secondly, they're a really weird shape.

Thirdly, guys stare when girls eat them, because of their weird shape. Fourthly, they taste like baby food and there is a reason why we no longer eat baby food. And finally, hello! They're yellow."

He flashed his dimples at her as they stopped to look at the mangoes.

"A weird shape, huh? I wonder what kind of dicks you've been looking at, because I promise there is nothing weird about my shape."

She choked. Plain and simple. On air. "Umm, no thanks. I've seen one already. Once you've seen one, you've kind of seen them all."

She picked up a random mango and put it in her basket, hoping he couldn't feel the heat of embarrassment coming from her. Or the heat of desire.

"Mm, I suppose it's like breasts, then," he said, as he picked up two mangoes and squeezed. "I mean once I've seen a pair of breasts they must be exactly like another pair of breasts. They probably feel the same, smell the same, taste the same. No difference in size, whether the nipples taste smooth or rough, whether when I suck or lick she goes from wet to crying my name."

Breathless, Reagan watched. Watched as his finger caressed the mangoes, as if they were actually breasts. Her *breasts*. When her eyes eventually left his hands and met his, she could see the wicked amusement in them. The jerk. He was fucking with her. She never could back down from a challenge.

"Maybe you're right. Of course, you're right. If breasts are different then cocks must be different. Some must be long and thin. Some must be short and thin. Or some might be long, thick dicks." She stepped closer towards him, gratified when his eyes turned cloudy with *lust. His mouth tight. His body rigid. "There must be a difference between size and whether when I suck or lick he goes from being hard to saying my name."*

In the middle of the grocery store, in the fruit aisle, surrounded by people, they stared at each other and she had never been so turned on in her life.

"Come with me," he said in a deep, husky voice. "Before I bend you over and fuck you in front of all these people."

Reagan didn't remember how or when they had dropped their baskets and hightailed it to his car. All she remembered was sliding into the back seat of his Lexus before he had hauled her into his lap and kissed her.

She knocked off his cap when her hands trailed into his hair and clung, not wanting to separate from his hard mouth. He shifted her over his erection until they lined up perfectly, grinding down as he thrust up. Mouth against mouth, they gasped, the ache between her thighs growing with each thrust, those big hands of his curled around her ass, kneading gently until she felt like she was going up in flames.

"Reagan. Reagan."

"What?" she said stupidly as the images of her and Zac finally subsided.

"I've been calling your name for the past five minutes," Letty said in her ear. From her phone. Right, she was in the middle of a conversation. "Damn, he must be really good to get you to join the space cadets."

"Sorry," she said, sincerely. "What did you say?"

"I said, why haven't you guys gotten together already?"

"Why else?"

"Your brother."

"Yes." She nodded, wrapping an arm around her bare legs. She was still in her girl boxers and blue tank top and it was creeping towards two o'clock.

"But it is not just about Aidan, it's about all of my brothers and even my dad. They all love him and consider him one of the family. One summer when I was sixteen, Aidan flat out told me to not even think about entertaining any feelings for Zac, because Zac was like a brother to me and nothing more."

"But, he was already too late," Letty whispered.

"Yeah," Reagan sighed. "I fell in love with him at fifteen and I've never managed to get over him."

"Then what's the problem? If you love him and can't stay away from him to hell with your brothers and your dad. They will come around when they see how in love with each other you are."

But was Zac in love with her? Reagan pulled her legs even deeper into her chest, resting her cheek against her knees. The only thing she was sure of was her own feelings for Zac that seemed to only grow and grow over the years. She loved his thoughtfulness. The way he always remembered the little things, like how she loved throw pillows so he always sent her crazy memes about giant pillows or got her eccentric ones whenever he travelled. Or how he could spend hours talking about Wayne Gretzky but if she gave him a single compliment about his own abilities, he would change the conversation very fast. She loved that mix of cockiness and humbleness.

"Reagan? I swear to god if you're having another Zac-induced fantasy, I am going to hang up on—"

"I don't know if he loves me, Letty."

"What do you mean?"

"He's never said he loves me. We've never even spoken about our feelings. I'm pretty sure though that he doesn't even *want* to want me. He was the one to suggest we stay away from each other after that scene at the parking lot."

"Then make him love you," Letty said bluntly.

Make him love me? Um, how the hell does one do that? Was that even possible? So, she asked Letty.

"He's attracted to you, right? Use that. It sounds to me like you haven't even been trying to attract him and you've had this explosive chemistry anyway. Imagine what could happen if you put some effort into it. He wouldn't stand a chance."

Reagan scrambled to her knees. Letty was right. She had never really tried to win Zac over, but he still found it hard to resist her. Instead she'd been letting the men in her life, her brothers, even Zac, dictate who she could be with. *Fuck that.* No more sitting back and no more passive Reagan. *I'm going all in and I'm going to show Zac that there's something between us and if it doesn't work out... Hey, at least I tried and I'll finally know it wasn't meant to be.* Reagan's heart thumped hard against her ribs and she almost reached up to caress the spot on her chest as if she could physically console it. *But that's not going to happen.* She smiled.

"You're right."

Letty laughed. "Of course, I am."

"No one likes a bragging friend."

"Who said that? You? Because I know that ain't true. You love me."

"Bitch, bye! *You're* lucky that I love you and put up with your ego!"

"Get your lazy butt out of bed and go use that devious mind of yours to drive that man out of his mind. Then into your bed."

Reagan's smile grew. "Oh, I will. Project Make Him Fall in Love with Me is a go."

Zachariah Quinn won't have any idea what hit him.

Chapter Six

Zachariah Quinn was fucked.

He had completely and utterly messed everything up.

Zac sat in an armchair in his living room, hands crossed and his head dangling down. Maybe the blood rushing to his head would help him start making better and smarter decisions. Decisions that didn't lead him to having sex with his best friend's little sister in the coatroom of the most prestigious party. If they had been caught both of their reputations would have been on the line. Not to mention he would lose the only family who had ever given a shit about him.

He groaned as he tangled his fingers into his brown hair.

The Thomas family had always been there for him. Ever since that fateful day when he was seven years old, in the cafeteria of his new school. He had been sitting in a corner by himself, stomach growling. He hadn't eaten since yesterday morning's burnt toast breakfast that he had made on his own and his mother had forgotten to pack him lunch again. Hands rubbing his stomach, Zac had contemplated what to do and was ashamed to think it, but he was seriously contemplating stealing from one of the other kids in his class.

And then a boy with short black hair and deep brown eyes had sat down in front of him.

"Hey."

Zac stared. "Hey."

The boy smiled. "We've all been wondering why you don't talk. Dean—that's my older brother, he's in sixth grade—said it was because you're a mute. A person who can't talk."

"I can talk."

"I hear that." He took out his lunch box and began to eat an apple. Zac watched him, confused.

"You're from Texas, aren't you?"

Zac nodded. "We moved here, because my dad got a job as the sheriff."

"Oh, cool. My dad used to be in the military, but not anymore. Not since he hurt his leg."

Zac dug his fingers deep into his stomach, silently begging it not to suddenly grumble and ruin one of the coolest things that had happened to him since he moved here last month.

And then the boy cocked his head to the side and asked the one question Zac didn't want to answer.

"Hey, why aren't you eating?"

Heart thumping so loud, he did the only thing he could.

"Left it at home," he lied.

"Oh. You want one of my sandwiches?"

"No. It's okay."

"Come on, man." The boy placed half of his sandwich in front of him. "It's PB&J. Malcolm—that's my other brother, he and Dean are identical twins—well, he makes them really good. Try one."

Slowly, Zac picked up the sandwich and nibbled a little.

"It's good, right?" the boy asked enthusiastically.

It was better than good. So good, before he knew it, Zac had devoured his half of the sandwich.

"The best PB&J I've ever tasted."

"Told you," he said smugly. "I'm Aidan, by the way."

"Zachariah, but my friends call me Zac."

"Do you wanna play softball with us, Zac?"

Meeting Aidan Thomas had changed his life.

He had taken him home that day and introduced him to his father. Lincoln Thomas had been and still was one of the most intimidating men Zac had ever met and that included his own father. Seven-year-old Zachariah Quinn had practically pissed himself when he shook the hand of the six-foot-six, broad-shouldered, dark-skinned, ex-military man. Even the cane Lincoln leaned on had just added to his imposing nature.

As the months and years went by, Zac had found himself spending every waking moment playing with Aidan, the twins and, the albeit-quieter of the Thomas siblings, Callum, teasing the younger by two years Reagan and avoiding home as much as possible. They had played every sport imaginable together, but both he and Aidan had been hooked on hockey. They lived and breathed it.

But Zac had barely been able to afford any of the ice-rink time, the coaching and not to mention all the equipment necessary for the only sport he wanted to play. It wasn't like his father would ever pay for him. The one time Zac had been stupid enough to ask, he'd had to stay home for a whole week, dodging Aidan and his brothers, so they wouldn't notice the bruises and scrapes on his back that came from being belted. And the accidental bruise on his face from when he'd fallen and knocked into the side of the table. By the time Zac had worked up the courage to go to the coach and let him know that he was quitting the team, he had received a letter saying he had gotten a scholarship that had paid for everything.

He had cried. Zac had flat out balled his eyes out like a baby. Hockey was everything to him, the one thing he knew he could do in his future, to get far away from all the other shit. And now he didn't have to worry that his father was going to rip it away from him like he did with everything else in his life.

Except, as he had discovered later on, Zac hadn't actually received a scholarship. There was no such scholarship for ice hockey in their town. Zac had confronted the only man who would have ever done something like that.

Lincoln had sat behind his large desk in his study room, watching Zac casually even when Zac told him he didn't want his charity. Aidan's father had walked around the table and come to stand before him. *"You are one hell of a player, Zac. I've seen you and I can honestly say you have a god-given talent. And, you shouldn't have to do this yourself, son. You're not alone. You have us. And I consider you to be like one of my sons."* Lincoln had ignored Zac's dismissals of his own talents and just said, grinning, *"If you're uncomfortable taking this scholarship then don't think of it as charity, but as an investment. Once you've become a pro hockey player, you can always pay me back. With interest."*

Zac had trained harder than anyone else on the team.

It had all proved worthwhile when he got a full ride to several of the top universities in the country and then recruited right out of college. He paid back all the money he had owed Lincoln and then some the first year he had gotten signed.

And how had he repaid the Thomas family for all the generosity they had shown him? Oh yeah, he had slept with Reagan.

Zac groaned again.

His fingers tightened in his hair, his scalp beginning to burn. Usually, when Zac had a problem of this magnitude he called up his best friend and hashed it out with him over a couple of beers. But since it concerned Aidan's sister, he didn't even want to imagine how that conversation would go. He couldn't even ask a hypothetical question without Aidan hounding him to death about it. Aidan was like a pit bull when he got his teeth sunk into something. He never let go.

Zac's head snapped up, an idea forming.

He'd call the one Thomas sibling who wouldn't ask him a million and one questions.

He reached over for his phone and dialed the number by heart. The dial tone clicked after several seconds.

"Yo, Zac. What's up, man?"

"Dean." He smiled. "I've got a hypothetical question."

"Please say this hypothetical question involves dirty sex and a hot woman."

And Dean is a mind reader.

Zac raised an eyebrow. "As a matter of fact, it does."

"Good," Dean said. "It's been too long since you got any pussy. We've been starting to wonder if you had taken a vow of celibacy or there was some girl you were pining for."

Offended, he replied. "I went out with that actress— what's her name? Lindsay! I went out with Lindsay like last month. And I just took Brandy as a date to Steven's party last night."

"And did you fuck either of these girls?"

How could Zac fuck another girl when all he could think about was Reagan, how was that fair to any of them? The only solution was to somehow get Reagan out of his goddamn mind.

Dean chuckled. "Doesn't count then. Shoot. What is this 'hypothetical' question of yours?"

Now, Zac was really questioning his sanity in re- cruiting Dean's help. But fuck, did he really have any other choice?

"So, hypothetically, let's say that after a couple of heated moments with this girl—"

"What kind of heated moments?" Dean interrupted.

"Just heated moments."

He clucked. "Come on, man, I need details to really give informed and good advice. I mean what the fuck does 'heated moments' even mean? It could mean any- thing from you going down on her, her going down on you, you fingering her, her kissing you, you kissing her...you catch my drift?"

"Yeah." Zac ran a hand down his face. "We've kissed a few times. Some heavy make-out sessions, always with clothes on."

"Okay. So, you're in the 'I want to fuck you, but I don't want to want to fuck you, but I can't resist at least touching you' stage. What happened?"

"I fucked her."

"Really? As in you took her back to your place and made sweet, sweet love to her all night, or…"

"As in, I fucked her against the wall in a coatroom without even taking off my pants."

"Wow." Dean whistled. "What's the problem, then? You got it out of your system, right? It sounds like you two have been working up to this for a while now anyway."

Zac sighed. The problem was that every time he saw Reagan now he would know exactly how it felt to be inside of her. He was *still* imagining being inside of her, though preferably with all their clothes off.

"Ah, I see. You still want her."

"But I don't *want* to want her."

"Why?" he asked. "Is she ugly? Daughter of a mafia boss? She has tits that sag down to her knees? Jeez, are you into cougars? I guess, each to their own."

Zac laughed. Typical Dean and his dirty mouth.

"Remind me why the fuck I called you again?"

"Because you wanted great advice from the smartest Thomas sibling?"

"The smartest Thomas would be Callum and then Malcolm and then Aidan and then—"

"Ouch." Dean pouted. "I'm smart."

"You just asked me if I was fucking an old woman!"

"Well, are you? Because I have to say, I'm not judging, but I'm still kind of judging, you feel me? Tell me the truth, Zac, I'll still love you, bro."

And this was why he called Dean, because he really wouldn't judge. Dirty mouth aside, he'd back him up in a minute and give him honest advice. *I need that right now.*

"Fuck, no. She's hot and younger than me. But not

too young, so get that out of your sick mind. But…let's just say that her family would not be happy if they found out I had touched her."

And that was the understatement of the year. If Dean knew that they were discussing his baby sister, he would break every bone in Zac's body. He might be the most laid-back of the Thomas siblings, but when it came to his baby sis's welfare, Dean didn't dick around.

"And besides, I don't think I even want to date her. I like her, of course, but she's not my usual type."

"Your usual type sucks."

"What?"

"Oh, come on, man." He could practically hear Dean rolling his eyes. "You pick the most perfect girls to date. Beautiful, smart and with impeccable manners. Perfect."

"What's wrong with that?"

"They lack character."

"They have character," Zac argued.

"Please." Dean blew a raspberry. "They bore me out of my mind when I talk to them for even a few minutes. I wonder how you manage to talk to them for months, not to mention fuck them. You need more of a challenge. A girl who makes you work for it. Now, this girl sounds like more of a challenge."

"She is too much of a challenge. I'm not kidding when I say her family would cause too many problems for us. What do I do?"

"If you think it's going to cause so many problems, stay away from her."

If only it was that easy. Zac stared at his reflection from his plasma TV. Reagan had been the first person he'd called when his agent had told him The Comets were thinking of drafting him. They'd got drunk that night and sat on his kitchen floor talking about the future. She was the person who got how much it had meant to him, not that the others didn't, but somehow being with her had filled Zac with hope that everything he'd ever wanted was going to come true.

"Been there, done that, it didn't take. What do I do?" he repeated.

Dean was quiet for a moment. "Find out if she's worth it."

Zac stood up and began pacing. "If she's worth it?"

"Yeah. It sounds to me like you need to find out if she is worth the risk, worth you trying to date her and worth you taking on her family. See if you even like her beyond wanting to bang her brains out."

He stopped pacing. See if he liked her? In theory, it sounded like an okay idea. Maybe if he spent time with Reagan, all this sexual tension would ease up when they discovered that they didn't even like each other in that way. Maybe it would work.

See if she is worth it? Spend time with the one woman that made his dick harder than stone? Zac smiled. He could do that. But *should* he do that was another question. And that was where he hesitated. Did he really want to risk his friendship with Aidan and everyone else? Not to mention his friendship with Reagan for something that was ultimately going to fade.

Zac's smile faded. *No.*

"I can't do that," he finally said. "I won't do that."

He wasn't going to risk it, risk losing everything for her to realize that he wasn't worth much anyway, and if Reagan thought last night changed anything, she was in for a rude awakening.

Dean sighed. "Okay. If you don't want to see if she is worth it, then why don't you just back away from this girl? Avoid her until the lust cools down?"

"We've been trying to do that for months. The distance, if anything, just makes us hornier when we do eventually see each other. And, I've got a feeling that she isn't going to back away this time either and give me space."

He remembered when Billy Malone had knocked Reagan to her ass, she had come up swinging. She'd broken his nose and landed in detention for the rest of the year. Not to mention the blistering she had gotten from her father and brothers. But as soon as she had left the room, her dad had turned to them.

"The girl's got a hell of a left hook, doesn't she?" Lincoln Thomas had said, grinning.

"Mm. So you guys can't be around each other without wanting to fuck each other, but you can't be away from each other without wanting to fuck each other. I guess that leaves you with only one thing you can do."

"It better be good."

He could hear the smile in Dean's voice.

"Oh, it's good alright. You ready for it?" Dean paused for effect. "You got to make her stop wanting you."

"That's it?" Zac asked, incredulously. The idea didn't even make any sense. Maybe, he shouldn't have called Dean. He should have picked a saner Thomas sibling, like Malcom.

"Now. Now. Hear me out. All girls want to date, right? But you need to convince her that dating you would be a bad idea. So, all you have to do is show her all the things she would hate to have in a relationship and voila. She stops wanting to date you, the magic goes out of the mystery and you can start being around each other without wanting to tear each other's clothes off."

"Silence.

"That is actually pretty good advice," Zac admitted.

"I know," Dean said smugly. "I am after all the guru when it comes to the ladies."

"Yeah, yeah, you're Casanova and Don Juan rolled into one."

"That's what all the girls tell me when I have them flat on their backs screaming, 'oh, Dean! Right there, Dean! Oh yes, Dean!'"

Zac hung up on Dean's manic laughter.

He leaned against his breakfast bar that separated his kitchen from his living room. *Show her all the things that would be wrong with dating.* Zac could do that. Who knew Reagan better than he did? And when she finally saw that anything romantic happening between them didn't live up to the fantasy, she would be dying to break things off with him.

He smiled.

Reagan Thomas won't have any idea what hit her.

Chapter Seven

Reagan tapped her fingers idly on her steering wheel. She sat at a traffic light, right in between the pharmacy and the grocer's in Carter Springs, the town she grew up in. The clock read 5:00 pm. Outside her window, it was still bright, with the sun high in the sky.

It was too damn hot, and her blue shirt stuck to her skin. *I should just open all the buttons and sit here in my bra and jeans.* But she couldn't be bothered to undo more than the top ones. Reagan tried to turn on the air-conditioning in the car, but it was busted. She should have fixed it in the winter, but she had used the money to get the best new, luxurious mattress money could buy. *Great.* On top of being nervous, she was going to arrive all sticky and sweaty. Not that it should matter; her brothers wouldn't care and Zac, he knew who she was. A hot mess.

She had spent most of the morning and afternoon driving out of the city to try and work through her nervousness, but she was still anxious. Project Make Him Fall in Love with Me had seemed like such a good idea when she'd been on the phone with Letty, but now that she actually had to put actions to her words? Not so much.

The light changed and she drove down the main street and took a left. It had been a week after the "incident" with Zac—that was what she was calling it, at least in her mind—and she had spent that time trying to figure out a plan to deal with him. But so far Project Make Him Fall in Love with Me was going nowhere fast. Rather than thinking about the future, she kept reliving that night over and over again. Especially at night. With her hand between her thighs. *Bad, Reagan.*

She had known sex with Zac was going to be explosive, but she could never have imagined just how delicious it had been. And now that she knew, it was hard to concentrate on anything else. She hadn't seen Zac yet. He was probably avoiding her, but he wouldn't be able to avoid her tonight: their monthly dinner at her dad's house. There were only three reasons why you missed family dinner: one, you were dying. Two, you were about to die. Or three, you were in a game—not *at* a sports game, but *in* the game—since all her brothers were athletes.

Reagan pulled up to one of the picturesque suburban homes at the end of a cul-de-sac, parking right behind a red BMW, a black Lexus and a green Jeep. The garage was closed and she knew it was probably full. Their cars alone took up half the street. She turned off the ignition and got out. *Okay, breathe, Reagan.* She shut the car door and walked up the driveway to her father's house, gravel crunching beneath her Converses.

She only had one goal for Project Make Him Fall in Love with Me tonight: act cool, calm and collected. She wasn't going to let Zac know that he'd ruffled her. She was going to pretend everything was normal—for now—and then step by step, she was going to make him see what he was missing. If she tried to push him too hard too fast, she'd lose him quickly, like when she had tried to get Zac to play games with her at the arcade. At first he had refused as a joke, but now he wouldn't play on principle. Sneaky was the way forward, to bombard Zac with the little things, like turning up to all of his games or getting him all the gummy bears he liked—especially the green ones. *That's the plan anyway.*

Reagan knocked on the large, white door and barely had to wait a few seconds before it was thrown wide open to reveal a tall, broad-shouldered man. Her father's eyes were the exact same shape and shade of brown as her own. While her skin was closer to that of Gabrielle Union (yeah, but no way was she actually comparing herself to Gabs), his was the color of midnight and onyx rolled into one, like Mahershala Ali. His black hair had begun to thin at the top, but there was still a lot of it. He held a cane in his right hand, but it did nothing to lessen his imposing figure. The man was six foot six after all and as big as a bear.

"Dad," Reagan greeted with a smile on her face.

Lincoln Thomas opened his arms and she went into them willingly. He enfolded her in his embrace. She breathed him in deeply, that musky smell of wood that was uniquely his. He didn't say a word and that wasn't surprising since her dad wasn't much of a talker and neither was Callum. Dean and Reagan were the aberrations—you couldn't get them to shut up.

She knew her father was ready to end the hug when he shifted back. Reagan let go. She wanted to hold on for longer, but there was no point. No matter how much she needed her dad, she knew how painful it was for him to even be in her presence. It hurt her that she was hurting him and that she didn't really exist as just her-self, as just Reagan. Like now. He stared at her for a mo-ment too long. His eyes going blank, looking beyond her. She tried not to tense, because you would think a girl would be used to having her dad see through her to only remember his dead wife who lay beyond. But she wasn't used to it at all. It still cut her up deep inside, but she didn't lose the smile on her face when he finally snapped back to reality.

"Sorry, did you say something?"

She didn't bother telling him that she hadn't said a word.

"How are you?" Reagan asked him as they stepped into the house together.

"I should be asking you that, baby girl."

Reagan blinked. "Why? I'm fine."

"We've barely spoken," her dad reminded her.

"We speak every day and I've been busy. With work and stuff."

"Mm," he huffed.

Before she could ask what that meant, they turned from the hallway into their open and large living room. Reagan had been born and raised in this house and mostly everything stayed the same year in and year out, except for the TV. Growing up with four older brothers who played and loved sports and a dad who was equally enthusiastic meant that they needed one that was usu-ally bigger than anything else they owned. Their plasma right now took up most of the wall, with couches and armchairs in front of it.

It was an open-plan space with the kitchen melding into the dining and living room. A dining table that could house eight people was directly in front of her and beyond that was the kitchen. It was much smaller, because let's face it—they were not a family that cooked very often. Only Callum could actually cook and enjoyed it, while Malcom did it out of necessity. The rest of them avoided it like the plague.

Aidan and Zac stood on opposite sides of the counter, talking to each other, not noticing her arrival. Reagan stopped in her tracks, forcing her dad to stop beside her. *Oh god.* She was helpless to do anything but stare.

Zac was leaning against the kitchen cabinets. Dangling in one hand was a beer. His dark blue short-sleeved top was stretched across his chest and his arms, showcasing his large tattoo. A series of writing that ran from his elbow up his forearm. It read: "Take one's adversity, learn from their misfortune, learn from their pain, believe in something, believe in yourself, turn adversity into ambition, now blossom into wealth." He'd gotten the quote from Tupac's poem the day he left Sheriff Jeremy Quinn's house and it was the only tattoo he had. Zac always said it was the only one he needed since it represented everything about who he was and who he was planning to be. She loved that about him.

Zac brought the bottle to his mouth and took in a deep pull of the beer. His throat convulsed as he swallowed. She tried not to let a moan slip out of her mouth. She followed the little droplet that leaked out the side of his mouth and the way his tongue licked it right up. Her nipples tightened with want.

Yeah, this was a bad, bad idea.

Zac chose that moment, when she was burning up with need for him, to turn his head and look at her. Even from here she could see his body stiffen. And the way his eyes darkened. Exactly the way it had before he kissed her, touched her and fucked her. Reagan wrapped her fist around the hem of her shirt and tightened. Zac placed his beer on the table, his eyes never leaving hers. *Be cool, calm and collected.* That was what she'd told herself on the ride over. Where the hell was this coolness and the supposed calm? She was panicking. She was absolutely panicking. Everyone in the room was going to be able to see what they had done. And Zac was going to want nothing—

Reagan's meltdown was cut off when someone stepped in front of her and blocked her view of Zac.

"Short-stuff!"

She barely had time to register who it was before arms wrapped around her and lifted her off the ground. Only one brother greeted her this enthusiastically and openly. *Dean.* Dean was all about creating the madness and seeing just how far and wild you could take things. He was one of her favorite people in the world.

Reagan forgot about Zac for a moment and laughed as she hugged Dean back.

"Put me down, you goon," she said.

"No, the goon would be Aidan," Dean joked as he set her down onto her feet.

His black hair was growing out and looked as if it hadn't seen a comb in weeks. He was wearing an over-sized football jersey—his of course—blue jeans and his customary grin.

Reagan saw Aidan shoot him the middle finger from where he stood.

"Anyway, why are you acting like you haven't seen me in years?" Reagan asked. "We talk more or less every day."

"If you count one sentence as a conversation, then

yeah, baby sis, we talk every day. You suck at long-distance communication."

She gasped. "I do not."

She looked around the room. Everyone was nodding, even her dad. *Traitor.*

"Reagan, you texted me the same thing every day the whole time I was away at training camp the first year I joined my team: 'good luck,'" Aidan pointed out.

"Even Callum speaks more than you do and I'm pretty sure that boy is mute," Dean said.

Reagan frowned. She didn't mean to do it. She just didn't want to get in their way too much. She constantly had to remind herself that although some of the people in her family liked to talk, they *didn't* talk. She missed them with such a fierce passion that if she let the floodgates open, she'd bombard them with so much their heads would explode. And it was so hard to not be frustrated that they thought she was the problem since it was totally them, not her, but trying to have that conversation again with them would probably not end well.

"Sorry. I'll try and call you guys more often."

"That's what I want to hear." Dean grinned as he threw an arm around her shoulders. "Now, let's get you a beer."

He pulled her towards the kitchen. Her dad went in the opposite direction and settled himself into his armchair in front of the TV, where of course a game was playing.

Aidan hugged her. Aidan looked exactly the same as he had a week ago. His hair was again curly on the top, with the sides shaven and a light gray pullover and jeans. He smelled lightly of some typical men's cologne.

"What's going on?" Aidan asked when he pulled back.

He was wearing a frown as his eyes searched hers. "What do you mean?"

"You disappeared from Steven's party a week ago and stuck me with Letty."

Oh shit. Reagan forced herself not to look at Zac, who she could feel watching them. She frantically racked her mind. *What can I say? What can I say? Oh sorry, Aidan, I had to leave because I just got fucked into oblivion by your best friend and my heart was breaking since I wanted more and he didn't?* Nope, definitely can't say that.

"Why? Did something happen?"

Dean handed her a beer, which she took gratefully. She gulped down half the bottle in one go, ignoring the burn. Liquid courage and all that.

"She asked me why do we say 'sleep like a baby' when a baby gets up every few hours? And then somehow we ended up talking about how we have to pretend to go to sleep before we actually go to sleep." Aidan shook his head in confusion. "It was the weirdest conversation I've ever had."

Reagan smiled. "Letty loves her random facts. She has this app that sends her a new one every day." They liked to spend morning coffee breaks laughing at how ridiculous but true some of them were.

"Aww, little Aidan is all grown up and having actual conversations with girls, is he?" Dean said, pinching Aidan's cheek.

Aidan slapped him away, and Zac sniggered, which made Aidan glare at him.

"Don't look at me." Zac held up his hands. "If you took a minute to actually speak to Letty, you'd realize how tame that convo was."

Dean nodded. "She once asked me why blueberries weren't blue. But then again, why aren't strawberries made of straw?"

Everyone groaned.

"Still tame," Reagan said. "I just learned that you can use your penis to unlock your iPhone if you set it up to think it's your finger."

Dean hooted in laughter. "Fuck me, I might have to marry your BFF if she keeps on giving me these kinds of ideas."

She turned towards Dean, who had come to stand beside her.

"You fuck my best friend, Dean, and I will castrate you," Reagan threatened.

Dean and Aidan both winced.

"Reagan, why did you have to go and say it like that?" Dean whined.

She smiled sweetly at him. "We're all adults here so suck it up."

Her eyes shifted and caught Zac's. His eyebrows were raised and she could read his expression perfectly: *you dare to chastise Dean when you fucked me only a week ago? Isn't that the pot calling the kettle black?*

Or something like that, with less Victorian words and more swear words probably. She didn't bother replying to his nonverbal question. Cool, calm and collected did not dignify things like that with a response.

"Anyway, where is Malcolm and Callum?" she said, changing the subject.

"Malcolm is—" Dean began.

"Right here," someone interrupted.

Reagan spun around. Coming out of another door into the open kitchen was Dean's identical twin. Malcom's hair was kept neater than Dean's and pushed back out of his face. He wore a maroon T-shirt and jeans tucked into big boots. She smiled as he walked towards her.

Unlike Dean's exuberant hug and Aidan's tight squeeze, Malcom put his hands on her cheeks and watched her carefully. A few seconds passed.

"Have I passed your inspection?" she asked, only half-joking.

"You look good, sis," Malcolm said, quietly. "And I agree with Dean though. You do suck ass at long-distance communication."

She lost her smile as all the boys hooted with laughter. She knocked his hands away.

"Bitch, bye. You're all such bullies," she grumbled.

This is what happened when you grow up in a household of brothers: they found it fun to gang up and tease you. But she wasn't twelve anymore. Not that it stopped them from treating her like that or for her to act like it sometimes.

"And Callum got delayed," Aidan answered her earlier question. "He just flew in from San Francisco and should be here in about an hour or so."

Callum was a professional baseball player and currently the only brother in the middle of his season. But even if he wasn't really busy it was still hard to see him since he lived so far away. Aidan, Zac and Reagan were the only ones to live in Scarlet, the city near their hometown, while Malcolm, Dean and Callum had been recruited to teams all over America. She missed them a lot, but she was kind of used to it at the same time. They hadn't all lived under the same roof for over ten years now. And she couldn't be anything but happy since they were all living their dreams.

Malcolm moved around the counter and came to stand shoulder to shoulder with Zac.

"How's training going?" Zac asked Malcolm, abandoning his half-drunk beer to fold his arms across his chest. Reagan noticed his abs contract and wished she could see his six-pack without the top in the way. The only time she ever got to see him half-naked now was on a billboard advertising shaving just like the rest of America. And how sad was it that he had been inside of her and she still hadn't seen him fully naked?

Malcolm shrugged. "It's going as well as it can be."

"Well, my training is going fan-fucking-tastic. I can't wait until we face off," Dean said, with a wicked grin aimed at his twin.

"Don't expect a different outcome," Malcolm said, mildly.

The twins were both football players but on opposing teams. Malcolm was a linebacker for the Paramount Tigers and Dean a defensive end for the Ravanna Seagulls. Whenever their teams went up against each other, like they had last season, the world went nuts for it. Brothers playing against each other, and identical twins at that? Yep, it made for an entertaining and highly competitive game. Last year, Malcolm's team knocked Dean's team out during the playoffs, going on to the Super Bowl before they too were unfortunately defeated. Reagan had literally been on the edge of her seat during that game. She had shouted herself hoarse by the end of it, screaming so much for both of her siblings.

Dean blew a raspberry. "Yeah, yeah, we'll see."

"I guess we're going to be the only ones with a championship under our belts then if your teams have to put faith in the two of you," Aidan said.

He bumped fists with Zac, while Dean booed loudly and Malcolm rolled his eyes.

Reagan laughed. "We get it. We get it. You guys won the cup. At some point it's going to get old."

"It's old right now," Dean grumbled.

"Nobody likes a sore loser," Zac said. "If any of you guys won, we would gladly give you the bragging rights until the next season began. Until that happens, suck it up."

"Okay," her dad said, standing up and walking over to them. "I think we've had enough trash-talking for one evening. Dinner."

"Callum isn't here yet," Malcolm mentioned.

"He'll join us when he gets here. Help me set the table, Reagan," her dad added in a commanding tone.

Reagan threw her empty bottle into the trash and went to help.

Once it was done and the food was placed, they all sat down in their usual places. Unfortunately, it meant that she was at the end, and Zac was directly in front of her again, with Malcolm and Dean on her left. She met Zac's gaze directly and held it for the first time that night.

He looked on impassively, elbows on the table. His knees brushed hers and sent shivers down her spine. No one would ever be able to tell that he had thrust his cock into her pussy and made her come harder than she had ever come before. But inside? Inside, she was an absolute and utter mess. And now she was thinking about it again. She resisted the urge to squirm in her seat, because then he would know.

Too late. His lips curved into a smile that screamed he knew exactly what was on her mind. Reagan was not a good enough liar to keep it off her face that she knew that he knew so now he knew that she knew he knew.

"Reagan? Reagan?" Dean called her name.

It was only when he waved his hand in front of her face that she snapped out of it.

"Huh?" She turned to look at him, stupidly.

Everyone at the table stared at her.

"You okay?" Aidan asked, eyes narrowed with concern.

She swallowed. "Yeah."

"You're sweating," Dean pointed out.

"It's hot in here," she shot back, glad for the excuse. "What were you saying?"

"We weren't saying anything, Dad was about to make a speech," Aidan answered.

"Sorry, Dad," she said, sheepishly.

Lincoln sat at the head of the table. He acknowledged her apology with a slight tilt of his head.

"I only have a few words," he began, meeting each of their gaze. Immediately, they all sobered at the seriousness of his tone.

"First, I want to say that it's nice having you all home, with the exception of Callum. But he'll be here when he gets here. I want you to know that all my boys and my girl have made me proud and that includes you too, Zac. You are like a son to me. And no matter what you all do, if you win or lose games, I'll always be proud of you. Having you come here whenever you can means more to me than you will ever know."

Wow. Reagan sat in her seat stunned. She wasn't used to hearing words like that coming from her dad, so when they did it left her feeling incredibly moved. Proud of her? She couldn't help the little seed of doubt that wormed its way in. Was he really proud of her? She wasn't a hockey-playing super-god like Aidan or Zac, or a multimillionaire amazing football player, like Dean or Malcom, and she definitely wasn't like her talented baseball-playing brother Callum, who was also a certified genius. At least her work was related to sports, right?

She wasn't like them. She knew what she had though. She had a good job that she enjoyed and loved. Good friends who were there for her whenever she needed them. And a family that might have some baggage but were at the core of who she was. Reagan needed to be grateful for that and stop wanting something that she could never have. Like having her father see her for her.

"Are you dying?" Dean suddenly demanded.

"Dean!" Malcolm hissed.

"What?" he asked. "Come on, it's not like you weren't all thinking it."

Their dad sighed. "No, I am not dying."

They all visibly relaxed. Thank god. For a moment there, she was left wondering too.

"Then, aww, shucks. Thanks, old man." Dean wiped away an imaginary tear. "It's nice of you to say you're proud of us all, but let's get real...we all know that I'm your favorite. Stick with me and I'll get you a gold cane like a real pimp. Where do you think they get canes like that? Does Pimps-R-Us exist?"

"Swear to god!" Aidan said over their laughter. "If

it wasn't for Malcolm, I would think you were dropped on our doorstep."

"Hey!" Dean said, offended. "I'm older than you! If anyone was adopted, it's more likely going to be you."

"Less talking and more eating," Malcolm said, reaching for a bowl of mashed potatoes and pushing it into Dean's chest.

"Thank god," Zac agreed.

They all dug in.

The food was good. Considering her dad had definitely ordered it from Mama Jones and had not attempted to cook it himself that was a blessing. Occasionally, Callum cooked, but they otherwise always got takeout. Not that she was complaining, but she wasn't going to be twenty-five years old forever. Maybe, she shouldn't have a second helping of pie.

She looked at the all-that yummy goodness. And before she realized it, there was another helping on her plate and her mouth was full of lemon pie. *Mm, now that is some seriously delicious stuff.*

A rich, deep laugh rang through the room. Reagan closed her eyes, pretending to be savoring the lemon pie she was chewing and not the sound of Zac's laughter. *I'm not going to look at him*, she thought desperately. Just pretend he wasn't there and if worse came to worst, she was just going to think of him as one of her family members. Like a distant cousin.

Zac was laughing at something Aidan said. He had a great laugh. Deep, but not too deep. If she was pressed against him, she'd be able to feel his laughter resonate through her. *Bad, Reagan.* The thought had her tingling. She made a move to bring the tray of vegetables closer to her, but the side of her arm caught her beer. It tipped over and the dark liquid poured out. Everyone jumped out of its way.

She gasped and made a quick grab for it. She righted the bottle, but it was too late. The damage was already done to the table.

"Oh crap," she said. "Sorry."

"Whoa," Aidan exclaimed.

Malcolm grabbed some kitchen towels quickly and passed them to her. She thanked him as she began to mop up the mess, not that it helped very much. Everyone was still looking at her.

"Sorry," she said again to no one in particular.

Shit, what is wrong with me? She didn't want to look at anybody, but the room was too quiet.

"It's okay, Reagan. Just take a breath," Malcolm said, quietly.

She looked up and found everyone staring at her. All with different expressions of worry. Except for Zac. He looked furious. And Reagan knew in that moment she could not handle another second in this room.

"I'm okay. I… Let me get some wipes."

Reagan hurried out of the room, ignoring the surprised comments from her family.

Chapter Eight

Zac sat at the table, stunned. His eyes were glued to where Reagan had just been sitting moments before. *What the fuck just happened?*

"What the fuck was that?" Aidan asked beside him.

"I was about to ask *you*," Dean said, frowning. "What's wrong with baby sis?"

"I have no fucking clue. She was fine when I saw her last week," Aidan growled.

Yeah, she was fine, until Zac fucked her that is. Now, everything was different. Reagan had barely looked him in the eye all night and she hadn't even said more than two words to him. Usually, they would spend monthly dinners at her dad's joking, trash-talking, playing video games before ending up where they'd ended up every time since their first kiss—taking a walk through Muckberry field. Just the two of them. But like he thought, he was an absolute and utter idiot. They couldn't just go back to pretending that he didn't know what her mouth tasted like when she was panting out an orgasm. Or how her ass had felt against his cock, so round and perfect he'd jerked off to the thought of it last night and the night before that and the night before that. Or how much she liked it when he spanked her ass.

Fucking her hadn't made him want her less; if any-thing he wanted her more. Watching her sit across from him with that fork in her mouth, her eyes closed in bliss while she swallowed that pie had been torture. This whole night had been torture. The only reason why he hadn't bailed out from the beginning was because he was determined to have everything return to normal. And it wasn't going to happen unless he did something.

Zac stood up, pushing his chair backwards. The guys all looked at him, stopping midway through the con-versation he hadn't bothered to listen to.

"I'll go speak to her," he announced.

"Maybe I should go?" Malcolm asked, looking at him.

"Let me. It's probably nothing, but I'll talk to her and find out," Zac said, hoping they would all just agree. He knew Reagan. No matter how upset she was, she wouldn't tell her brothers the truth, and fuck, wasn't that just a kicker? He knew she'd lie for him. *I need to be the one to clear the air between us.* Or else if he let this go on for too long, they might never be able to go back to the easiness that used to exist between them. And he'd hate that, to never be close with her again.

Malcolm looked as if he wanted to argue further when Lincoln spoke.

"Let Zac go. We all know Reagan listens to him more than the rest of us. He was the only one who could get her out of the tree house after she spray painted the Hersheys' wall for being racist assholes. Zac will find out what is troubling her."

Lincoln nodded at him with approval. Fuck, he re-ally wished he could take back what'd happened now, but there was no ignoring the guilt that crept up on him with Lincoln's words.

Zac dropped his napkin and began to leave the room.

"Women," Aidan muttered behind him. "Why are they so hard to understand?"

"See here, Aidan, it's because women have a different biological structure. They have this thing called estrogen pumping through them that makes them act irrational and completely crazy," Dean replied.

"When you get married, I will not be surprised to learn that your wife strangled you in your sleep."

"Just don't finish all the fucking pie. Ree will kill you guys if you do," Zac said over his shoulder, knowing it was useless, because even as he said it he caught a glimpse of Dean stuffing his face with another slice that was as large as his fist.

Zac left the room.

Reagan made her way to the cleaning closet down the hall, hoping to find something to clean the table, but to also calm down. The room was dark, but she didn't bother turning on the light. She knew where everything was. Going to the last rack, she squatted down and pushed a few bleach bottles out of the way to get to the wipes.

Get a grip, Reagan. If she kept acting like this everyone would guess there was something up with her. She clutched the wipes. *You can do this.* She took a deep breath. *All I have to do is spend the next hour or two making chitchat, finish my food and get the hell out of here.* And when she got home, then she could think about how exactly she was going to proceed with Zac. It was easy to tell Letty that she was going to make Zac fall in love with her, but she didn't have any idea of how to actually do that.

You couldn't *make* someone love you. Either they did or didn't. And from everything she had seen so far, Zac did not love her. He never told her how he was feeling, never shared his most vulnerable parts with her and if he did, he quickly backtracked and acted like he'd made the biggest mistake of his life. Reagan had parts of him, but she didn't have all of him. But she had to try, didn't she? She didn't want to spend the rest of her life wondering "what if?" What if Zachariah Quinn was the one for her? She was pretty sure, but then again, they had never dated.

Reagan brought the wipes to her chest. She had been imagining what dating Zachariah Quinn would be like since she was fifteen years old. Almost like an extension of their friendship right now, but more. Better. Infinitely better, because they would be able to kiss and touch whenever they wanted to.

The sound of the door opening and closing brought her out of her contemplation. She stood up quickly, dropping the wipes to the ground.

"What the—" she started.

Zac prowled towards her. She couldn't see his face clearly, but she could practically feel the anger radiating off him. He stopped a couple of inches away from her.

"What the fuck was that, Ree?" he snapped.

She opened her mouth, unsure of what she was going to say. She closed it again and then swallowed.

Finally, all she could say was, "I don't know."

"If you keep acting so nervous and skittish, your brothers are definitely going to know that there is something going on!"

"I know!" she snapped back.

Her hand curled into a fist. How was it that she was a mess after having sex with him once and, yet, he acted like barely anything had happened between them? She could feel his eyes on her, but she refused to meet them.

"Look," he sighed. "You need to stop acting so nervous."

"Don't you think I would if I could?"

Zac stood close enough that she could smell him, his woodsier, masculine scent filling her lungs every time she took a deep breath. The racks on either side of her felt closer, the room suddenly a hell of a lot smaller and the calm she had been feeling a few moments ago was now disappearing fast.

"And why did you follow me in here?" She groaned.

He really needed to stop following her into enclosed spaces or she could not be held responsible for her actions. Namely when she pushed him up against the wall and had her wicked way with him. *Don't lick your lips. Do not do it.*

"What happened between us at Steven's party—" Zac said, as he took a step forward.

"We don't have to talk about it."

No, no, that's not what I mean, I just don't want you to have a heart attack at the age of twenty-seven if I told you how crazy in love with you I actually am. So here I am acting like a complete moron, hoping you might feel even a bit of what I'm feeling for you.

"I think we do," he replied. "Or else you wouldn't be acting this weird. I don't want things to be weird between us, Ree," Zac said quietly.

Yep, too late for that. How exactly was she supposed to act around him now? Was there a manual for people who banged their brother's best friend and childhood crush out there? No? Maybe she could use her discomfort to make millions, then.

She looked at him and saw his blue eyes watching her, waiting for her to tell him that she felt the same way.

"I don't either," she admitted.

"Then, can we go back to being friends?"

Hadn't she agreed with Letty? Hadn't she decided to fight for Zac and stop letting him push her away? Well, there was no time like the present to test the waters.

Taking a deep breath, Reagan took a hesitant step forward on her Converses.

"Is that what you really want?" she whispered.

He said nothing. Not a good sign, but not a bad sign either. She took another step forward, until they were so close her nipples grazed his chest. She shivered.

"What are you doing, Ree?" he asked, his voice a little deeper, a little rougher.

"Do you really want to go back to being friends?" Reagan whispered, coming onto her tiptoes so she could say the words closer to his mouth.

To help with her balance, she reached out and grasped his shoulders. She leaned into him a little more, every inch of his chest and her chest now pressed together. She gasped from the heat of his body and stared at his lips. The full biteable bottom one had her aching to take it between her teeth.

He steadied her by placing a hand on each side of her waist. She wanted him to slip his hands under her top and touch her skin. She was dying from wanting.

"We can't do this again, Ree," he said, some of his desperation leaking out. "We need to go back to being friends."

Oh. Her eyes flickered up to his blue eyes. *He wants me*, she thought with shock. She knew that he wanted her but she didn't realize that he couldn't resist her just as much as she couldn't resist him. Letty was right. *This, I can work with this and make him see that there's a reason why we can't stay away from each other.* As soon as she thought that, all of her fear seeped out of her.

"Zac," she said with a smile. "I hate to break this to you, but I don't kiss my friends at night. I don't make out with them in my car or dry hump them on a sofa. And I definitely don't fuck them against the wall of some party."

She leaned forward and bit into his bottom lip. *Give in.* She wanted him to give in so badly. To not just desire her, but to love her too. He let out a guttural sound that had blazing heat and relief trailing down her spine. He stroked her back lightly up to her shoulders, to her nape. Gently clasping her hair, he tilted her head back, away from him. His eyebrows were furrowed, but she couldn't tell if he was angry or upset. *Have I gone too far?* Maybe he didn't want to—

Her mind short-circuited when he dragged her upwards, until she was on the very tips of her toes, and took her mouth. *Yes.* Everything inside of her whispered and yearned. Her fingers dug into his shoulders. *If I could kiss him forever, I'd die happy.* His tongue swept in, bold and strong. She whimpered as he shifted between her legs, pressing his growing erection into her. I *want him again.*

He walked her backwards. Some distant part of her heard something crash to the ground, noticed it was too loud, but she really didn't care when Zac was basically fucking her mouth. She smacked into the wall behind her. Zac pressed her deeper into it. She was hotly aware of how much bigger, heavier, taller he was, his masculine scent surrounding her. He pulled back a little from her mouth and they both took deep gulps of air.

"What?" Reagan whispered when he paused to stare at her.

He shook his head. "I don't know. You're…"

The intensity between them heightened.

"I'm amazing? I'm beautiful? I'm what?" she said, trying to ease the sudden tension in him.

Reagan traced his smile with a finger. "There you are."

She felt proud that she could make him happy, even if it was for a moment.

"You're so modest."

"You mean like you're modest, Mr. Champion?" she teased.

"You're such a vixen."

A vixen—ooh, she had plenty to say to that, except Zac reached for her shirt and made short work of her buttons. It lay forgotten and tangled around her waist when he plumped up her breast, holding it up like an offering, before his mouth descended and enveloped her bra-covered nipple. She cried out, her clit throbbing in unison to the pull of his lips. God, the way he could have her go from laughing to mad to crazy with desire astounded her. No one affected her the way Zac did. She shifted restlessly. He pressed his hip into hers and stopped her lower half from moving.

"Zac." She tugged on his T-shirt.

He stopped sucking and as much as she wanted him

to continue doing what he was doing, the results were well worth it when he whipped his top over his head.

Reagan went immediately to stroke the bare skin of his stomach. His muscles were tight and ripped and gorgeous. *I'm in awe of him.* He'd worked hard to be where he was and it showed on his perfect body. Except it wasn't perfect she noticed when she looked closer. A smattering of light brown hair circled his belly button, not much, but what caught her attention was the faded brown scar right below it. Asking what happened would be pointless, because she knew what had happened. Sheriff Quinn. And this probably wasn't the only scar Zac had, she realized angrily. How many others were there smattered across his body that she had never noticed? Was it—*Nope, nope, I'm not going to let that selfish, horrible bastard ruin this moment for me or Zac. I want to stay in the here and now.*

"Reagan," Zac said, drawing her attention to the fact that she stood frozen, with her hands on his chest. "Is this too much for you to handle?"

"No!" she said, quickly. "Have I told you how pretty you are?"

He rolled his eyes. "No and I don't want to hear it."

"Pretty, pretty—"

She giggled as they kissed. Short, drugging kisses that had her head spinning and her laughter dying in her throat. *Oh.* Her hands ascended upwards to the smooth edge of his nipples. She pressed down on them and he gasped. It was so sexy she decided to do it again. Or better yet, her mouth drifted away from his to lick at the small tight nub, as her hair fell over her shoulders.

"Oh fuck," he gritted out.

She hummed with pleasure when he unclasped her

bra. She slipped out of it, letting it drop to the ground. With her tongue, she traced his chest, felt him smooth and rough beneath her, until she reached the cords of his neck. His throat convulsed when she nipped at the skin. She loved how sensitive he was, like he was aware of her every touch just as she was of his.

He squeezed her right breast, rolling her nipple between his fingers. She dug her fingernails into his back as everything inside of her throbbed and light sparked behind her eyelids. *Too much, not enough, more, more.* He kept rolling her nipple, sending tingles of pleasure down her spine. She craved relief more than her next breath.

Reagan rocked into him, hoping that the friction would help. If anything, it was worse. Zac must have felt the same way, because he attacked the button and zipper of her jeans. She helped him undo it, just as frantic. She moaned into his mouth, her lips bruised from the exquisite pleasure. Without preamble, he dragged her jeans and panties down her ass, before they got caught around her ankles. She managed to kick them off with desperate, jerky movements.

Zac dipped his finger into her pussy and began to thrust. Reagan couldn't breathe. She stopped giving him her mouth, throwing her head back. She reached for his wrist, not to stop him, but to just hold on. She didn't know how empty she'd been until he'd filled her and she felt close to too full as he added another finger. *I can't even think of how much better it'll be with his cock inside of me.* She knew how good it could be.

"Zac," she cried out, feeling him shift as he continued to finger-fuck her.

He buried his face in her neck, lips sucking on her

skin. Her chest was tight, Reagan's breath coming out in pants as she built fast towards a pleasure that was going to be so intense, she was already shuddering with it.

"Zac!"

"I've got you, Ree," he murmured against her neck.

"Oh god. I can't." She caressed his wrist.

She was right on the edge.

"Don't come yet," he said, but added, "I want to feel you come around my cock."

She tightened harder around his fingers, close to going off the edge. *How am I supposed to stop now,* she felt like wailing.

"Fuck, fuck, Ree," he gasped, before pulling his fingers out of her.

The only reason why she didn't curse him out was because he went to work on his jeans. Zac lowered his zipper while pulling out his wallet from his back pocket. He got out a condom and threw the wallet behind him. Hands shaking, he ripped the packet open and then shoved down his jeans and boxers. His cock was so hard and thick. He gripped the base of it and stroked upwards. Her clit throbbed as she watched him. He slid the condom down his length.

Yes, finally. His eyes fell on her. Zac pushed apart her knees and stepped between them. It was a tight fit. He bent his knees and used his fist to angle his cock upwards into her pussy.

The head was broad as it pushed inside. So good. It burned as inch by inch, he got deeper inside of her, until he let go and all of him was in her. So full. He was a lot bigger and longer than two fingers. He gripped her waist and pulled her up the wall. She slid up the length of his cock as he did that, until only the tip remained and then he slammed her back down.

"Ah! Zac!" She made a sound that would have embarrassed her at any other time. Something between a whimper and a moan.

He cursed softly as he began to thrust shallowly into her.

And because of the tight fit, his pelvic bone ground into her clit.

She clung to him, gasping. Blindly, she peppered kisses down his cheek until she found his mouth. He groaned, his hands on her waist like a vise as he bent his knees even more and thrust up harder into her. *Oh shit. Oh shit.* It felt incredible. Her body shook with need and Reagan knew she was seconds away from having the best orgasm of her life.

"Zac, I'm going to come," she told him, desperately. She ground down into him, tightening around him.

"Fuck. Fuck."

She knew he'd given up on prolonging the inevitable when he used his thumb to rub her clit as he fucked her again and again.

"Come."

And that was all it took.

Pleasure, unlike any she'd felt before, overtook her. She yelled out her orgasm into his mouth, babbling nonsense. She didn't even feel the wall as he kept thrusting, his chest rubbing against hers, his muscles rippling and sending bolts of pleasure through her. She could feel it in every part of her body.

He planted an arm on the wall beside her head while the other went to her knee as he pushed her legs even further apart. He throbbed inside of her as he moved deeper still. Once. Twice. Until he groaned and shuddered. She felt his orgasm and she couldn't stop herself from clamping down harder around him even if she wanted to.

"Fuck, Ree."

He released her mouth and dropped his forehead onto her shoulder. He straightened his knees and lifted her further up the wall. Her hands drifted into his dirty blond hair slowly. Out of breath, her heart beat wildly. His did too. They were sweaty and plastered together. And though Zac had done most of the heavy lifting, she could begin to feel the effects of what they had just done. Not that she cared.

I can't believe we just did that, Reagan thought. Again. She twirled his hair around her finger, dropping a kiss on the cord of his neck. He was softening inside of her, still half-hard. She smiled.

Zac straightened his arm over Reagan's head and pushed himself off. He didn't look at her as he pulled out. Reagan gasped a little.

"You okay?" he asked, lowering her carefully to the ground, but not letting go.

That was definitely a good thing. Reagan didn't think her legs could support her yet.

"I'm okay," she said. "Just… I can still feel you."

He made a noise from the back of his throat. "You can't say things like that, Ree."

She rolled her eyes. "Why the fuck not?"

Zac pulled up her jeans and panties roughly, but she swiped his hands away and he let go, stepping back. Reagan zipped and buttoned her own jeans while he removed the condom and righted his clothes. Only when he got rid of the condom did he look at her again.

They stared at each other. Oh Lord, this was eerie.
This was almost exactly like last week. Sex in a closet,
check. Sex in a place where other people were in the
building, check. Regret on Zac's face, double check.

"Hi," Reagan said, trying to inject some humor into
the situation. "We really need to stop meeting like this."

"Reagan—" Zac began, managing to infuse so much
regret and dismay into just her name.

She smacked her hand over his mouth.

"No, it's okay, Zac. I get it. You don't need to say anything more."

Oh boy, did she get it. She pushed down the hurt
deep into the pit of her stomach. *I knew this was going
to be a long road and I'm still only at the beginning.*
She was not going to get discouraged just because Zac
was having regrets. Again.

He took hold of her wrist and moved her hand off his
mouth. She wanted to hold on to him, but he let her go.
Zac rarely touched her anymore, outside of sex, that is.

He looked at her solemnly.

"No, I don't think you do get it."

"You want me to forget this ever happened and for
us to go back to being friends. You think this thing between us is just a phase and if we keep on ignoring it,
it will eventually die. And you think if this happens
again between us, someone—namely one of my brothers—could find out and that might mean my family
will never talk to you again. How am I doing so far?"

He didn't say anything, but he didn't lose that look.
She sighed.

"We're good, Zac," she said.

"And what does being 'good' mean?" he asked.

"It means I'm not going to let you shove me into a

compartment in your mind that you can conveniently forget about. If you think I'm going to let you do that, you don't know me."

"Oh, I know you," he scoffed. "You only think you want me."

She gasped. "What the fuck does that mean?"

He laughed grimly. "You, Reagan Thomas, are one of the most persistent, bullheaded women that I know."

She poked him in the chest. "Take that back, Zachariah Quinn!"

"Nope." He shook his head. "You and I both know that the only reason why you want me is because you're so fixated on this idea of what it means to be with me."

Of all the idiotic things to say! She didn't know whether to stomp her feet or scream or cry.

"Is that what you think?" she asked quietly.

"It's what I know."

"You're so stupid."

She couldn't tell if Zac just had a really low opinion of her or if he just didn't believe anybody could ever want him for him. Either situation just left her feeling exhausted.

Zac opened his mouth to say something, but they were interrupted.

Knock. Knock. Knock.

"Hey. Are you guys okay in there? It's been a while." Aidan's voice floated through the door.

Oh shit, they had definitely been in here for too long. Reagan was lucky that Aidan had knocked. If it had been Dean who had come for her, he wouldn't have bothered. Zac gave her a look that said, *See what I mean? A few minutes earlier and Aidan would have heard you crying out in pleasure while I fucked you.*

So maybe they needed to learn the definition of discretion, but it still didn't change her feelings or her plan.

"This isn't over between us," she hissed under her breath.

She walked towards the closet door.

"Oh yes, it is," Zac said, behind her.

Reagan yanked open the door and stepped outside, forcing Aidan to take a giant step back.

Aidan raised an eyebrow when he looked at her.

"Are you feeling better?" Aidan asked.

"No," she said honestly. "But I will."

She wasn't going to take no for an answer anymore. She fell into step with Aidan as they made their way back to the living room, with a quiet Zac following. Reagan forced herself not to turn around. She was only going to look forward. And that meant it was time to go after what she really wanted: Zachariah Quinn. No more defense. She was going on the offense.

Chapter Nine

"Zac, we need to meet." Reagan stood beside the window in her office, phone to her ear.

"Yeah, we do need to talk. Where are you? I'll come to you."

She was hoping he'd say that. "I'm at my office."

"Working on a Sunday, Ree. I hear being such a workaholic is bad for you."

She sighed, wishing it was just about being addicted to her work. Ever since she signed Trent as a client, Daniel had been acting, well, like a dick. A shoe company had just approached her wanting Trent to be the face of their brand, which would theoretically be great exposure for the rookie. But Reagan had finally decided it wasn't the right move for a number of reasons. First and foremost, the money being offered had been insultingly low since Trent was just starting out, but he was projected to go on to be one of the best players of his generation. So yeah, Reagan was not going to stand for her player being disrespected. Her hand tightened around the phone. Too fucking bad that Daniel didn't think the same and would not shut up about how her decision was the wrong one. So now she had to write a five-page report for her boss, Alan, outlining her plan of action for Trent to cover all her bases. A report that she wished she could shove up Daniel's patronizing, egocentric—

"Reagan?"

She cleared her throat. "I'm here."

"I'll be there in fifteen. Don't work too hard."

Zac hung up.

She was ready to confront him and this thing between them. Shivers of excitement and apprehension racked her body. She had been holding the phone for more than an hour, trying to work up the nerve to call him when she'd finally taken the plunge. But now that it was happening, there was only one thought going through her mind.

He's coming to me.

Taking a deep breath, she walked to her desk. *Sit down, or remain standing?* After a few minutes of hyperventilating, she finally decided on standing, but behind her desk. Available, but not too available. Intimidating, but not too intimidating.

It had practically taken all her energy to figure out what to wear. In the end, Reagan had settled on a pencil skirt that reached just above her knees. A white, soft, buttoned-up blouse that was tight around her breasts. She left her black hair to cascade down her shoulders. Minimal makeup, except for the nude lipstick that she had bought with Letty last week. She smoothed a hand down her skirt. She was ready. Ready to fight for what she wanted. She repeated the mantra over and over again as time slowly ticked by. She was still saying it as his shadow filled her doorway.

He leaned against the wall, arms crossed. He didn't say a word, just took her in. And she did the same.

Zac was dressed a hell of a lot more casually than he usually was and more than her. But he looked just as delicious. Black jeans clung to his narrow hips and were tucked into his large black boots. A similar blue shirt to the one he wore at family dinner and that matched his eyes perfectly stretched over his toned chest and showed off his well-muscled biceps. She really did like guys with impressive arms and she knew that Zac liked to work that part of his body. His dirty blond hair that was just a little too long to be labelled fashionable looked messy and windswept. But when didn't it? He had the habit of running his fingers through his hair whenever he was nervous or agitated. A tell she loved that he had. It made him seem so much more…approachable, like maybe he wasn't entirely out of her league.

He stepped into her office.

"Reagan."

"Zac," she said. "Come in. Sit down."

He sprawled in her visitor's chair, fingers tapping away on the arms. She swallowed at how comfortable he looked, at the way his energy seemed to make the room smaller, even though she was the one standing and he was the one sitting.

"Look, Ree, I don't like—"

She cut him off, the words rushing out of her mouth. "I have a proposition for you."

"A proposition?" He said the words like he had never heard of them before.

Moment of truth. Could she make this work? *No, I have to make this work.*

"I think we can safely say that we can't stay away from each other. Last night being a prime example of that—" she began.

"Last night was a mistake."

His words stung. Not unexpected, but they still stung.

"And what about the time before that?" she asked. "Or the time before that? You keep making the same mistake over and over again."

He stretched out his legs further, touching the edge of her desk. "Which is why we should stay away from each other."

"You and I both know that's impossible. We run in the same circles. You're part of my family." She rolled her eyes. "We can't just ignore each other and we were stupid to think otherwise."

"I guess you have a better idea, then?"

It was the perfect opening, but still she hesitated. Once she spoke, Reagan could never get the words back. Things from here on out would always be different. There would be no more burying their heads in the sand.

He wants me and he likes me. Even if it might only be friendship right now, she was sure of that if nothing else and relationships had been built on less.

Here goes nothing. She put her hands on the desk and leaned forward.

"As a matter of fact, I do have a better idea," she said firmly. "I think we should date."

His fingers stopped tapping. "Excuse me?"

She raised her chin. "You heard me. We should date."

"As in go out for dinner, hold hands, have an awkward conversation getting to know one another, a platonic kiss at the end of the night followed by me sending you flowers the next day. As in that dating?"

If she wasn't so wound up, Reagan would have laughed at his description.

Zac shook his head. "You're not going to let go of

this idea of dating me, are you? I've already told you, Ree. It's not a good idea."

"Why?"

"Why?" He snorted. "I can think of a million reasons to why us dating would be a bad idea. Not the least of which, you and I don't suit."

Ouch. She tried to keep her face blank, but good god he was bad for a girl's ego. *Nobody said this was going to be easy, Reagan. Pull up your big girl panties.*

"We suited last night when you fucked me. You want me, don't deny it," she said, sharply.

He shrugged. "Was last night good? Yeah. Do I want to have sex with you again? Of course, I do. I'm not dead. But it's not worth losing everything over. I've realized that I want you as a friend more than I want to have sex with you."

"And having sex with me would mean that we could no longer be friends?"

When he nodded so casually, she felt the brief spike of pain. Her hands curled into fists, her nails biting into her palms. Could he really get over her, them, so quickly? Had that moment been just sex, nothing less, nothing more?

Breathe, Reagan. She was finding it hard to breathe through the pain though. *What is the point of doing this?* she thought. This was a terrible, terrible idea. She needed to stop listening to her heart and start listening to Zac's words. Again and again, he told her she wasn't what he wanted. And again and again, she ignored him because of what? She couldn't imagine him not feeling the same way that she did? That was her own arrogance speaking. No more.

Reagan opened her mouth, determined not to let the

jerk see how much he'd hurt her, to give him exactly what he wanted. But then she noticed what she hadn't before.

Zac was still clenching his jaw, his fingers gripping the arm of the chair and she knew it was to stop himself from running his hands through his hair. If this was such an easy decision for him, why was he so tense? His blue eyes never looked at her directly, focusing on some spot over her shoulder. He couldn't even look at her. Oh! She was an idiot. She wasn't going to listen to his words; she was going to listen to his body.

Her lips curved into a smile.

"Liar," Reagan whispered.

"What?"

"I said that you, Zachariah Quinn, are a liar." She walked around the desk, taking her time doing so, and came to stand in front of him.

He watched her with that same look he had last night. Like he couldn't decide whether he wanted to be angry with her or keep on eye-fucking her.

"You are such a liar," Reagan said, triumphantly.

"I'm lying? Why would you think I'm lying?"

"Uh, maybe because your eyes are currently glued to my legs?"

Said eyes finally flickered up to meet hers. The amount of heat she saw in them made her stomach clench in excitement and made her wonder how she could have ever doubted whether he still wanted her. At least physically. She brushed that thought aside. He might only want her body for now, but her plan would work. He desired her and she was going to use that to show him that there was a fine line between lust and love. She needed to stop second-guessing herself and move forward.

"Who's eye-fucking who now?" she taunted, smugly.

He laughed. She soaked it in.

"You do have great legs," he finally acknowledged.

"Thanks," she said lightly, boosting herself up to sit on the edge of her desk. "I like them myself."

"I've never denied wanting you, Reagan. I just don't see how wanting you and dating you amount to the same thing."

She lifted one leg up to place it on the arm of his chair. He moved his hand out of the way and her lace-up open-toe heel took its place. Her pencil skirt had climbed up to her thighs. She was wearing white stockings that were being held up by garters. From the way she was sitting, the thin straps were all that he could see, but it was enough. A muscle in his jaw ticked.

She had rolled her stockings on in the morning, imagining his reaction. She had turned herself on just thinking about it. And now she could hardly resist the urge to look down at the bulge in his jeans and see if he was getting hard. She was definitely wet and getting wetter thinking about Zac touching her.

"One month."

"One month?" He raised an eyebrow.

"One month," she reaffirmed. "Give me one month to prove to you that wanting me and dating me doesn't have to be mutually exclusive. That we just might work."

She watched as he thought about it, trying hard to maintain the cool and unaffected look on her face. If he only knew that his response meant everything to her… oh god, she wanted to shake so badly and take back every single thing she had just said.

"And what if I get bored before the month is over?"

Taken aback, she didn't know what to say. She'd never imagined he could get bored of her when every moment with him felt too short. Like it'd never be enough. *And if he can get bored of me...* Her heart stuttered with the pain of that thought.

"We'll wait until the month is over and I guess," she said slowly, "if you are still bored by the end of the month, then I will have my answer and you would get the satisfaction of proving me wrong."

"One month is too long," he said.

"Three weeks."

He shook his head.

"Two weeks and a half?"

He shook his head again.

"Two weeks," she said, desperately. "It can't be any shorter than that."

Zac stood up. About to lower her leg to the ground, he stopped her by putting a hand on her stocking-clad knee. Reagan's heart rate kicked up a notch. His body screamed desire and it was all aimed wonderfully at her. His callused hand slid upwards, leaving goose bumps in its wake. He pushed up her pencil skirt even further, until he touched her bare skin and the straps of her garters. His fingers played with her buttons. She fought the urge to moan.

"Or," he started, as he stepped closer in between her legs, while simultaneously putting his hand on her ass and pushing her further to the edge of the desk.

She lifted her other leg onto the arm of the chair to stop herself from toppling over. It had the effect of caging him in and pressing them together from hip to chest. All his delicious heat and hard body against her.

"We could make this even more interesting."

"Interesting, how?" she said breathlessly.

She could barely pay attention to his words, not with him touching her the way he was touching her. Especially when he began to caress her other knee.

"I think we should define exactly what you mean by dating. And how often would we be dating anyway? Will we be seeing each other every day? Will I be deciding where we go and what we will do or will you? Will we have sex or are we going to pretend that the last couple of weeks didn't happen?"

Oh, this I have an answer to.

"Since I only have two weeks, I think I should be allowed to capitalize on every moment, don't you think?" She didn't wait for him to answer but plowed on. "Here are the rules: we will go on a date every other day starting from tomorrow and I will arrange all the dates. Dates that will involve going out and doing things a normal couple would do. Whatever happens, happens. We will be a couple in every sense of the word. At least for the next two weeks. So that's a definite yes to the sex."

Her thin stockings were no barrier against the warmth of his palms.

"That doesn't seem fair," he murmured.

"What doesn't seem fair?" She tipped her head back a little, already feeling drunk on his proximity.

"That you get to arrange all the dates. If you want us to date, then you need to experience what it truly means to date me and that means *I* should arrange the dates."

She shook her head. "No way."

"Fine, you can arrange one of them."

"Fuck no. You can arrange one of them and I'll arrange the rest of them."

"Seventy-thirty, then."

"Seventy me and thirty you. I will agree to that."

"Nope. Seventy me and thirty you."

"I repeat myself, fuck no. Sixty-forty."

"Let's just go fifty-fifty. I have one week and you have one week."

"Okay," she said slowly. "That seems fair."

They stared at each other.

"Two weeks?" he asked again.

"Two weeks," she confirmed, resolutely.

"And once those two weeks are up, no hard feelings, right?" He watched her carefully. "I mean it, Ree. If I agree to this, you have to promise that you won't act weird in front of your family and that they will never, ever find out about this."

She swallowed. "Would it really be the end of the world if they knew?"

She was desperate for the answer. She understood why her family was so important to him—she knew the basics of how he had been raised. Had seen some of it firsthand when he would come around her house limping and with a busted lip. Not to mention that night at Muckberry Field. She had also once bandaged his hand when he had punched a wall in their corridor. She had never told anyone the truth and had gladly taken the blame for the sudden hole in the wall.

"How do you think your brothers would react if they found out we had kissed? Had sex? Or that we were even having this conversation?"

She gave him a weary smile. "They would go apeshit."

"Exactly."

She leaned into him. "I've known you my whole life,

Zachariah Quinn, and for roughly half my life you've annoyed me, filled me with more anger than I thought possible. Confused me beyond belief and teased me mercilessly. Especially, when I made the stupid mistake of dyeing my hair red."

He twined a strand of her black hair around his finger. "You, Reagan Thomas, are not a redhead. You looked like a science experiment gone wrong."

"See! You make me so mad! But even when you are driving me mad, I can't forget that you are the person who made sure Anna Liu in eighth grade stopped picking on me. Or that you helped me move into my dorm freshman year and stayed with me all night, talking and eating pizza. Or that kissing you sets my whole body on fire."

Reagan couldn't decipher the look in his eyes. But Zac didn't step back, so she took it as a sign that she hadn't completely freaked him out yet.

Suddenly tired, she shook her head. "I understand that you don't want to think dating me would be a good idea, but I think a part of you is at least intrigued. Don't you want to see if all this combustible sexual tension between us could be more?"

Chapter Ten

Zachariah Quinn was fucked.

Every inch of his body was pressed against Reagan. He could feel her heart beating against his own. Could feel her breath tickling the side of his neck as he stared down at her.

All his plans to resist her had gone down the drain the moment she had opened her mouth. Hell, the moment he had walked into the office and laid eyes on her. And now, she was enticing him to spend every waking moment with her for the next two weeks to… what? Date?

Wait. Wait. He thought fast. This could be a good thing. What had Dean said? *"All you have to do is show her all the things she would hate to have in a relationship and voila. She stops wanting to date you, the magic goes out of the mystery and you can start being around each other without wanting to tear each other's clothes off."*

This was the key to getting Reagan to back off. To stop having this delusion of a happily-ever-after between them when it would never happen. He didn't need to convince her, he needed to *show* her. And let her come to the right conclusion herself. If he kept trying to push her away, she only dug in her heels more, so he needed *her* to be the one to give up. To make her realize that dating him was the worst mistake of her life. She might have one week to arrange their dates, but the first week would be his and that was all he needed. One week where he could be in the driver's seat and show her the truth. *That we're not meant to be together and all I'll ever do is hurt her.* A guy like him, with a background like his, was not built for a relationship.

"Fine," Zac announced suddenly.

She blinked slowly, deliberately. Looking owl-like with her big, brown eyes.

"Fine?"

"Yes, fine. We'll date for two weeks, but I've got some rules of my own."

When she would have spoken, he placed a single finger on her lips.

"Uh-uh. You told me what your rules were and now I am going to tell you what mine are. Are you listening?"

She nodded.

"Good. Here's the deal: for the next week, while it is my turn, I decide what we do, where we go and what we see on these dates. That means if I decide we're going to a zoo, then we're going to a fucking zoo. And…for the next week, I'm in control of our sex lives."

"What?" she squeaked behind his finger.

God, she's cute. He shot her an amused look. "You heard me. If we're feeling it at the zoo to have sex in one of the stalls, we'll do it. If I tell you to bend over and let me fuck you, we do it. If we're going to date then you're going to let me try out every single fantasy I've ever had over the years of you and me."

He was going to kill two birds with one stone: have

Reagan realize the impossibility of things working out between them and achieve what he had always wanted to achieve—to purge Reagan out of his system. It has to work, there's no other option and no other way. He heard Dean laughing maniacally in the back of his mind and he pushed it roughly away.

"That…" She licked her lips. "That isn't fair. Maybe I have fantasies I want to try out."

Holy shit.

Zac stared. He was hard just thinking about Reagan thinking about sex-induced fantasies.

"That's good." He cleared his throat. "I'm willing to entertain any fantasies you might want to try out—"

"How kind of you," she said dryly, her cheeks stained red.

I'm being an asshole. He opened his mouth to apologize, but stopped. *The whole point of this is so that she stops liking you romantically.* And no matter how much it might suck, if he didn't stop treating her like she was the most precious person in his life, she wasn't going to stop. So he gritted his teeth.

"But you can do that in your week," he finished. "During my week, it's my rules and my decisions. Are we in agreement?"

Reagan looked like she wanted to say something more, her eyes shifting away from his as she thought deeply about everything. He waited patiently, letting his hands caress her soft and gorgeous skin. And those stockings and garters… *She is trying to kill me.*

"Okay," she said, nodding.

Fuck yes. That meant for the next week, he wasn't going to think about their family, or whether or not they could ever come back from this, or if this was right or wrong. For the next week, he was going to think about touching Reagan as much as possible, without feeling guilty about it. But he wasn't just allowed to think about sinking his cock into her, or kissing her, or hearing those excited moans from her mouth, he could actually do it and he was going to enjoy having her, over and over again. Which reminded him.

"I want you. Here and now."

"Here?" she said, breathlessly. "Now?"

"Yes."

Zac ran his hands up her legs, until he reached her skirt, pushing it further up her thighs, making a sound when he saw her white thong. *I can't believe I get to touch her again.* His hands trembled slightly. It was like the sweetest dream that never ended or a fantasy come to life. Things like this didn't usually happen to him. Zac was more used to disappointment, not being able to buy that console because his mom was too scared of his father's reaction, or not going to the class sleepover at the library because his dad decided he needed another lesson in discipline. His hockey career was the only thing he'd ever succeeded in and he wouldn't have that if it wasn't for the Thomas family—*Fuck, don't think about that.* Think about her, think about Reagan. There was going to be no guilt in what happened between them.

She reached up and grabbed his shirt between her fists.

"Fuck me," he whispered. "That is hot."

She stared up at him. "Thanks."

"But the thong has to go."

And he didn't waste any time getting that done. He pulled it down.

"Lift up," he told her.

She lifted up and he easily slid it off, dropping it to the ground. He stroked Reagan's inner thighs, coming close to her center, and almost smiled when her breathing deepened.

"Stop teasing me," she whispered.

"Am I teasing you?" he asked, amused.

"You know you are."

He could see glimpses of how wet and puffy her pussy looked. Fuck, he knew exactly how he was teasing her, but did he care? Not particularly, no, because he wanted her on the edge of her seat, literally and figuratively. *I want her out of her mind with pleasure and her thoughts to be consumed with nothing but me.* And when she was right at her peak, he'd leave her, cursing him out and spitting mad.

"Tell me exactly what you want me to do, Ree, and maybe I'll consider doing it."

She opened her mouth to answer the question, but he stole the words from her mouth. He kissed her. She moaned, kissing him back enthusiastically. She tasted like *her*—brilliance and sunshine all rolled into one with a hint of cinnamon, her favorite flavor in her coffee. He broke the kiss, not because he wanted to stop, but because he was dying to taste her somewhere else. *Just a little*, he told himself, *and then I'll stop and she'll see how much of an asshole I am.*

Her eyes were still closed as he pressed a hand to her stomach.

"Lean back."

He dropped to his knees before her, gripping her waist as she did what he asked and leaned back, legs wide open, her feet still on the arms of the chair. Tipping her hips upwards using his hold on her waist, it gave him his first full look of her. His cock thickened and grew. Fuck, so pretty. Completely bare. And so fucking wet. He breathed in deep, her musky and sweet smell. He groaned, so good and so damn addictive, it washed away all of his other plans.

"Do you know how fucking perfect your pussy is?"

She let out a startled laugh. "Um, no?"

"Well, it is. Just fucking perfect."

Zac pressed his mouth gently on her right inner thigh. The scent of her was strong here and he wanted more and more. He ran his tongue downwards, until he reached the lips of her pussy. He licked her and she shook.

Her hands slid into his hair, clinging, crying out as his tongue brushed her clit. *Don't worry, I'm not going anywhere, not until you give me exactly what I want.*

"Zac!"

He had no thoughts in his head other than pleasuring her. He forgot about her family and his and that he never planned to go this far. He wanted her a quivering mess, to be left wrecked by him. Zac caressed her thighs as he enjoyed the taste of her. He hummed against her and she cried out his name again, his cock throbbing in his jeans. Fuck yes, nothing got him going more than having Ree say his name like he was giving her so much pleasure she couldn't contain herself. *I love knowing that she craves me as much as I crave her.*

He plunged his tongue inside of her and her core tightened. She rocked into his mouth as he flicked his tongue, before pulling out and then into her again. He pressed his palm desperately against his jeans to stop himself from shooting his come like a teenager. His body felt hot, his leather jacket separating him from what he truly wanted, which was to be skin against skin. To feel her heart beating beneath his.

He used his teeth, scrapping her clit, before sucking her into his mouth as he ate her out in earnest. Her hands fell away from his hair and she fell backwards onto her desk, spine arching, legs quivering. When he felt her pussy tightening even further around his tongue, he knew she was close and even though he couldn't reach in deep enough, to really hit the spot that would make her come, he was determined to make her go over. *Come on, Ree, give me what I want. Fuck, all I want to do is to unzip myself, pull out my cock and thrust into her.* He was so desperate for it, he could already imagine and feel her coming around him as he gently coaxed another orgasm out of her. Except that wasn't the plan. It'd only hurt her more if he let her assume this was more than the physical between them and he'd already given in to her more than he was supposed to. Right now, he was in control and he needed to keep it that way. He gave one last swipe of his tongue before he finally pulled away. Pulling down her skirt, he covered her up, noticing that she wasn't moving anymore, completely wiped out.

Zac got to his feet, wiping his mouth with the back of his hand. Not that he couldn't still taste her. He stared down at her lying flat on her back, her hair a mess around her face, chest rising and falling rapidly, eyes dilated. He was going to be jerking himself later at home, remembering her smell and taste and the way she looked. *She is gorgeous.*

"Um…" she started, before her voice trailed off.

"I'll pick you up tomorrow at 7:30 pm. Text you more

about it tomorrow," he said, smiling. "You don't need to see me out."

He was about to walk away when he noticed the white thong on the floor. Without even thinking about it, he picked it up and stuffed it into his back pocket.

"This is mine," he told her.

"Okay," she said, nodding.

He grinned. "If I had known all it took to get you to be so agreeable was to put my mouth on you, I would have done this a long time ago."

Reagan didn't even reply as Zac left.

Shutting the door behind himself, he walked two steps when he heard the unmistakable sound of Reagan's head hitting the desk and her whispering "stupid, stupid" over and over again.

Zac grinned as he walked down the hall. Oh yeah, Reagan Thomas had no idea what she had gotten herself into. By the end of the week, she was going to realize just how "stupid" it was to date him.

Chapter Eleven

Reagan stood in her bedroom, in front of her mirror. She stared at the dress she wore with a grimace. It was a cream-colored dress with a one-shoulder strap. It was loose around her breasts and then grew tight around her ass and thighs, before it ended at her calves. She pulled her hair up in an elaborate bun that had taken her most of the day to master—thank you, internet tutorials! And she paired the dress with laced open-toe stilettos, quite similar to the ones she had been wearing at her office yesterday, but these were white to match her dress. Overall, it worked, but still there was something missing. And she had no idea what it was.

She let out a squeal of frustration.

"I don't know! I don't know!"

She didn't even have an idea of where they were going tonight. Zac had only sent her one text: I'll be over at 7:30 pm. Dress formal. And that was it! No hint or clue about where they were going, beyond "dress formal." But what did that mean? Were they going to an event? An opening of some sort? To a restaurant? To a party? There were so many places he could be taking her to, and the possibilities were killing her.

Reagan was not the best at getting dressed for a normal event, but when she had barely any information to go on, she was terrible.

Her phone rang. She looked over her shoulder, to where she had left it on her bed. She reached over and grabbed it. She answered it on the second ring.

"Are you freaking out?" Letty asked immediately.

She laughed, going for confident, but instead sounding manic.

"No."

"Yeah, you are. I can hear it in your voice."

"Okay, yes. I'm freaking the fuck out. Help," she urged Letty. "I have no idea what to wear and Zac's meant to be here in…"

She looked at her alarm clock on her bedside table (luckily, she managed to fix it, so now Callum would never know) and groaned.

"Thirty minutes. I'm so screwed."

"What are you wearing now?"

"Here, let me send you a pic."

Reagan took a picture of herself and sent it to Letty. She waited for a few seconds, while Letty received it.

"Girl," Letty said, "that dress is hot! And it does amazing things for your ass."

"You think so?" Reagan asked, hesitantly.

"Yes! Stop worrying, Reagan."

Letty was right. Zac was going to see that dating her was the best decision of his life and that he wasn't going to be disappointed. Or bored. She needed to stop worrying.

"It's going to be okay," Letty assured her. "Now go and have fun. Can't wait to hear all about it tomorrow!"

Reagan was still laughing even as she hung up.

She threw her phone back onto her bed. She looked at

herself in the mirror again. Okay, so what if she didn't have the biggest boobs or ass in the world? Zac seemed to like her body well enough. He had sex with her both at Steven's party and at her dad's house like he couldn't get enough of her. And that sound he had made when he was eating her out on her work desk? Oh, that had turned her on almost as much as what his mouth was doing. And not to mention, *she* liked herself.

She cocked her shoulders back. Tonight, she was going to relax and have fun and let Zac show her what "dating" him meant. And for the first time since the morning, she was excited.

Half an hour later, exactly at 7:30 pm, the doorbell rang.

Reagan walked out of her bedroom, down the hall-way to the front door. She smoothed her dress, taking a deep breath. *You can do this, Reagan. You've only been waiting for this day to come for ten years. This is your moment.*

She opened the door.

"Holy shit."

She hadn't even realized she had said that aloud. She was too mesmerized by the sight of Zachariah Quinn in a suit. But where the one at Steven's party had been a charcoal gray, this was a gray that was essentially black. It was form fitting, showcasing his slim waist and broad shoulders. His hair was perfect and slicked back so she could see his face in all its natural glory. Unlike the shadow he had been rocking yesterday, he was clean shaven. His piercing blue eyes met hers.

"Good evening, Reagan," he said, smiling. "These are for you."

She only noticed the bouquet of roses he was holding when he held them out to her.

"You got me flowers?" she whispered, a small line forming between her eyebrows.

She took them from him and—because isn't that what everyone is supposed to do?—she pressed her nose to one of the roses and breathed in deep. *Mm, roses smell like roses. Good to know.*

"I hope you like them."

She nodded at him. "Thank you."

No one had ever given her flowers before.

"You're welcome."

"I didn't think you were the kind of boy who gives a girl flowers."

"This is a date." He shrugged. "And every girl deserves flowers."

"Way to make me feel special."

When he said nothing, Reagan's frown deepened.

"Okay, let me just put them in a vase," she said. "Come in. It will only take a sec."

He stepped into her house as she spun away and went to find a vase. She found one in her kitchen. She dumped the roses in it, filled it with water and left it sitting on her windowsill. Reagan hurried back to the living room. Zac was in the middle of the hall, waiting for her. Could the man be any more gorgeous? *Be still, my over-beating heart.*

"Okay, I'm ready."

She grabbed her coat and was about to put it on, when he stopped her.

"Here, let me help you."

He took the coat from her and held it out. She put her arms in and Zac helped her into it. She shivered when his fingers skimmed her bare neck. He held out an arm and she placed her hand gently on the inside of his elbow.

"I didn't know you were such a gentleman," Reagan murmured as they exited her house, shutting the door behind her.

They walked out of the apartment complex together, arm in arm. At 7:30 pm, during summer, it was warm evening though the sun had just set. The sky was a navy color and there was barely a single cloud. A perfect still summer night.

"I've always been a gentleman," he replied.

"Mm, I guess you were a gentleman yesterday when you ate me out without asking for anything in return," she teased.

Zac said nothing. *Okay, then*, she thought, biting her lip. She glanced at him, but he didn't look angry at her comment. He looked calm. *I guess he has nothing to say or he's nervous*? This was a huge step for both of them.

His black Lexus was parked right out front and they made their way towards it.

"Have I told you how beautiful you look yet?" he suddenly asked her.

She shook her head.

"You look beautiful."

Wow. She almost melted entirely from his words.

They reached his car and he opened the door for her. Yeah, definitely a gentleman. She could get used to that. Reagan slid inside. He walked around the car and into the driver's seat.

"Where are we going?" she asked.

She expected him to say something like "it's a surprise," but he shocked her by telling her the truth.

"We're going to La Maison restaurant," Zac said, as he drove them down the road.

"La Maison? That's a really fancy restaurant."

He shot her a small smile.

"You know," she said, "I wouldn't mind just hitting a burger joint or that little pizza joint we went to last year near your place—what was it called?"

He shrugged. "Can't remember."

"Nigel's Pizza!" Reagan recalled, clapping her hands together. "Their pizza was amazing!"

Her mouth watered just remembering how the cheese had tasted and how fresh the ingredients were. And the way Zac had teased her about her pizza choices: he didn't think pineapple counted as a topping, but it definitely did. And when it was paired with prawns, it was wonderful.

"Reagan," Zac said, calmly, pulling her out of her memories. "I already made reservations for La Maison."

"Oh."

She slouched in her seat, deflated.

The rest of the journey was taken up in silence. It took them thirty minutes to get there. It was a long time of just dead air and it gave Reagan a lot of time to think. What the hell was going through Zac's mind? *Is he angry with me?* He had seemed fine yesterday and usually when he was quiet, it was because he'd lost a game or it had something to do with his parents. Since Reagan didn't think it was the latter—surely she'd know if his dad or mom were up to something—then it must be because he had a bad practice. *Yep*, she nodded to herself, *that must be it.*

"We're here," Zac announced.

He stopped the car right in front of the restaurant. Reagan reached for the handle.

"Wait! Let me get that for you."

He got out of the car and, before she could tell him there was no need since she had been opening and closing doors for far longer than she had been tying her own shoes and brushing her own teeth, he had rounded the car and helped her out. He shut the door.

"Thank you. I've always needed a strong man to help me with those pesky little things." She grinned at him.

Zac stared at her. "A gentleman always helps a lady."

The grin slowly slipped off her face. "I just meant... Never mind."

The restaurant was so fancy it had valet parking. Zac handed his keys over to the man standing behind the podium. He pressed a hand to Reagan's back and walked them into the restaurant.

A woman wearing one of those sophisticated waitress outfits greeted them.

"Good evening, Mr. Quinn and Miss Thomas, could I please take your coat?"

Nice, they knew who they were. *Talk about celebrity status.* She wanted to say that to Zac, but something made her swallow her words. If he was upset because of practice, maybe it would be best if she gave him a while to get out of this funk. Again, Zac helped her with her coat and handed it over to the woman.

"Simmons will show you both to your table," she told them.

A man appeared out of nowhere. He indicated for them to follow and began walking. Simmons pushed open the double doors and escorted them to a table tucked away in the corner. The restaurant was mostly full, but no one turned and looked at them. Most people were preoccupied with themselves.

La Maison was decorated in shades of white and orange with a chandelier in the center, dripping crystals. The lights were dim. There was a single candle in the middle of their table and it was mostly there for ambience. It was so romantic and perfect.

"Thank you," she said to the waiter, with a smile as she sat down.

Zac got into his seat across from her.

"I'll leave you alone for a moment while you decide," Simmons said, before disappearing.

"This place is fancy," she said, ogling the tableware. "Look, isn't that Michelle McFadden, media mogul?"

"Most of the people who come here are famous or semi-famous," Zac said, casually as he flicked through the menu. "That's why this restaurant is really well-known. They're very good at privacy."

Mm, that would make sense. Reagan opened her menu and looked at her choices.

"What are you planning on getting?" she asked. "I was thinking of getting steak. Everything else seems a bit too fancy."

Zac closed his menu and looked her right in the eye, suddenly very serious.

"Do you not like the place, Reagan?"

She shook her head. "No. I love it! It's perfect."

It looked like every romantic date night scene from movies so it definitely ticked all the right boxes. But… Reagan didn't want to whine. She had hoped that being somewhere like this would mean that Zac would loosen up, not go the opposite way.

He smiled. "Good."

Simmons returned.

"We'll have one steak and one lemon cockerel. And a bottle of pinot noir," Zac told him as he handed back his menu.

She held out hers and Simmons took it.

"Very good choices, sir. They will take a few minutes to prepare."

"Not a problem," Zac said.

Simmons disappeared before coming back a second later to pour them their drinks and leave them the bottle and then left again.

"Not going for red meat tonight? Feeling sick, Zac?"

"I'm on a strict diet."

Zac sat straight up in his chair, taking a sip of his wine.

"I didn't know you liked wine," she said, intrigued.

"I only drink it in places like this."

"You could have ordered beer. I'm sure they wouldn't have minded. I'm kind of tempted to get beer myself." She said the last few words in a low voice as if she was confiding in him a secret.

Reagan expected him to raise an eyebrow at that and give her a mock-lecture about what a place like this would do if they ordered beer instead of vintage wine.

"Would you like me to get you one?" Zac asked instead.

"Um, no, it's okay." She took a sip of her wine and wished desperately it was beer. Or something stronger, like vodka or tequila.

"So…" she started.

He didn't say anything, just watched her.

"How was practice?"

"It was good. Normal," he answered.

Okay. Great. Reagan's eyes narrowed. If it wasn't work, then what the hell was going on? She wanted to shake the boy and ask him what was with all the awkward silences. They never ran out of things to say to each other, which was why she considered him to be one of her closest friends.

"How was work?"

She smiled gratefully. "It was good. I really enjoy working at Mitchells. The people are great and working with some of the biggest names in sports is really exciting. It's taking a lot longer to build my own client list of course, but I'm getting there."

"How's it going with your new client? Trent?"

"Yeah! I just started working with him! He's great. There's this shoe brand that wants him, but I don't think it's a good idea. I'm trying to find one that would be a better fit for him, except… Daniel, he wants Trent to take the deal. He's really not listening to me when I say it's a bad plan—what do you think?" she asked.

Zac shrugged. "I don't really have an opinion."

"Nothing? Do you think I should listen to Daniel, since you know he's been doing this for a lot longer than me, or should I listen to my instincts?"

"I think that it's your decision."

Reagan stared at him in disbelief. Well, that was helpful—not! The waiter interrupted them at that moment—thank god—to bring them their food. He placed their plates before them.

She cut into her steak and took a small bite. She groaned.

"Holy shit," she sighed. "This is really good. I don't think I've ever had steak that's tasted this amazing."

"Yes, it is really good."

"How's yours?"

"Good," he answered, looking down at his own dish as he cut into his vegetables.

And that was the end of all conversation. They ate their food in silence. Once their plates were devoid of food and they were cleared away, they both sat there. *Oh shit, oh shit.* Reagan racked her brain desperately, trying to search for something to talk about. This whole dating thing was on her and she did not want Zac already getting bored with it all.

"Should we get some dessert? Their chocolate cake looked to die for," she finally settled on.

"Sounds good. I can't eat too much, since I'm in the middle of conditioning," Zac said, tapping his fingers on the table.

"We could share it." She smiled.

"I'd prefer getting the lemon cheesecake actually."

"Oh, okay."

They ordered their individual cakes and ate them, while continuing on with their small talk. Eventually, they asked for the bill, picked up Reagan's coat at the front desk and left. The valet gave Zac his keys and they got into his car. During that whole time, a feeling swirled around in the pit of her stomach and her chest. She had no idea what it was, had no name for it, but it made her feel itchy beneath her skin.

As they were driving back home, Reagan turned and looked at Zac.

"That was nice," she said.

"It was."

"You had a good time?" she pressed.

"What was not to like?" he asked back. "You looked beautiful. The restaurant was good. The food was good. The conversation was good. And everything ran smoothly."

She gripped the top of her seat belt. Shit, everything *had* run smoothly. Everything had been great. No, everything had been perfect. But wait—the date wasn't over yet.

"You heard me. If we're feeling it at the zoo to have sex in one of the stalls, we'll do it. If I tell you to bend over and let me fuck you, we do it. If we're going to date then you're going to let me try out every single fantasy I've ever had over the years of you and me." Zac had said that to her last night and remembering that promise had her shifting in her seat in anticipation for some sexy time. She peeked at him from the corner of her eye.

Zac gripped the steering wheel with his right hand, his left lying on his powerful thigh. She didn't understand fully her fascination with his arms but watching his forearm flex made her pussy clench.

She was so deep in her fantasy world she didn't notice when they parked outside of her apartment. Not until he took off his seat belt and got out of his Lexus. Zac came to her side door and helped her out. Her fingers tingled, hypersensitive to every touch and movement of his.

They walked together to the front of her building. She was slightly unsteady on her feet but tried to shake it off. *Breathe, Reagan, you are going to need every breath during all the hot sex you're about to have.*

They paused outside of her door, facing each other. He stared down at her and she saw a flicker of something in his eyes. Yes, yes. He was going to kiss her. He stepped closer to her, but he didn't touch her. His face descended towards hers slowly.

Reagan leaned in, her eyes already fluttering shut with anticipation. But the kiss to her lips never came. Instead, she felt a slight brush against her cheek. Her eyes flew open. Zac stared down at her, with a smirk.

"See you later, Reagan."

And then he sauntered off, hands in his pockets. Reagan stood there, one hand on her cheek. *What the fuck just happened?*

Chapter Twelve

Three days after their first date, Reagan slid her phone into her pocket.

"Sorry," she said as she sat down at the corner table in the small, quaint coffee shop opposite their agency.

"It's cool," Letty said. "I know you have to always take your dad's call."

"Not always." She took a sip of her hot cinnamon latte.

The shop was half-full, but it was only the beginning of the lunch hour. Soon people would be coming by the truckload to feed their caffeine addiction.

Letty rolled her eyes. "Come on, I have never seen you reject a call from anybody in your family and if they ever need you to do something, you're down for it no matter what."

Reagan shifted uneasily in her chair. "That's not true."

"Last year, you helped Callum decorate his house even though you were in the middle of juggling three clients and that boy could have done it himself. You flew four hours to help Dean break up with his stalker girlfriend! Admit it, girl, you got a problem."

Do I have a problem? She shook her head. This was

just what families did. So maybe her dad was more protective than others and maybe she spent a lot of time cleaning up her brothers' messes. How else was she supposed to show them she loved them and that she was grateful for everything they've done for her?

"Enough about your family, give me the true deets. How did your date go last night? Was it better or worse than the one you had with him the night before last?" Letty leaned forward, her golden eyes bright with excitement.

A few days had passed since she had propositioned Zachariah and they had already been on two dates. Both had taken place at different expensive and upscale restaurants and had ended with Zac leaving her in front of her apartment with nothing more than a kiss on her cheek. And he kept giving her flowers—what was up with that? The first time it was sweet, but now it was just getting annoying. What was she supposed to do with all of them? Make a shrine? Reagan had a sinking feeling that tonight was going to be much of the same.

"It was perfect." She thought back over the night. Over every gesture, every word spoken, every move made and it just left her feeling bewildered. What had happened to the boy who wouldn't shut up about hockey stats or wouldn't let her make comments about the gaming world without a teasing reply? *And I can't believe I'm about to quote Charlie Puth, but: "we don't talk anymore."* What was worse than feeling bewildered though was feeling horny. Knowing how much pleasure Zac could give her was making the sexual tension between them worse than normal.

"If I had to rank it on a scale of one to ten, I would definitely say it was a ten. Hands down one of the most perfect dates I've ever been on. Both of them were... absolutely perfect."

"If they're perfect, why do you look like someone's just ran over your imaginary dog?"

Reagan sighed. She didn't feel as if someone had run over her imaginary dog. Maybe just scared it a little.

"I can't explain it to myself, explaining it to you might just give me an ulcer. All I know is that it was... perfect."

"You're going to have to give me more than that."

"Everything went perfectly. The food was perfect. The conversation was perfect. Hell, last night is a perfect example of why romantic clichés are such clichés."

Letty crossed one leg over the other, her black work skirt riding up a little to expose the tops of her tights-clad thighs. "All clichés have to start somewhere, right? And you got to experience the clichéd dream: the romantic candlelit dinner that every girl wants."

"But this is me." Reagan pointed to herself for extra emphasis. "Nothing ever goes that perfect when I'm involved. High school graduation? I tripped and fell on top of my principal. First time I tried alcohol? I threw up on my date and ended up in the hospital. I accidentally fed my date last month strawberries, even though he had told me he was allergic! We ended up in the ER for six hours. Are you sensing a theme here? Do you really want me to keep going, Letty? Because there are so many more awkward and embarrassing stories in my arsenal."

"So, what you are saying is that you would have been more comfortable if something had gone wrong?"

"Yes. No. Yes!"

Letty laughed.

"Look." Reagan breathed. "Nothing between me and Zac has ever gone perfect or easy and last night and the other night everything was. The candlelight. The flowers he gave me. The way he opened doors for me and tucked me into my chair. He was the perfect date and I'm…"

"Dissatisfied?" Letty nodded. "Have you ever thought Zac might be fucking with you?"

Reagan blinked.

"Maybe there is a reason why your dates have been going so perfectly?"

"That doesn't even make any sense. I know he doesn't think us dating would be a good idea, but what would be the point in making the date so wonderful when he could have sabotaged it…?" She trailed off as she started to think. "Because he knows me. He knows that if the date had started to go wrong, I would have guessed he was doing things to fuck it up and I would have dug my heels in. Instead, he did the opposite."

Letty snapped her fingers. "Bingo."

"That devious, crazy son of a bitch!" Reagan banged her fist against the table.

People around her jumped. Some gave her looks like *bitch, you cray cray* or *who let the mad person with the really expensive shoes in here?* Damn right, she was. And she was getting crazier by the second thinking over everything that had happened the night before now with this new information in mind. The way he smirked at her at the end when he leaned in and kissed her cheek? He was most definitely fucking with her!

"What are you going to do about it?"

Reagan glared. "What do you think I'm going to do about it? I'm going to nail his balls to the wall."

Letty grinned. "I want to say I feel sorry for him, but... I really don't."

"Don't feel sorry for him. By the time I'm done with the boy, you best believe there'll barely be anything left."

"Now, now," Letty said. "Do remember you love his dumb ass. The aim is not to cause any permanent damage or to even maim him. Just destroy his ego and make him remember who's boss."

No, the aim was to make him love her and look how well that was turning out. She guessed it was too much to hope for Zac to actually "date" her without coming up with some plan to ruin it all. She thought he had said yes too quickly to her proposition, but then he put his mouth between her legs and it was bye-bye to her brain cells. Had he done that on purpose? To make sure she didn't think too deeply on why he had agreed? God, she was so stupid! And to think, she'd actually been excited!

"Make him love me, my ass," she said softly to Letty. "As soon as we stop having sex, he remembers exactly why he doesn't want to be with me again."

She couldn't help the hurt that leaked into her voice. Letty grabbed her hand and interlaced their fingers.

"I know it hurts, Reagan," she said. "But if you really want to be with Zac, you got to think beyond that and think about *why* he doesn't want to be with you."

Why he doesn't want to be with me? Reagan snorted. She knew exactly why: he was scared, because... Her eyes widened. The only relationship he had ever known growing up was his parents' own dysfunctional and abusive one. And the only family he had was her family. Why would he want to jeopardize that when he didn't believe love could last or that love between a man and a woman didn't even really exist?

"I think you're starting to get it," Letty murmured.

Yeah, she was starting to get it. Of course, Zac was going to be wary. It was up to her to stop letting him push her away, to stop doubts from creeping in and making her forget her objective: him.

"I'm going to show Zac," Reagan said, determined. "I'm going to show him that we are meant to be together. No matter what it takes."

"You go get him, girl!"

She stood up and was about to throw away her coffee and head back to the agency when she remembered something. She sat back down and pointed a finger at her best friend.

Letty took a calm sip of her mocha.

"Don't think I've forgotten," Reagan accused. "What was that shit you said about my brother not going for someone like you?"

Letty sighed. "Let it go."

"Nuh-uh, we've just spent all this time talking about me, Letty. Now we're going to talk about you."

"There's nothing to talk about." Letty set down her drink.

Reagan stared her down. If Letty thought she was going to let this go, then she had another thing coming.

Letty sighed again.

"Okay, okay, don't get your panties in a bunch. I just think…love isn't for someone like me."

"Someone like you?" Reagan asked slowly. "What the fuck does that mean?"

"Come on, Reagan. You don't need to pretend. I

know exactly what kind of girl I am," Letty said with a sad smile.

"And what kind of girl are you?"

She shrugged. "The party girl. The easy girl. The girl a boy wants to fuck but doesn't want to take home to his mother. A girl who can be a mistress, the side-piece, but never a wife. I'm the girl people call if they want to have a good time but won't remember to call if they need a date for a charity gala. I'm the girl who has a body like a porn star, which is why boys want to fuck me and exactly why mothers hate me. But I'm not competition, not truly. 'Cause they know it and I know it that I'll never truly occupy their world. I'll always be on the outside looking in."

"I'm really getting pissed off at the way you're insulting my friend," Reagan said, mildly.

"I don't mean—"

"I know what you mean," she cut her off.

Reagan leaned forward over the table. She cupped Letty's cheeks and looked her right in those brown eyes of hers.

"Are you listening, Letty?" She waited for Letty to nod between her palms. "You deserve love. You are the most beautiful person I know. And I'm not just talking about your looks, but, god knows, if I was a guy or a lesbian I would totally fuck you and take you home to meet my dad, proudly. I'm talking about you as a person. You are giving, kind and unbelievably smart. I grew up with all boys and when I met you, I knew you weren't just going to be my closest friend, but you were…you *are* my sister. And I know it's going to take more than this to make you believe that, but I'll be here for the day you realize that you deserve more than just love: you deserve it all."

Letty stared at her. Tears filled her eyes.

"You're going to make me cry," she whispered hoarsely, before clearing her throat.

A few of those tears trickled down her cheeks. Reagan rubbed them away with her thumb. Letty knocked her hands away.

"But I'm not going to, because I don't want to ruin my makeup. So, no more touching. And quick, tell me something that doesn't make me want to bawl my eyes out. Like sports statistics!"

Reagan laughed, but then sobered quickly.

"Will you tell me next time you feel this way?" she asked Letty, seriously.

Letty nodded.

"Good." Reagan breathed out in relief. "Okay, I think our lunch break's over. We better get back to work."

Chapter Thirteen

Zac sat in his living room, watching a Tom Cruise movie. *Whoever doesn't think the man is an action genius is out of their goddamn mind.* He was killing time before he had to pick up Reagan for date number three—the last of the ones he had control over. Sitting in his armchair, with his legs spread out and a bottle of water before him, he was completely chill.

He tried to stay focused on the explosions happening on the screen, but he couldn't stop thinking about the way Reagan looked on their last date. That dress. It was hard leaving her standing on her doorstep with only a kiss on the cheek. What he had really wanted to do was take her back to her room and fuck her all night long.

His lips curved into a smile just remembering Reagan's confused face at the end. It had been well worth curbing his tongue the whole night just for the last image of her standing there, swaying towards him, eyes closed before they opened and realized no kiss was coming.

The plan was coming along nicely. All the dates so far had been nothing but boring. Oh, he was definitely going to fuck Reagan again, but outside of the bedroom he was going to show her nothing but Mr. one-word, unfunny, un-teasing Zachariah Quinn from the previous nights. And that was all she was getting from him, other than his cock, mouth and fingers, until she threw in the towel and cried quits on the whole dating thing. Who knew fucking with Reagan—and not in the biblical sense—would be this much fun?

And what was even better was knowing that ultimately he was saving Reagan from the true pain of ever dating him. Sometimes as he sat across from her in a restaurant, thinking about what it'd actually be like to be able to listen to her talk about her colleague and tell her Daniel was an asshole. That she should stop second-guessing herself since she had brilliant instincts. *But I can't.* It might be okay this date or the next but eventually though he'd disappoint her, hurt her when he didn't give her the right answer or give her the romantic gesture she so desperately wanted. He'd show her that he had no idea what love looked like.

Zac frowned when his phone vibrated and he fished it out of his pocket.

Mom flashed on the screen. He didn't think. His thumb swiped the red arrow. *Why won't she leave me alone?* He ran his hand through his hair. The calls had started yesterday and since then she had called maybe three times. Every single time, he rejected her. It wasn't like they didn't speak. He always left tickets for her to his games. Games she never came to. He spoke to her on her birthday, his birthday and every major holiday. But outside of that, they had nothing more to say to each other.

Nothing.

Zac stared unseeing at the TV. He could feel it at the edge of his mind, all the images he had been pushing away that emerged at nighttime, but had slowly been creeping up on him even in the daylight. He saw his mom, not like the last time he saw her at that little cafe just over a year ago, but when she was standing in the bathroom, faucet running, hand over her bleeding mouth. He'd been six at the time, or was it five? Fuck, he could barely remember since it was a constant in his life.

What did his mom want from him, and why now? His gut twisted with guilt. Maybe it was something serious and he should call her back. If it was, she'd text him though so she was probably just calling to chat, six months ahead of their usual catch-up period. Yeah, it was probably nothing. *And this is why I shouldn't be doing this with Reagan*, he thought as he ran a hand through his hair. He was too fucked up and all he'd do was drag her down with him.

DING DONG! Zac pulled himself to his feet and went to the door, shaking off the mood his mother's unwanted call had thrown him into. Fuck, he hoped he hadn't promised to hang out with one of the boys or something.

He opened it and stared.

"What are you doing here?" He frowned. "I'm supposed to be picking you up in an hour."

Reagan stood on his doorstep wearing a thin black coat that fell to her knees, and heels. Her black wavy hair was loose around her face. She smiled at him and Zac's frown deepened.

"I need to talk to you about something."

"Something that couldn't wait until an hour from now?"

She nodded.

He crossed his arms, leaning against the door. What the fuck was her game?

She blinked up at him, innocently. Fuck yeah, there was some kind of angle he was missing. She never looked that innocent unless she was up to something bad.

"Aren't you going to let me in?" she asked softly.

No. Yes. This was definitely a bad idea, but he did it anyway. He stepped aside and let her in.

Her heels made that clicking sound as she walked into his house, with him following close behind.

Reagan stopped in the middle of his hallway and turned around to face him. Her fingers went to her waist and unwound the knotted trench easily. He was about to say something, something about why she was here, but the words died in his throat when her coat fell to the ground.

"Fuck." The word slipped out of his mouth without conscious thought.

She stood before him, wearing clothes—if they could even be called clothes—that were so provocative they should be illegal. Her breasts were cupped by black lace that was so sheer he could see the outline of her deep brown nipples. The lace baby doll was molded to her skin and revealed the outline of the baby blue thong she was wearing.

Zac swallowed, his eyes glued to her pussy. "What the fuck are you wearing, Ree?"

"Do you like it?"

Do I like it? He wanted to ask whether or not she could see his hard cock, which was ready to burst out of his jeans. But when he looked at her, he saw the teasing glint in her eyes. The little vixen.

"Answer my question, Ree. What are you doing here?"

She walked to him, one long leg in front of the other, stopping right in front of him, the top of her head just coming up to his mouth. He wanted to step back, but he couldn't move; he was transfixed by her. He could handle this. Of course he could. Sweat trickled down his spine as his eyes continued to skim her luscious body. *Fuck, she is gorgeous*.

"Isn't this what you wanted?" her red-painted mouth whispered. "To fuck?"

"No. Yes. No."

How was he supposed to think with her dressed like this? With all his blood pooling straight out of his head into his cock?

"We're supposed to go out—"

"I like staying in."

"I had plans."

"So un-plan them," she said. "I'm here. You're here. What more do we need?"

"Ree," he said desperately.

Come on, do not give in. He was supposed to take her on another boring date and only then would he allow himself to taste her, but this right here was not part of the plan. *Think of penalties, think of anything that isn't Reagan.*

"Zac," she sang.

Her nipples brushed his shirt. He groaned. Zac wanted to look away, but she was a feast for the eyes. And she knew it. But he had to try.

"I don't think—"

She cut him off. "Come with me."

He nodded, like his head wasn't attached to his body, unable to help himself.

She laughed like the little vixen she was. Her hand reached out and touched his. Their fingers tangled. She pulled him forward and walked backwards towards his bedroom door.

They fell into it together. The light was off, but he had left his bedside lamp on. It cast a nice glow. His eyes never left her legs and the way her hips swayed while she dragged him towards his king-sized bed. At the edge of the mattress, she turned them unexpectedly. She pressed two hands to his chest and pushed him back. He fell onto his ass, on the bed.

She stepped in between his spread legs.

"Fuck," he murmured.

"We'll get to that," she laughed.

Slowly, Reagan got to her knees. Whatever thoughts he had of resisting went out of his mind then and there. He was fucked. There was no other way to put it. But, did it matter? *It's just sex.* And for the next week, he was allowed to indulge as much as he wanted to with the girl who had always been off-limits, before they had to go back to being platonic. He wasn't giving in to her forever, he was just not going to deny himself anymore. Boring, blue-balls Zac could wait for another day.

Zac swallowed, his hands curling into fists on the bed. Reagan watched him from beneath her eyelashes. Her lips curved in a seductive smile. Her hair had fallen forward and covered her nipples from his view, but that only added to the allure.

"I think this is one of your fantasies, isn't it? Having me on my knees?" she whispered. "I'm not breaking a single rule. It's just a bonus that what you want and what I want align so well."

It was definitely a fantasy of his. And he couldn't believe it was coming true.

"You've thought about being on your knees before me?" he asked.

She nodded. "Doing more than just being on my knees."

Oh fuck. He tensed. He knew exactly what she was going to do when her hands touched his thighs. They skimmed up his legs until her fingers grazed his fly. She unbuttoned his jeans, then unzipped him slowly. He helped her pull his pants down, until they were thrown somewhere over her shoulder. The cool air did nothing to take away the fierce desire in him. He was so hard, he was tempted to squeeze himself at the base with the hope that the bite of pain would stop him from prematurely ejaculating. The way Reagan was staring at him wasn't helping.

Her eyes were wide and filled with heated lust. Her cheeks flushed and her hips wiggled a little as if she was getting turned on just from staring at him. She did nothing for a moment longer and he let her look her fill. Until her eyes flicked up and met his.

"A present, just for me." She licked her lips, reaching out to him.

He was already close to coming when she finally put her hand on him. Her soft palm was warm against his cock as she wrapped her fingers around his length. His eyes fluttered closed, trying to block out the added stimulus of watching her as she touched him. Strands of her hair brushed his knees. She ran her hand up and down him gently as if she was deliberately learning the feel of him. Too gently. Before he could ask for "harder," she tightened her grip. He grunted. He clutched the covers in fistfuls as she jerked him from base to tip. And then again. His cock leaked and she used the lubrication to better grip him. *Oh fuck, that feels so good*. She squeezed him tighter. His hips came off the bed a little, chasing her touch.

Suddenly, she let go.

Zac peered down at Reagan, just as she brought her finger to her mouth and tasted him. Fuck. Fuck. She let out a small whimper and he wondered if he was going to come. Reagan nestled in closer to him, lifting up higher on her knees, and tucked her hair behind her ears. If she was about to do what he thought she was going to do, he didn't know whether to beg for it or to beg for mercy. All he knew was she was going to kill him.

Sure enough, he watched her mouth descend towards his cock, before he felt the brush of air and her wet mouth engulf the tip. His head tipped back. He groaned, low and deep. Fuck. Her tongue licked at him, like she was licking up cream and she didn't want to lose a single drop.

"You're killing me," Zac ground out through clenched teeth.

"Mm, that's the idea."

He huffed out a laugh, which turned into another groan when she opened her mouth wider and took him in deeper while continuing to stroke him with her hands.

The way Reagan was lost to blowing him turned him on. She was totally into what she was doing, her tongue laving attention that had his cock glistening with her saliva. She even made little noises that he felt in his balls.

Zac lost the battle with himself. His hands slid to

the back of her neck. He thrust into her mouth. She hummed against him. She didn't fight him, letting him fuck her face for a few moments, before she took over again. The urge to come was too overwhelming. And fuck, hearing the sound of her mouth on his cock? He was about to go off the edge.

"Ree, I'm going to come," he told her in warning.

She didn't let him go as he thought she would. Instead, she took his cock deeper into her mouth. Her hands drifted to cup his balls. She squeezed. All it took was a couple more sucks and he was coming. Hard. He yelled out his pleasure.

"Ree!"

His hands tightened in her hair. His body jerked with his release. Fuck. Her throat swallowed around his cock and he lurched again. Fuck. *Fuck.*

When his shaky hands fell out of her hair, Reagan released his cock with a small audible pop. He fell backwards, onto the bed, completely spent. Blinking up at the ceiling, he had no words or thoughts about what had just happened beyond *holy fuck that was good* and *when can I do it again?*

Reagan's hands pressed into his bare thighs. She crawled up onto the bed, until her face was hovering over his and her knees were on either side of his waist. He was still riding the high of the orgasm so even with her nipples against his chest and feeling the heat of her pussy against his cock, it barely twitched.

"Hi." She smiled shyly at him.

He somehow found the energy to lift up his hand and twirl a strand of her hair around his finger.

"Hi."

Zac ran his thumb over her bottom lip. *Oh, fuck it.*

He could sleep when he was dead. Without hesitation, he kissed her. They rolled over so she lay beneath him. They slid into the kiss, their tongues tangling. He ran his hands up her thighs, under her baby doll, to caress both of her breasts. She whimpered as he played with her nipples. Squeezing, rubbing. She undulated restlessly beneath him.

"Fuck me, Zac," she said against his mouth.

"Vixen," he whispered back, amused. "I might be an athlete, but even I don't have an instant recovery time."

"Oh." She pouted.

And it was so fucking cute, he kissed her again. He ran his mouth over her cheek to bite the lobe of her ear. Reagan gasped.

"But we can do other things in the meantime."

So, he ate her out and *then* he fucked her.

Hours later, Reagan's naked body was lying on top of his naked body and they were both breathing hard. When she giggled, her body shook against his.

"What are you laughing about, Reagan Thomas?" Zac raised an eyebrow.

"We…" She was giggling so hard the words weren't coming out.

Finally, she took a deep breath and said, "We made it to a bed. Does this mean we're boring now?"

"Ree, we could never be boring."

He rolled them over again and showed her exactly how non-boring they were.

Chapter Fourteen

Zac's eyes flew open.

He didn't know what woke him. Was it the sound of heavy breathing? Was it the sound of loud whispers in the air? Or was it just the heavy feeling in his gut? He crawled out of bed and out of his room. He knew where he would find them: in the kitchen. It was always the kitchen.

Dread had him walking slowly. Had his heart beating too fast and his thoughts a jumble. He stood outside of the door, hand on the doorknob. I should go back to sleep. He had practice in the morning and then school. But he didn't. He never did.

He could hear them now. Louder and clearer.

"I've told you! Over and over again!"

"Please—"

"Fucking hell, I mean look at this."

Zac flinched as something shattered. A plate or a cup.

"I can make something different if you—"

Laughter cut off the woman's words.

"You say that every night, bitch, and every fucking night, it's the same. What do I gotta do to teach you how to do it right?"

"I'm trying—"

Skin slapping against skin. A body thudding against tile floor.

Zac didn't hesitate; he pushed the door open. His eyes swept past the man heaving in the center of the room and the woman crying on the floor. Instead, he noticed the time flashing on the microwave: 2:16 am. The same time every night. He noticed the shards of glass and the remains of the destroyed dinner on the floor. I'm going to have to clean that up, *he thought.*

He couldn't look away from it. His father grabbed his shoulder in a punishing grip. His fingers were going to leave bruises. Zac looked up at the sheriff. His spit turned to dust in his mouth. His father was apparently a good-looking man and apparently, he shared his features, but, to him, he looked like a monster. More so because of the blood splatters on his face, the hard look in his eyes and the sneer of his lips. And the smell—the stink of whiskey and beer—clung to him like a second skin. It bled out of him.

His father shook him to get his attention.

"Clean this shit up," he spat. "You hear me, son. I don't want to see any of this tomorrow."

And then he left, pushing past him.

Zac didn't care about the glass on the floor or the splattered food. He walked across them to the only thing that mattered. His mother was curled into a ball, sobbing silently to herself. She was bleeding from a cut across her forehead and a few other places. She didn't notice him standing there.

"Mom," he whispered.

He fell to his knees and gathered her up in his arms. But suddenly she stopped crying. She looked up at him

*and his heart stopped. Something was in her eyes that
he had never seen before.*

"Zac," *she said in a flat voice.*

"Mom."

"I want to die."

Zac gasped awake.

His eyes opened to darkness. He was in his bedroom, breathing hard. A nightmare, he realized. Zac shuddered. A fucking nightmare. He ran his trembling hands over his face, into his hair.

"I want to die."

It was the same nightmare he used to have in college and it had started back up again about two nights ago. He was twelve years old again, watching his father hurt his mother. Zac never dreamed the moments when his father beat him, which had happened frequently. No, it seemed his consciousness wanted to torture him with the worst moment of his life.

He rubbed his eyes. *Why now?* he thought angrily. *Why the fuck now?* He hadn't had a nightmare like this in years. It was supposed to be buried and *stay* buried, but if anything, it was getting more intense. He could barely sleep, afraid to close his eyes and see her lying there surrounded by blood and glass. He didn't want to see—

A little snore interrupted his thoughts. His head snapped to the left to look at the woman sleeping beside him. *Ree.* He'd forgotten she was there. Fuck, he was so lucky Reagan was such a deep sleeper. Even now, she was still sleeping beside him, face buried in his pillow, oblivious to his struggles. Good. She would never know just how fucked up he truly was.

She was so goddamn beautiful. That long black, curly hair of hers that was pulled up in what she had called a pineapple bun. Perfect skin. That gorgeous mouth. Waking from a nightmare straight into her arms felt strange. Like the two shouldn't exist but somehow this was his fucked-up reality and damn was he glad for it. In this moment, while she was asleep, he could admit that having her here calmed a part of him that would have otherwise been a festering wound for the rest of the day. *But Reagan's here with me and I'm not alone.*

He reached out and touched her cheek with the back of his fingers, her warmth seeping into him. Desperate for more of it, he pulled her towards him. She snuggled in deeper. *A few minutes*, he told himself as he closed his eyes. And then he would get up. But hours went by and he didn't move.

Zac felt the moment when Reagan woke up in his arms. Her breathing changed and he could feel her eyelashes fluttering against his chest as she blinked. Her hands skimmed his lower back and she rubbed her thigh against his. His morning erection pressed in between them, resting on her soft stomach.

Having Reagan in his arms was nice. Too nice. Usually, the women he fucked didn't sleep over, which was why he avoided having them over in the first place. It was just too messy. But with Reagan, everything was in the gray area. They were friends and friends came over to friend's houses, except they were dating, which meant she shouldn't be here, right? He groaned mentally. He was not awake enough to be having this conversation with himself.

Reagan unwound herself from him. He didn't open his eyes or tense. He just let her slide out of bed. He heard the bathroom door open and close. He rolled in deeper to her side of the bed, facedown on the pillows. And waited.

A few minutes later, he heard it open again and heard her walk around his bedroom, probably collecting what was left of her clothes. The bed suddenly tipped. Her body curled over on top of him. He slowed his breathing even further, faking sleep. He had no idea what he wanted to say to her. If he was truly being honest, he was more likely to pull her back into bed and fuck her again rather than have a rational conversation, which is what had got him into this mess in the first place. Thinking with his cock rather than his head.

She leaned towards him. Her lips brushed his cheek.

"See you later, baby," she whispered.

She left the room. The front door slammed a moment later.

Zac opened his eyes. With the sunlight seeping in through the curtain, he could see the *Die Hard* poster above his bed. There was no way he was going to be getting any sleep after that. He looked over at his watch, sitting on his bedside table. Oh fuck, sleep was definitely not in the cards. If he didn't move now, he was going to be late for practice.

Practice had been brutal.

He played like shit, because for the first time, his head wasn't in the game. *Shake it off*, he told himself as he pulled out his street clothes from his locker. But, fuck, he hadn't played this bad since he was in high school and what was happening at home kept throwing him for a loop.

"You okay there, Quinn?" goalkeeper and resident

smart-ass DD asked, as he opened the locker beside Zac. "You're looking a little pale there. You starting to feel it in your old age?"

Zac flipped him off as he dropped his towel. He wasn't getting old. He was only twenty-seven years old, but he couldn't deny that he was going to feel every bruise tomorrow. Coach had worked them hard all day. Only allowing them a short break before he made them run plays again and again.

"Seriously, man, where was your head today?" DD shook his head, referring to the easy passes Zac had missed and the frequent body slamming he had endured for his inattention.

His head? Oh, yeah, his head had been with a certain black-haired, brown-eyed girl who had enjoyed teasing him all day with texts about the night before. He had almost swallowed his tongue when she had sent that first one.

I really enjoyed having your cock in my mouth. I've been thinking about it all day.

Or the text that had followed.

Can't wait to show you the lingerie I have for you tonight. Green's still one of your favorite colors, right?

The messages had shifted from graphically sexual to light teasing.

Zac had no idea how to deal with this side of Reagan. The geeky, hesitant Reagan? He knew what to do. The determined, tomboyish Reagan was not a problem at all. But this sexually confident, daring vixen? Fuck, he had no idea what to do with her. He'd rather focus on that than on the other reason why he had barely gotten any sleep last night.

"Nowhere," he said in reply to DD's question.

"You better get your head out of your ass, we got a game coming up."

Zac rolled his eyes. "It's a charity game, so back off. And I could still skate rings around you, DD, you know why? My shit day is always going to be better than your best."

Aidan miraculously appeared between them before DD could hit Zac with one of his infamous punches.

"Stop being such a dick, DD. And don't be an ass, Zac, or next time, in practice, I'll let you get body-checked by Rick the Prick."

And he would. He so totally would. DD snorted and turned back to his locker.

"But DD's got a point. Where the hell was your head today in practice?"

Zac groaned as Aidan leaned against the locker beside his. Aidan was like a German shepherd when he sunk his teeth into something; eager to get to the bottom of things and loyal beyond anything. He was semi-dressed in blue jeans that hung low and showed that he hadn't bothered to put underwear on.

"It's nothing. I'm just a little distracted," he repeated.

Aidan's eyes narrowed. "Bullshit."

"My money says it has to do with a girl," Taylor, another teammate, contributed as he sauntered over, wearing nothing but a towel around his hips. "Only a girl has the power to fuck with a guy's mind."

"Thank you for that, Dr. Phil," Zac said, dryly.

DD pointed a finger at him. "Evasion tactics, which means we're on the right track."

"Does it have to do with that girl you took to Steven's party—Whiskey or Scotch, right?" Aidan asked.

"Who?" Zac said blankly. Then it clicked. "You mean Brandy? Wrong alcohol, man. No one names their kid Whiskey or Scotch."

"So, if it isn't Brandy who has you all distracted, then? Who the fuck is it?"

All three men looked at him expectantly.

Zac slammed his locker shut.

"It's no one important." He ran a hand through his hair. "Just some girl I'm casually dating. I'm going on a date with her tomorrow night."

"Oh, Quinny has a date," DD mocked. "Tell us what you're wearing to this date, Quinny? Planning on wearing your expensive thong in case you get lucky?"

Taylor howled with laughter. Even Aidan's lips twitched. Zac, on the other hand, was not amused.

"Fuck off, DD."

"Yeah, fuck off." Taylor snickered as he started to put his clothes on. "You know Quinny here doesn't wear a thong unless it matches his bra."

He walked out, flipping them all off as he did, their howls of laughter following him.

Outside, he found Simon Caron, The Comets' most recent transfer from Vancouver. He sat at the end of the hallway, back to the wall, head in the palm of his hands. Zac could see the defeat written all over his body. Even though he wasn't in the mood for this, he couldn't just leave the rookie to wallow after that clusterfuck of a practice.

"You okay there, rookie?" Zac asked, crouching down to his level.

Simon shook his head, mumbling something. It was hard to hear with his thick French accent but it sounded like "I think I'm going to be sick."

Zac clasped the kid on the shoulder—and really when the fuck did he get so old? The rookie was only a couple of years younger than him, but that might as well be decades in ice hockey.

"You're going to be okay," he assured him.

"I played like shit," Simon said.

"Yeah, you did." Zac nodded. "So did I. But do you see me having a breakdown? Why? Because it's over. I can't fix that. You know what I can fix? The next practice. The next game. Stop focusing on what you can't change and focus on what you can."

Simon finally looked at him with his bloodshot eyes and clean-shaven baby face. "I don't want to let anyone down."

"Then, you won't. Just show us what you got. This charity game is the best opportunity you're going to get, rookie. If you fuck up—" Zac smiled "—it won't be that big of a deal, you feel me?"

Simon laughed. "Yeah."

"Cool. Why don't you—"

"QUINN!"

They both looked up to see the assistant coach waving him over.

"Coach wants to speak to you."

Fuck, that isn't good.

"That isn't good." The rookie echoed his exact sentiment.

"Catch you later." Zac gave him another squeeze on

the shoulder, before ambling to his feet and down to the coach's office, his bag slung over his shoulder.

A million thoughts ran through his head. Fuck, would Coach bench him for one terrible practice? *No, that's crazy. Maybe a transfer?*

He knocked on the door and walked inside when a voice told him to enter.

"You wanted to speak to me, Coach?"

Coach Bryan used to be one of the best forwards in the league for twenty years, before a puck to the eye took him out of the game. It was rare, but it happened. His eye was mostly healed, but his perception was fucked. It didn't stop him from seeing all.

"Take a seat, Quinn."

Zac took the only chair opposite Coach Bryan's desk in the small office cramped with playbooks, a TV and a sofa.

"If it's about today's practice, I'm sorry—" he began.

"It wasn't." Coach waved his words away. "But you did seem distracted. Anything you need to tell me?"

Zac shook his head quickly. "Nope. Everything's good."

Coach raised a single bushy eyebrow. "You sure? I know it's just a charity game and I don't expect you to give it one hundred, but all eyes will be on us as the reigning champions."

"I know," he said sharply and then took a deep breath. "I know, Coach. I let myself get distracted, but I promise I won't let that happen again."

"Good. I need you at the top of your form, Quinn, especially since the team will be looking to you as their captain."

Zac's mind went blank. Captain? Him? That didn't

make any sense. He knew that with Boucher's retire-
ment last year, they were in need of a captain, but it had
never, never crossed his mind that they were thinking
about him. A swirl of panic made his chest tighten.

"With all due respect, Coach, why me?"

Coach Bryan sat back in his oversized chair, hands
interlocked over his slightly pudgy stomach. His hair
might be gray and there might be lines on his face, but
his brain was as sharp as his eyes.

"You're a great team leader, Quinn, I don't need to
tell you that. For god's sake, you were MVP and you had
the most assists. People look to you for hel—"

"Aidan should do it. He's better than me." Zac's fingers tapped a beat on the arm of his chair. He wanted
to comb his fingers through his hair, but he resisted.

Coach tilted his head. "At what? No denying he's
a fine defenseman, but you're the glue that holds the
team together. This isn't a request, Quinn. I'll give you
until next week to get your head on straight and then
I'm telling the team."

Throat closing up, Zac nodded.

Coach smiled without humor. "Do you know how
many people would kill to be in your shoes right now?"

"I'm grateful. Don't get me wrong. I'm grateful. I…
just don't think I'm the right person for this job." *And I
don't want to let you down when you finally realize that.*

"You're exactly the right person."

Zac was shutting Coach's office door, stomach
churning, when his phone buzzed. It wasn't Reagan
like he suspected. It was his mother. *Fuck. Not again.*
Why didn't she take the hint? He didn't want to talk
to her. He hit the decline button so hard he thought he
might've cracked his screen.

He made it to the parking lot and saw Aidan waiting for him next to his car. Zac swore to himself. *I definitely don't need this.* Immediately, he felt guilty. What kind of person was annoyed to see his best friend?

"What did Coach want?" Aidan straightened, arms crossed.

Zac opened his trunk and threw in his bag. "He asked me to be captain."

Aidan's whole face lit up and he grabbed Zac in a bear hug.

"That's great!"

He pulled back and took in the expression on Zac's face.

"You're not happy about this?"

"You don't think I'm the wrong person for this?"

"Who would be better than you?"

"Ah, you." Zac pointed to him.

"Why would you say that?" Aidan shook his head.

"Because! You're calm, you're smart, you'd do a much better job than me."

"That's horse shit," Aidan growled. "Look, Zac, Coach chose you for a reason. Everyone looks up to you in this team. You're the reason we won last year. Yeah, we all worked hard, but you worked the hardest. We all see that."

Zac looked away as he leaned his shoulder against his passenger door. He heard Aidan, but it didn't change anything for him. It was like everything was going wrong at the same time. Too much change at the same time and he couldn't shake the feeling that this week and next would change everything. He didn't want to lose Aidan, Reagan or the Thomas family.

"What else is going on?" Aidan pinned him with his intense brown eyes.

"Mom keeps calling." The words spilled out.

Zac hadn't planned on saying them, but he didn't want to keep them in any longer. Aidan said nothing for a moment.

"What?" Zac finally snapped, running a hand through his hair. "I can feel you thinking."

Aidan shrugged. "You should talk to her. More for you than for her. It's eating at you."

"I don't want to talk to her," he said through gritted teeth. "I can speak to her at Thanksgiving."

"Zac—" Aidan started, his voice dripping with pity.

"No! No. Can we just drop it?"

Zac pushed past and opened the front door of his car. He was about to slide in when Aidan stopped him with a hand on his arm.

"We can drop this, but I have one more thing to say." Aidan stared at him. "I'm here whenever you want to talk about it. Whether you decide you want to talk to her or not. We're all here for you."

Zac let out a breath. "Thanks, man."

Aidan held out his fist. Grinning, they bumped knuckles.

"You wanna grab a beer tomorrow night?"

"Can't. Sorry. I'm…going on a date." He hesitated with the answer, but decided the semi-truth was better than a flat-out lie. Not that telling Aidan he was going on a date would be a problem. He dated enough during the year that it was pretty normal. Now, if he showed too much interest in the girl *that* would be a problem and Aidan the tenacious guy would make an appearance.

Aidan's eyebrows rose at that. "No shit? Is this

the same girl you were talking about before? Really? Weren't you the one who invented the three-day rule for after a date? No contact until those three days were up?"

"That was Dean. And Dean's an ass."

"He might be an ass, but he gets more pussy than all of us combined and still manages to do so without having girls wanting to maim him," Aidan pointed out.

"Probably because he doesn't refer to women as 'pussy.'"

"Well, for what it's worth, I hope your date goes well," Aidan said as he took several steps back, hands stuffed in his pockets.

Zac didn't think Aidan would be saying that if he knew who he was about to go out with. But he managed to drum up a smile.

"Thanks, man."

"But you still coming over for game night, right?"

"Fuck yes, I wouldn't miss it."

All the Thomas siblings and a few of their other friends all came over whenever they had the time for a huge game night that involved fun games and lots of alcohol. They held three games during the year, going up in level from mild to lightly seasoned to spicy. It was the best thing ever. Tonight, Callum was hosting Mild Game Night at his house in the city, the one he kept just for when he was staying over to see family and for emergencies even though he didn't live in Scarlet anymore.

"See you in a few hours," Aidan said, as he got into his Range Rover, which was parked two cars down.

Zac nodded as Aidan drove away. In a few hours, he was going to be in a house with the one woman who had him wound up so tight that he was going to go home and jerk himself off before having to see her again later that night.

Determined, Zac got into his car. His mind was already on tomorrow's date. He was going to make sure this date went according to plan—he wasn't going to play by her rules, she was going to play by his. And if she didn't think he knew what she was doing, she was in for a rude awakening. He thought with more than just his dick. If she wanted to fight dirty, he was going to fight dirty too. Starting with game night. By the end of tonight, Reagan would see that there was nothing special about him and she wouldn't even want to date him for one more day, let alone for another week.

Chapter Fifteen

Callum's house was crawling with people. The noise was almost deafening with everyone spread out in the games room, in the theater or in the Jacuzzi, drinking, laughing and generally having a good time.

Letty and Reagan were at a secluded part of the bar. Behind them, people danced to a hip-hop track. The music was louder here, but they could just about hear each other.

"Beer?" Letty offered, holding out a bottle to her.

Reagan took it. She popped it open and took a sip. Ice cold. *Yum.* She focused on her drink but felt Letty taking peeks at her while making a cocktail.

"You're glowing."

"Shut up. I am not glowing."

Reagan put her right hip to the counter. She hadn't bothered to dress up for game night and was in a shirt that had the words *I game, deal with it* across her chest, blue jeans and her trusty Converses.

"You are *so* glowing." Letty grinned. "The sex between you two must be phenomenal."

Reagan blew out a breath. Letty had no idea. *Except...*

"That's the one area we are not having a problem

with. It's when we leave the bedroom, or the sofa, or the wall—"

"Okay, bitch, we get it. You're having lots of sex," Letty grumbled.

"Sorry," Reagan said, sheepishly.

Letty made a gesture with her hand to continue with her story.

"I feel like we've made practically no progress. He still won't talk to me or even seriously entertain the idea of us being together. The first week is almost up and I still have no idea where we stand."

"Have you thought about asking him?"

Reagan gave her a look.

"Bad idea, I'm guessing."

"I can't just go up to him and be like, 'Hey, Zac, I know a week ago you thought it was the worst thing— worse than the apocalypse—to date me, but since we've been spending this time together, talking, having fun, having amazing sex, I was wondering if that had in any way influenced you and that maybe you've changed your mind? Wait—what's with that look? Why are you breathing funny? Zac! Zac!'"

Reagan pretended to go limp.

Letty laughed. "I get it, Miss Drama Queen. You don't want to freak out the boy any more than you already have."

"Exactly."

Reagan straightened.

"So just keep doing what you're doing," Letty said, with a sly smile.

Reagan looked at her.

"The plan is going to work, Reagan."

They had come up with "the plan" after she had realized how Zac was trying to sabotage their dates and their idea was so simple it was either genius or utter shite. She wanted to believe it was pure genius, because of optimism and all that. Step one was to throw herself at Zac, have sex with him and leave him wanting more. That was last night. Step two was to play aloof, basically ignore him and not give in to the attraction between them. This was the stage she was in right now. In theory, it was supposed to have Zac feeling confused, but unable to keep his gaze and mind off her. Which is where step three came in. When he inevitably cracked under the pressure of trying and failing to resist her, he would come to her begging and she—being the awesome person that she was—would make him grovel first and then eventually let him back into her life and maybe go watch that *Die Hard* marathon with him he wouldn't stop talking about. He would be so grateful for it that the armor around his heart would start to crack. Ah, the things she did for love. She didn't get his obsession with action movies, something about it being mindless fun, but he definitely didn't get why going to Comic-Con every year was a must and still he had gone with her a few times. Laughing and teasing about the costumes, but still he went. And one day, he'd give in and dress up as Captain America, because seriously the boy had the body for it. Finally, step four would be them hopelessly in love with each other and both parties acknowledging this fact. That was the plan.

"Is it? Stage two, he was supposed to be drooling all over me, dying for my attention, but do you see him anywhere? Is he even looking this way?"

Letty's eyes wandered over her shoulder. Her brown eyes widened.

"Uh-oh."

Reagan spun around and she knew instantly what had Letty looking worried. Past all the grinding bodies, she could just about see Zac standing in a dark corner of the room, leaning against the wall, but he wasn't alone. Ashley, a super pretty blonde and an up-and-coming actress, was standing next to him.

"Okay, Reagan," Letty murmured in her ear. "Don't lose your cool."

"Lose my cool? Why would I lose my cool?" It was not as if she felt hurt or betrayed that he was flirting with another woman. She clutched her beer and downed it. Okay, maybe she was losing her cool a little. He was standing awfully close to Ashley, while here Reagan was thinking and pining over him. *Don't lose your cool, he could just be doing this to mess with me, like those dates. That makes total sense, right?*

"FYI, I think this is the definition of losing your cool."

Ashley lifted her hand and rested it on Zac's chest. Reagan's eyes narrowed. Her blood boiled, especially when Zac did nothing. Just kept letting her touch him when he knew that they were dating!

She watched as Ashley said something—probably something flirty—and Zac smiled back at her.

Oh, he wanted to fight dirty, did he? He had no idea who he was messing with.

"You're going to go over there, aren't you?" Letty asked.

Reagan ignored her and sauntered over to Zac's side, but she did manage to catch Letty's muttered curse in Spanish.

She pushed through the throngs of bodies. The music

pounded and made her already heated blood boil. When she finally made her way to their side, she was raring to go.

Zac and Ashley both looked at her in surprise.

"Reagan," Zac said, the warning implicit in his voice.

Reagan held out her hand to Ashley. Ashley looked down at it, confused.

"Hey, Ashley," she greeted.

Ashley took her hand and shook it.

"Reagan, it's nice to see you again."

Reagan turned her head.

"So, Zac," Reagan said, "how's the groin injury?"

Ashley's eyes widened comically.

"You have a groin injury?" Ashley gasped and then realized how that must have sounded. "I mean, I'm so sorry. Are you okay?"

Reagan patted Zac's arm. "He doesn't really like talking about it. It's left him…how should I put it? Less sensitive down there."

Ashley's eyes followed Reagan's hand as she pointed to her own crotch.

"That can happen?" Ashley asked in a whisper.

Reagan sighed sympathetically, while continuing to pat Zac's arm. "Unfortunately, it is really rare, but it does happen. A groin injury like this means that a lot of things just won't be working the same way anymore. A shame, really."

"I'm so sorry, Zac." Ashley's face was full of pity.

"Can I talk to you for a second, Reagan?" Zac sent a forced smile at Ashley. "Sorry. If you'll excuse us."

He grabbed Reagan by the arm and dragged her out of the room. He pushed her into the first room he saw, which happened to be one of Callum's many bedrooms.

As soon as the door closed, they were thrust into blessed silence.

"Ow." Reagan glared at him, rubbing her arm. Okay, he hadn't hurt her, but dramatics and all that.

Zac slammed the door. The lights were dim and the room was mostly empty, except for a bed, a closet and a table.

"What the fuck was that, Ree?"

"Ah, I don't know. Except, while Ashley was pressing herself up against you like a cat in heat, did you maybe forget one important detail? Like the fact that you are supposed to be dating me?"

"I've forgotten nothing," he insisted. "But this thing between us is secret. And we're not really going out either."

Ouch, she winced, taking a step back. He might not be thrilled about this, but did he have to say it like that? As if the idea was crazy and wrong? They were dating and she was going to make him realize that it was time to put up. Reagan took a determined step forward.

"Oh yes, we are. Or are you telling me that you haven't been taking these dates seriously enough?"

"I'm not saying anything. And that is not the issue here. The issue here is that you told Ashley that I have a groin injury. What if she tells people?"

She waved her hand. "It'll be okay."

He clenched his hands. "How can you say that for sure?"

"Because Stacey never said anything."

"Who the fuck is Stacey?"

Oh shit, she should not have said that.

She shook her head adamantly. "No one. Nothing. It isn't important."

Retreat, Reagan. Retreat. She tried to walk by him, but Zac wasn't having any of that. He grabbed her by the arm again and pulled her towards him. She collided with his chest. He stared down at her, his eyes narrowed in anger.

"I'm going to ask you again, Ree: Who is Stacey?"

Reagan bit her lip to try and stop the words from spilling out, but she couldn't hold them in. "Stacey was my freshman college roommate. She was the one with the really big—"

"Yeah, I remember," he cut her off. "What did you do?"

"Stacey had this huge crush on you. She talked non-stop about you during the whole year we lived together, until she finally decided that she was going to make a move on you."

"What did you do, Ree?"

"I might have told her an eenie-weenie white lie."

He groaned. "You told her I was gay, didn't you?"

"No," she huffed out. "How would I have gotten away with that when you were constantly surrounded by your adoring fans? No… I just told her that you had a thing for toys."

He looked at her, confused. "Toys? What kind of toys?"

Cheeks bright red, Reagan whispered, "Paddles? I might have said you couldn't get it up, unless you were spanking the girl and she was calling you Daddy."

Zac dropped his hands.

"Let me get this straight, you told your college roommate that I had a fetish for spanking and being called Daddy?" he asked slowly, as if he didn't comprehend what she was saying to him.

"Basically," she squeaked.

"What the fuck, Reagan? What would have happened if she had told people that?"

"But she didn't! I told her that you were talking to a therapist about your addiction and that you were abstaining from sex in the meantime. Jeez."

He shook his head. "You're crazy."

"I know." She groaned. "I'm certifiable. Trust me, I didn't mean to do it. It just kind of happened."

"What the fuck were you thinking, Ree? Seriously!"

"I get it."

"Of all the fucked-up things you've pulled, this has got to be one of the worst."

"I said, I get it. And it's not like you haven't done dumb shit before."

"Like what?"

She put her hands on her hips. "One word: Paul."

"Who is Paul?"

"My boyfriend in junior year."

She watched as Zac tried to think back. She saw the moment he remembered.

"Oh, you mean Pete the douche."

"His name was Paul," she said, jabbing Zac in the stomach.

"Paul. Pete. Who the fuck cares?" He stopped her from drilling a hole into his stomach by holding her hand captive.

"I care!" she told him. "I especially cared in junior year when my boyfriend of six weeks suddenly broke up with me and avoided me like the plague, with no explanation. And I know it was because of you. Fess up, Zachariah Quinn. What did you do?"

He ran a hand through his hair.

"Oh my god, what did you do?" Reagan asked, trying not to hyperventilate or let her imagination get the best of her. "You told him I was gay, didn't you?"

Zac laughed. "If I told him you were gay, he would have asked for a threesome, not broken up with you."

"What did you do, Zachariah James Quinn?"

"Oh, my full name." He winced. "That is never good."

"What did you do?"

"I might have told him you had a few restraining orders from previous boyfriends. That you were a brilliant girlfriend during the first couple of weeks, but then you started to get really paranoid about what the guy was doing so you kept tabs on him. Checking his phone, hacking into his email, turning up everywhere he went. Stalking him until he couldn't breathe without you being there."

Reagan closed her eyes. "You told my college boyfriend I was a stalker."

"You told your roommate I was a pervert!"

"At least now I know that it wasn't anything I had done to make him suddenly act like a douchebag."

"And now I know why Stacey could never look me in the eye whenever I ran into her."

"We're crazy," Reagan whispered to herself.

But Zac was definitely crazier. She opened her eyes and glared at him.

"And don't think I don't know what you've been doing," she accused.

"And what *have* I been doing?"

"The candles. Opening doors for me. The restaurants." She glared at him. "You think you can get me to say that this whole dating thing is a bad idea. It is not going to work. I'm onto you."

"And I'm onto *you*, Reagan Thomas."

"What does that mean?"

"The heels. The lingerie. Showing up at my house and blowing me." He glared right back at her. "Oh yeah, I know what you're up to, Reagan Thomas. Trying to use sex to control me. Somehow make me believe that us dating is a good idea."

"It is a good idea!" she argued.

"No," he hissed. "It's not. Look at us right now. We should be out there having fun, but instead we're in here arguing. And about what? About petty shit. We never used to argue like this before when we were just friends. You can't deny that."

Reagan threw up her other hand in the air, letting out an air of frustration. Friends argued, that was a fact of life, and she definitely remembered spending a whole evening arguing about whether pineapple on a pizza was a topping or not. It is. Unlike that conversation, this one was not her fault; the blame lay solely on his shoulders.

"Because you weren't fighting me every step of the way."

"And you weren't fighting me back?"

"I'm not going to stop."

"Oh, for fuck's sake. Why do you have to be so stubborn?" he burst out.

She lifted her chin. "I still have one more week."

"One week isn't going to make any kind of difference, Ree. You have to see that."

"No. All I see is that you *want* me. You can't stay away from me. You'd rather fight with me than admit that you love having sex with me and—"

"We've already fucked enough times," he said.

"And how is fucking me out of your system working for you, Zachariah?" she shot back.

He fell silent at that. He let go of her hand, but they were still pressed together. Chest to chest.

"Do you want me less? You aren't thinking about pushing me up against the wall and fucking me?" she pushed, staring up at his beautifully bitable lips. "Have you gotten enough of me?"

She moved in closer to him, their thighs touching. He was wearing a tight blue shirt and when she put her hands on his stomach, she could feel his muscles tense. She licked her lips. Suddenly, Zac grabbed her chin with his forefinger and thumb, tipping Reagan's head back to look at him.

"Is this what you want?" he whispered, his eyes staring straight at hers.

She didn't think she could unravel her tongue long enough to untangle that question. All she knew was that she wanted him. Always. Any way that she could have him. *The plan*, a desperate voice in the back of her mind screamed at her. But it was drowned out by the lust in Zac's eyes. *I'm not giving in and letting him distract me with sex*, she reassured herself. Except, it was okay to give in a little, to remind him why they were perfect together. That's the only reason why they had come this far, because she'd been using their physical attraction to push him. So Reagan had to keep pushing him even further.

"Is this what you want?" he asked again.

Zac slipped his hand under her T-shirt and stroked up her stomach before pushing the cups of her bra under her breasts. He rubbed one of her nipples between his forefinger and thumb and squeezed. She moaned. As if her nipple was attached to her spine, her whole body arched. He squeezed harder and harder. She strained to her toes. The pain-pleasure making her dizzy. His grip on her chin never slackened. Never allowed her to move away. He completely controlled her. And just knowing that brought her to the edge of an orgasm, quicker than any orgasm she'd ever had.

"Zac," she moaned.

"Are you wet for me, Ree?" He plumped up her breast, before squeezing her nipple again. "Hmm? Tell me just how wet you are for me, right now."

"I'm wet. So wet for you."

His mouth was reaching for her again when the *Mission Impossible* theme song blasted. *Zac's phone*, Reagan realized. He released her suddenly and stepped back and kept moving back until there was distance between the two of them. Reagan swayed and almost fell. Somehow, she managed to stay on her feet. They were both breathing hard, staring at each other. Reagan's panties were soaked through and the bulge of Zac's erection was obvious beneath his jeans. An erection she remembered moving deep and hard inside of her.

His phone kept ringing and he finally pulled it out. He took one look at it and his eyes darkened. She opened her mouth to ask, but shut it when she saw how tense he carried himself. Oh! Only a few people had the power to piss off Zac that much. *It must be his parents. Oh god, that's not good.* Her heart ached with how bad she wanted to comfort him.

Zac took a deep breath as he looked away from her. He ran a hand through his hair.

"I made a promise to you, Ree," he said, quietly. "And I'm going to keep it. One more week. But I want you to remember that you made a promise to me too. When all of this is over, we're still going to be friends. I'm holding you to that."

He didn't wait for her to reply but walked out.

Reagan sat down on the edge of the bed.

Okay, that did not go the way she had been planning. Reagan ignored the painful arousal still coursing through her body to focus on the important issue at hand. She thought after last night, Zac had taken a step closer to seeing her side, but instead of moving forward he took a giant step back. And it didn't help that the unexpected phone call was probably from one of his parents. *Is this why he is having nightmares?* He thought she didn't know, but she did. She could see the lines beneath his eyes. She had so many questions, but if she pushed him too hard too fast, he'd shut down even more than he was already.

"Patience, Reagan," she murmured to herself.

You knew it wasn't going to be easy. You planned for this, remember? She still had tonight and one more week to show Zac. And she had a few more tricks up her sleeve. Zac had been right about one thing. They were doing too much fighting; there was fighting and then there was *fighting.* They needed to get back to doing more of the last one.

Her phone vibrated in her back pocket. She pulled it out and saw that it was a message from Aidan. Right on time. Excitement had her rubbing her hands together like a cartoon villain. She stood up quickly and high-tailed it out of the room.

Things were about to get interesting. *Let the games begin.*

Chapter Sixteen

Reagan sat on the sofa, watching Aidan, who stood in the center of the game room. Aidan was wearing a bandanna across his forehead to signal that he was the referee for the night. He was staring down at his clipboard—yep, they were that serious. The room had been divided into two teams, with six players on Reagan's Blue team and six players on Malcolm's Red team. And right now, they were waiting for Aidan to tally up the scores on their recent game.

Her middle brother, the host of the games, was sitting silently beside her. Callum was not as tall as Malcolm or Dean and not as bulky in size as Aidan. He wore his black hair long, just a bit under his chin and his dark chocolate eyes—nearly black—were at half-mast, like he was high 99% of the time. Many people had been fooled into thinking that nothing much was happening inside of Callum's mind, but they were very wrong about that. *Silent people have the loudest minds, after all.* It just took a lot longer to figure that out with Callum. It was one of the reasons why he was such a good pitcher. No one had any idea what he was planning to do or where he was going to throw the ball because they usually thought he wasn't that bright.

"And at the end of that round, Blue team, you have a total of six points. But, unfortunately, Red team is still in the lead with eight points."

Red team jumped up out of their seats, their voices rising into a triumphant shout as they hugged and high-fived. The Blue team sank lower into the sofa, shoulders down, moaning in defeat. Well, some, not all.

"Fucking A," Dean grumbled on her other side.

Letty, who didn't particularly care about the game, just took a sip of her cocktail. And Callum said nothing.

Fucking A. Reagan was right there with Dean. She slouched in her seat, groaning. She hated losing. It didn't help that they had dumb and dumber on their team as well, or as their parents christened them, May and April. Sisters who didn't have any talent. She wasn't exaggerating. If they spent even half as much time as they did on reapplying their makeup, maybe they'd be winning. Reagan had met some incredibly intelligent models over the years, but April and May were not some of them.

It didn't help that the Red team had Zac, Malcolm, DD, two kickass Olympians Lennox and Rachel, and Mandy, an amazing singer.

Reagan knew the plan for tonight was to ignore Zac. She knew that, but her eyes kept straying to the other side of the living room to him.

Zac barely glanced at her at all. He sat in between DD and Mandy, chatting amongst them with a causal smile on his face, acting like he wasn't even aware of her presence. That smile was anything but real. It was brittle at the edges and his shoulders were so far up, they might as well be sharing a zip code with his ears. Her epic plan was turning into an epic disaster.

Aidan tapped his clipboard, drawing all their attention back to him.

"The next round is charades. You have two minutes until it begins so get ready," he announced.

Yes! That was a game she was good at. They were going to win this one. Reagan could feel it in her bones.

"Everyone huddle around." She beckoned her team with two fingers.

They all did as she asked, with May and April sitting on the floor beside her.

"I can't believe you play these games three times a year." Letty shook her head, her brown ringlets raining down.

"Believe it, sugar." Dean grinned. "Wait until you play the Spicy game at the end of the year. Now, that's what you call epic fun. Whip cream, leather—"

"Are these games or are you just saying your BDSM fantasies out loud?"

Reagan sniggered at Letty's comment. "It's weird you haven't been to any, Letty, it feels like you've been around forever."

Although they had met three years ago, Letty's own drama with her family had kept her too busy to come to one of their game nights.

"Yeah, who would ever turn down charades?" Letty said, sarcastically.

Reagan held up her finger. "Girl, don't mock our games. Charades are awesome and we need to decide which signals we should use for—"

"Wait—which one is charades again?" May asked, flicking her blond hair behind her shoulder.

April raised her hand. "Can you explain the rules to me too?"

Reagan's mouth dropped open. She had no idea what to say to that. She looked at them closely, maybe they were joking? Except they didn't seem like they were.

Letty let out a laugh, crossing one leg over the other. "Are you guys for real? I didn't know people like you existed outside of TMZ and reality shows."

"Did she just insult us?" April whispered to May in indignation.

"If you have to ask—" Letty rolled her eyes "—then we're really going to have a real problem."

"Now, now, girls," Dean said with a shake of his head. "I'm happy to explain the rules to you both."

He explained the rules to them and then finally Dean passed the puck back to Reagan.

"Okay, so if it is a sentence we have to act out I was thinking we could—" she began.

"Time," Aidan said.

No, no, how could it be time already? They hadn't done anything!

"Dean, you're up first for the Blue team. Lennox, you're up for the Red team."

Dean stood up. "Don't worry, sis. I've totally got this."

He held out his hand. She high-fived him.

"We're going to lose, aren't we?" Letty murmured as they watched Dean and Lennox talk to Aidan and receive the words they would have to act out.

"Oh, we're definitely fucked," Reagan said back.

Dean turned to them; Lennox faced the Red team.

"You have ten seconds," Aidan told them. "Three. Two. One. Go."

Dean exploded into action, immediately flapping

his arms around. The room grew in sound as each team tried to guess what their teammate was acting out.

"I don't know what you're doing!" Reagan cried. "Is that the chicken dance?"

"No!" Dean said, before doing exactly what he was doing a moment ago.

"You're having a seizure?" Letty guessed.

"Ooh, I know." April threw her hands up. "You're doing the Running Man!"

Reagan gave her the stink eye. "Have you ever seen the Running Man? You don't flap your arms like that."

April waved her hands, still above her head. "I don't know. He could just be extremely bad at it?"

"No! No! And no!" Dean said again. "Come on, guys. You're not even trying. Watch what I'm doing and tell me what you see is happening."

Callum shifted in his seat beside her.

"A baby bird trying to fly for the first time," he said, softly.

Dean pointed at him and then pumped his fist.

"Yes!"

Red team cheered suddenly.

"And Red team gets the point," Aidan declared.

"What?" Dean turned towards Aidan in outrage.

"Callum said the answer first!" Reagan jumped up.

Aidan shrugged, uncaring that Dean towered over him by a few inches and was not happy.

"If the referee doesn't hear it, then it didn't happen."

Letty tugged on Reagan's shirt and Reagan fell back onto the sofa. Aidan was damn lucky that Letty saved him, because she'd been one second away from punching him in the face. She took her games seriously.

"The game isn't over yet," Letty reminded her gently.

"Next up, we have Malcolm for the Red team and Letty for the Blue team," Aidan said, looking at his clipboard.

"See. It's my turn. Watch me show them how it's done." Letty stood up and walked across the room to Aidan.

She was wearing skinny white jeans and a loose red blouse that looked amazing against her caramel skin complexion.

Letty smiled at Aidan. "Are you going to whisper the sentence in my ear?"

Aidan leaned down and put his mouth close to her ear. Letty's eyes closed. She nodded at whatever Aidan said.

"Want me to repeat that back to you?"

She didn't wait for Aidan's reply, but touched his shoulder and tiptoed to reach his ear. Her lips moved.

"What's going on between those two?" Dean looked at Reagan.

Reagan shook her head helplessly. "Have no clue."

Letty was definitely fucking with her. *Right?*

"Okay. I'm ready," Letty said.

Aidan repeated the words to Malcolm, who nodded. Both players turned to face their team.

"Three. Two. One. Go."

"Come on, Letty!" Reagan encouraged. "You can do this!"

Letty spread her legs apart and put her hands on her hips. Reagan frowned. Okay, what the fuck was she doing?

"You're a superhero!" May guessed.

Letty shook her head. She clapped twice, before putting her hands back on her hips. Then she raised her hands and wiggled her fingers.

"Do you have any idea what she's doing?" Reagan whispered to Callum.

Silence was his answer. Oh shit, they were most definitely going to lose.

"Spirit fingers!" Dean suddenly cried out.

Aidan blew his whistle. "And Blue team gets the point."

"Yes!" Blue team said in unison.

"I am a genius!" Dean grinned. "I knew watching cheerleaders closely would pay off."

Reagan laughed. "I think you're confusing *genius* with *pervert*."

Dean and Letty high-fived as she came back to the sofa.

The game of charades continued with May, then Callum, followed by Reagan going up. It wasn't a surprise when May had no idea how to act out *villain* and that Callum and Reagan were really good at charades. Aidan called an end to the games and was now taking a moment to figure out the scores.

Dean threw his arm around Letty's shoulders. Letty glanced at it and then at him.

"Can I help you?" she asked coolly.

"So, Letty—" Dean began.

"Whatever wildly inappropriate thing is about to come out of your mouth, let me stop you right there, Dean Thomas. I'm not interested."

He leaned in closer to her, smiling that gorgeous smile of his. "But, baby, trust me, my Cocoa Puffs need your Cheerios. You don't know what you're missing."

"What? Herpes?"

Everyone burst out laughing.

"Hey!" Dean exclaimed. "I do not have herpes! I take care of my junk, thank you very much. Wrapping it is always the way to go."

Aidan blew his whistle again. "As interesting as it is to hear about Dean's latest bout of herpes, we are reaching the end of the games. Before I announce the final scores and declare the winners, does anyone want to challenge any contestants?"

The Red team and Blue Team stared at each other, each side equally daring the other to try something. Except Zac barely glanced over. He was too busy looking at his hands and whatever mystery they held. She couldn't take it anymore. She needed him to look at her and realize that she would not be ignored. *Get ready, Zac, you don't know what's about to hit ya.*

Reagan rose slowly to her feet.

"What are you doing?" Dean hissed.

She ignored him. Heart in her throat, she stepped forward.

"I, Reagan Thomas, challenge you, Zachariah Quinn, to a face-off."

Silence reigned for a moment. Everyone stared at Zac, gauging his reaction.

Zac's eyes narrowed. He rose to his feet, towering over her in almost an intimidating way. But Reagan refused to be intimidated.

Zac raised an eyebrow. "You sure you want to do that, Ree? You do remember what happened last time, don't you?"

She smirked at him, secretly thrilled. "Keep acting cocky, it's only going to be so much more rewarding when I take you down."

"Don't forget you asked for this."

"Whatever."

"The challenge?"

"Wii. Boxing."

"Knock-out?"

"Of course."

"Stakes?"

"Ten extra points?"

"Make it twenty."

She shook her head. "Fifteen."

"Eighteen points."

"Seventeen."

She thought about that.

"Okay. Seventeen." She held out her hand. "May the best woman win."

He laughed and her stomach clenched, a blush rising up her chest and to her neck. He shook her hand, his thumb caressing her skin slightly before letting go.

"Oh, we both know who's going to win."

She didn't say anything to that, but just kept that smirk on her face.

"Don't get cocky," Reagan whispered low enough that no one else could hear them. "I have a side bet for you. If I win, you have to date me for real. No more of Mr. Boring Zac. I want the real you."

He lost his smile. "Fine. But if I win, we'll call off this whole deal once and for all."

Okay, she hadn't expected that. She licked her lips. *Oh shit, what if I lose and I lose him?* She didn't want this to end, not yet, not ever and it seemed like Zac was determined to push her away. *Then don't lose,* she told herself, *for you and for him.* Show him that you're willing to fight against him and his sneaky tactics. No, not sneaky, *dirty* tactics.

"Fine," she said.

I'm not going to back down now.

Aidan tapped his clipboard again to draw their attention back to him.

"I'll set up the game."

Reagan turned back to her team, who all stared at her.

"What just happened? What the fuck is a face-off? Can someone please explain to me what is going on?" Letty asked, sloshing her drink around.

"A face-off is when two opposing players are allowed to go head-to-head in any game to try and win back some much-needed points," Reagan explained.

"Like a Hail Mary," Dean added.

"Exactly. When I win, we'll get an extra seventeen points added to our total score."

"Nice." Letty smiled.

"That's *if* we win though," Dean pointed out.

"We'll win," Reagan said, confidently. Or she tried for confident.

You're not going to lose. You got this. She pushed everything out of her mind, except for the game. Her earlier intention might've been to knock that sad look off Zac's face, but now it was to knock Zac out. *What? I love him, but I'm still competitive.*

"Players," Aidan called out, "get ready. We're about to begin."

Reagan high-fived her team members as she moved to in front of the TV. Zac stood to her side, throwing her a grin. Aidan gave them each a controller. Reagan's hand tensed around it.

"Let's make this interesting. I bet twenty Zac beats Reagan," Malcolm said, holding up a twenty-dollar bill.

And just like that the betting started.

Dean blew out a raspberry.

"That's easy. I bet twenty on Zac too."

What the fuck? Reagan turned around and glared at him.

"Bitch, you forget that you're supposed to be *my* brother?" Reagan spluttered as everyone laughed.

Dean shrugged. "Sorry, sis. Bros before hoes."

"And you just called me a hoe!"

Letty rooted through her bag.

"I'll put twenty on Reagan." She slapped the money into Malcolm's hand.

"You got this," Letty whispered to her on her way back to her seat.

I so totally got this.

She jumped from foot to foot, shaking out her arms. *So totally got this.*

"You ready for this, Ree?" Zac murmured to her as the number *3* flashed on the screen.

2.

"You are so going down," she murmured back.

1.

Fight!

Reagan threw out her right arm immediately, but Zac was ready for that and blocked. For a minute, they both parried and tried to feint each other, but neither could seem to get the upper hand. Until, finally Zac's right hook connected. Her avatar on-screen fell to the ground.

"Ouch," the crowd groaned together.

Get up, get up, she told her character. Her character,

a sweaty man in boxers, stumbled to his feet. *You got this. You got this.*

The same song and dance began again. She tried to hit him, he blocked. Her arms were getting tired—she really needed to go back to the gym!—and a sneak peek at Zac's determined face told her he could do this all day any day. *Oh shit.*

"Come on, Reagan! You got this!" Letty called out.

"Come on, Reagan! Crush him!"

The support of her team sent a much-needed surge of energy through her. Her jab suddenly connected with Zac's avatar. With his guard down, she was able to land another punch and then another. The Blue team screamed their encouragement. She kept punching and Zac's character fell back in an exaggerated fall to the ground.

Oh shit, she did it. He's down.

And he's staying down. Still, she held her breath until the screen flashed "You win." Yes!

"And victory is mine!" She threw up her hands in tribulation.

They turned to each other. Zac held out his hand. Laughing, she took it, but he didn't let go of her immediately.

"What?" she asked.

"That wasn't bad."

She laughed again. "I crushed you."

"Let's not go that far," he scoffed.

"A win is a win, no matter what." She grinned as she threw the words he had been saying to her over the years back in his face.

"A very wise saying."

"Shut up." She smacked him in the chest. "By the way…"

Zac raised his eyebrow, waiting for her to continue.

She dropped her voice as she moved in closer. "We might occasionally fight, Zac, but fighting with you and by your side is always a pleasure."

His eyes darkened, his mouth opened, but she never got to hear what he was going to say.

"And you know what that means! Blue team wins!" Aidan announced.

Blue team leapt to their feet and let out a collective "whoop" of excitement. Dean grabbed Reagan and spun her around, making her dizzy with laughter.

"Put me down, you lunatic!"

He finally set her down, only to throw his arms around Callum.

"Fuck, can't believe we lost," Malcolm grumbled.

"Believe it! And start getting used to it, because that's all you're going to be doing this year," Dean crowed.

Malcolm held up his middle finger. This led to a lot more bickering between the two groups.

Reagan turned when she felt Zac's gaze on the side of her face, instantly snared by him. They stared at each other from across the room. She didn't know what his eyes were saying, but there was a world of emotion in them. She felt like she could drown and never find her way to the surface and she didn't want to. Oh god, she was so in love with him. She had to swallow down the emotion, because it threatened to bubble up. The air seemed to crackle between them as they faced off. It wasn't just physical, it was personal. She wasn't going to rest until he knew exactly what he meant to her.

She looked away.

* * *

Hours later, the party was finally unwinding.

"I think this is my cue to go home."

Letty had already gone and all her brothers had left as well. She hadn't seen Zac in a little while. The house was almost empty, with only a few stragglers left behind.

Reagan said goodbye to the girls she had been hanging with and went to find Callum.

She found him out on his balcony, leaning over the railing, his head down. It was pretty warm outside, which was a good thing since Callum wasn't wearing a jacket. His colored tattoos were beautiful against his dark skin. She'd always thought so. She touched him on the shoulder, trying not to startle him.

Dark bleak eyes met hers when he lifted his head. There was so much pain in his eyes she gasped and wondered for a moment if he was physically hurt.

"Callum, what's wrong?"

He didn't say anything, but it seemed like he wanted to. Like he was wrestling with it. She stroked his wavy hair softly.

"You don't have to say anything if you don't want to, or if you can't. Whenever you are ready to talk, I'm here, okay?"

He nodded.

For a moment they stayed like that. Her stroking Callum's hair and him letting her. Then he shifted away from her and his attention wandered to the cloudless dark sky. She knew that was her cue to leave, but…

"Are you going to be okay?" She hesitated.

He didn't look at her. Reagan really wanted to push him into talking to her, but that was the wrong move.

Once, when she was fourteen, the week before Callum had gone off to college, she'd found him sitting outside the house, back against the wall. She'd asked him what was wrong then too, but he'd only shaken his head. She'd sat with him for hours, but it was only the night before he was about to leave that he told her.

"I'm scared of being by myself. Away from the family. What if...?"

"What if what?" Reagan asked him.

"I don't know. What if I don't know who I am, never find out who I am, or I do and I can't come back home anymore."

"Nothing, there's no reason in the world why you'd never be allowed to come back home. And if you tried to escape, we'd all come and drag your ass back, kicking and screaming."

"Goodnight, Callum."

"Night, sis."

She walked away.

Chapter Seventeen

Reagan held her phone in her hand as she walked out of Callum's house, making her way over to where her car was parked. She was wondering if she should text Callum. Something was really wrong with him. She couldn't imagine what it could be. Was he injured? Or was it something else? She sighed as she put her phone in her back pocket, taking out her car keys. No matter how much she wanted to reach out, she didn't want to nag him. She needed to give him space.

She froze mid-step.

Zac leaned against his Lexus.

"You're still here," she whispered.

He straightened. She wanted to ask him what he was doing here, but she knew. One look into his blue heated eyes and her body shivered All the teasing over the last couple of hours had left her revved up. Oh god, she was about to break her own rule.

He opened the door.

"Get in, Reagan."

"What about my car?"

"We'll deal with it tomorrow." He raised an eyebrow.

She got in. He shut the door and got into the driver's seat.

Reagan didn't say anything. She was too busy trying to control her breathing and resisting the urge to rub her thighs together and ease the ache. And the vibrations were not helping either. Neither were the glances she kept stealing of Zac. He was too gorgeous for his own good.

Zac waited until they were moving to speak.

"Take off your panties," he said.

Reagan's head turned sharply towards his. He didn't look away from the road. Both hands were on the steering wheel and his knuckles were slightly white.

"Um…"

"That wasn't a suggestion. Take off your panties, Ree."

She blew out a breath. Her trembling hands reached for her buttons and zipper. She undid them and drew her jeans down, unlacing her Converses and kicking off both her jeans and shoes. Sitting in her baby blue panties with the world slipping by left her feeling very self-conscious. So much that she didn't know if she could do it, but she couldn't deny that she was excited as hell. The proof was in the slickness of her pussy.

"Come on, little vixen." Zac's voice dropped low. "I want to see how you make yourself come."

"I don't know if I can do that," she admitted. She was feeling way too self-conscious.

"Don't think about anything. Just focus on me and you. Touch yourself for me, Reagan."

Her hand slid under her panties. Her fingers brushed her clit, then down to her center where she was slick.

"Have you ever done this, by yourself, thinking about me?"

She nodded. She was embarrassed for him to know how often she had done it over the years.

"Me too. Fuck. Just knowing that is enough to make me hard."

His groan echoed around her, reaching deep and embedding itself under her skin. Her eyes drifted to his crotch. Yep, he was hard beneath his jeans. She felt the cool breeze of air against her heated skin and it made her pant in desperation. Her palm was smooth as she rubbed it back and forth over her clit, breathing in and catching hints of his masculine scent. *Oh shit*. She bit her lip, the pulsing between her thighs intensifying.

"I'm going to come," Reagan gasped out.

She barely noticed when the car swerved and they suddenly parked. She was so focused on riding her intense orgasm. She did notice however when Zac grabbed her by the waist and pulled her over the console. He settled her in his lap, pushing the car seat back as far as it would go so they were reclining, before kissing her senseless. Her hands touched his neck.

"This is crazy," she gasped when he finally let her breathe.

He answered by tightening his grip on her hips and grinding his erection against her.

"We should stop," she tried again.

He yanked her T-shirt over her head. She pulled his shirt off and threw it into the back.

"Don't tell me to stop, because I don't think I could."

"Stop? Are you crazy? If you stop now, I'll kill you, Zachariah Quinn."

He laughed, which turned into a moan when she finally pulled out his cock. Hard and heavy just like she wanted him. She ran her hands all over him. Her mouth watered and she was tempted to get onto her knees and suck him off again.

"Nope," Zac said, pushing her hands off him. "I need to be inside of you right now."

"Condom." She remembered in the last second.

He flicked open the glove compartment and rooted around, bringing out a foil packet. She took it from him, ripped it open and fitted the condom.

He helped her lift up over him, until her pussy was aligned with his cock. She lowered herself, taking him slowly. They both groaned. Until, finally, thank you god, she took all of him. Head tipped back, Reagan paused for a moment.

"You feel so good."

She had no answer for that, but another moan.

She rode him fast and she rode him dirty.

He cupped both of her breasts in his hands and squeezed her nipples.

"Faster."

He thrust up into her. She cried out. They fell into a rhythm with her grinding down and him thrusting up into her. Reagan's orgasm swept over her in shocking waves of pleasure, her pussy squeezing his cock, sending him right over the edge.

Her head fell onto his shoulder, exhausted. Zac wrapped his arms around her, breathing just as hard in her ears.

"Mm, is the sex supposed to be getting better and better?" She wanted to know.

"I have no idea." He stroked her spine. "But if it gets any better than this I might not survive."

She giggled. Reagan lifted her head to look at him, running her hand down his face. *So pretty. And all male*, she thought as she felt his stubble beneath her fingers.

"Come home with me tonight?" she asked him, the words emerging from a deep part of her.

She felt him tense beneath her. His eyes darkened.

"I'm not sure if that's a good idea, Ree."

"Why?"

He shook his head. "I just—"

She kissed him, stopping whatever hurtful words he was about to say. She rubbed her lips gently over his. Mm, this was an okay tactic, kissing everything better, but she was onto him. He might have won the battle, but she was going to win the war. He had promised he was going to try from now on and she was going to hold him to it.

"Come home with me, Zac," she whispered again. "I need you."

His arms tightened around her. She prayed desperately he gave her the answer she wanted. He swallowed before he gave her his reply.

"Okay."

Chapter Eighteen

The next night Zac stood outside Reagan's door.

Reagan had given him no clues as to what tonight would entail. All she had told him was the time and place: 6:30 pm and her apartment. Other than that, he had no fucking clue what he was about to walk into.

How the hell did we get here? He'd spent last night in Reagan's bed, not doing much but lying under the covers—oh, and arguing about the X-Men.

"You can't possibly say that Magneto is the best char-acter, he's the villain," she hissed, her arms wrapped around his neck, nose against his.

"And you can't say that Professor X is anything but boring," he retorted.

"But the comics—"

"Nope." He rolled her onto her back. "What did I say about the comics?"

There was only one rule: he hadn't read them so she was not allowed to bring them up.

The way she'd grumbled and bitched was honestly the cutest thing and he had not been able to resist kissing her. *Why am I resisting her?* No matter how much of an asshole he acted like—and he'd done some dickish things—she refused to give up on him. Why? *Why the hell is she working so hard to be with me?* He pressed his forehead against the cold wooden door. Maybe, fuck, maybe it wasn't the worst idea if they tried to... He lifted his head and let it fall, the sound of the thud echoing in the hallway. Some much needed pain helped him remember exactly why he couldn't give in, why spending the night had felt great at the beginning, until the nightmare came. They always came.

Now it was Reagan's turn to pick and decide their dates. So far, they were tied, if he was keeping score of who had the upper hand. *Ree might not back down*, he thought, straightening and moving back, *but, as soon as things become sexual, she loses her train of thought quickly.*

As was tradition, Zac was holding a bouquet of flowers. Oh, he knew how much the flowers annoyed Reagan, but he just didn't give a fuck. That was a lie—he did give a fuck. He *enjoyed* seeing the flash of irritation in Reagan's eyes every single time he handed them over and it might be perverse just how much he liked it. He was going to like it even better when she finally lost her temper and called him on it. Maybe then, he would bend her over the couch and fuck her—

Reagan's door opened and he was confronted with the woman of his thoughts.

"Hi," she greeted him.

Her eyes drifted down to the flowers he was holding. And there it was: that little flash of ire, before she pushed it down.

"For me?" she said through clenched teeth. "You shouldn't have."

"I know how much you love flowers," he murmured as he handed them to her.

Zac looked her up and down. Hair braided past her shoulder. Minimal makeup. Casual clothes. No shoes. Even now, she was so goddamn beautiful it hurt to look at her, but he couldn't look away.

"We're staying in?"

She nodded. "Yep. We're going to be eating at home."

"What are you up to, Reagan?"

"Wouldn't you like to know?" she said, throwing a smile over her shoulder as she disappeared inside.

He hadn't bothered to put on a jacket, and was only wearing a black shirt and his black jeans, so he followed her into the kitchen after kicking the door shut. He watched as she dumped the bouquet of flowers in a vase.

"And FYI, *we're* going to be making dinner," Reagan told him.

She moved to her counter, where there was a chopping board, a knife and bowls of different vegetables. He stared. Shit, she was serious about this.

"So *why* are you cooking?" Zac asked, hesitantly.

Reagan shrugged as she began cutting up some tomatoes. "Because I thought it would be nicer than going to another restaurant."

"But you hate cooking."

"Hey! I do not hate…" Her voice trailed off when she saw his raised eyebrows. "Okay, it's not my favorite thing to do, but I thought it would be romantic."

Romantic? He wanted to scoff. It wouldn't be romantic when she burned down the house and they had nothing to eat. Zac opened his mouth to tell her just that when she pointed her knife at him.

"And before you start with me, this is my week. So,

that means we do whatever the fuck I want. No exceptions. And I want us to make dinner. Not me. *We*."

She lifted her chin as she said that, getting that stubborn look. Too bad she was about to be disappointed.

"Babe, no."

"This is my night!"

"Yeah and you can do the cooking while I make sure you don't burn down the fucking house."

"I'm not going to burn it down!" she snapped.

"Ree."

"Zac!"

He sighed. "How about I set the table and wash the dishes, but no cooking?"

She took a moment to think about this before speaking.

"That would be acceptable," she said, glaring.

"Glad you think so."

She didn't bother to reply and instead turned back to cutting. He almost huffed out a laugh but managed to swallow it in the last second. He didn't want to set a new world record and get into another fight in the span of ten seconds.

"What are we making, then?" Zac conceded, crossing his arms and moving closer to her.

"Zucchini, sweet potato and tomato pasta."

Reagan smiled when he grimaced.

"Sorry, there's no meat. I know how you big men feel about your meat," she said.

"My meat is big," he purred, coming up behind and pressing himself against her.

Zac wrapped his arms around her waist.

She giggled. "That was so lame."

"Got you laughing, didn't it?" he pointed out.

He kissed the underside of her ear, his talented and dirty mouth drifting to her neck.

"Stop distracting me," Reagan whispered.

She loved his form of distraction, especially when he nuzzled the space between her neck and shoulder. She shivered.

"I mean it, Zac," she said again.

To show him that she was serious, she pushed him away. He leaned against the kitchen counter beside her. She peeked at him as she put all the vegetables she had chopped into the pan that was simmering on the stove. He didn't shy away, but watched her boldly, his mouth quirked but not enough to show off those dimples of his. Her heart beat fast; part of it was nervousness and another part of it was anticipation. She had something to give to him and she had no idea what his response was going to be.

"Um… I just remembered something," she said nervously. "Let me go and get it."

She ran out of the room, speaking over her shoulder. "Keep stirring for me."

Reagan grinned at the panicked look on his face as she skidded out of the kitchen to her bedroom. She found what she was looking for relatively easily since she had left it sitting on her bed. And just like that all the amusement was gone and every single paranoid thought came rushing back. What if he didn't like it? Oh shit, what if he hated it? What if he found it super weird that she had done this? What if he—

Stop, stop. Remember, cool, calm and collected. Cool, calm and collected.

"Is it meant to be doing this?" Zac asked her when she returned.

The sauce was spitting and turning a darker shade. Hell if she knew. Rather than reply, she turned off the heat.

"Here you go." She plopped the little gift box in front of him.

"You know my birthday isn't for another three months, right?" he teased, as he reached for it.

"I know that, smart-ass. I got you this because I was thinking about you and I wanted to."

She got him a gift and it wasn't even his birthday.

Zac had no idea what to say to that so he focused on the present. He opened the gift box. Inside, there was decorative paper that he rooted through until he touched something soft, feathery and long. He brought it out of the box and held it out in front of him.

Zac stared at it. It was a dream catcher. But that wasn't what had him stunned, it was the fact that the dream catcher was chocolate brown—his favorite color—and engraved with his jersey number. She must have had this made, because he was pretty sure you couldn't just find this in any store. His jersey, yes. They sold that merchandise everywhere, but this? Nope. And that meant she'd thought deeply about getting him a gift and it wasn't a spur of the moment purchase.

"It's supposed to help with bad dreams," she told him, quietly. "Protect you and keep you safe. I know you're only a quarter Native American on your mother's side, but I remember you used to have one a couple of years ago, and I thought you would like one again."

He looked into her bright brown eyes and saw the

apprehension in them. His heart stuttered. He put the dream catcher and its box down on the table and, unable to resist the urge anymore, he ran his hands through his hair. Fuck, fuck. She *knew*. He could see it written all over her face. She *knew*.

Reagan had always known about his fucked-up childhood. It was impossible to grow up in their town and not know who Sheriff Quinn was and *what* he was. And Reagan had unfortunately seen him right after some of his father's more unforgettable moments, like when he had gotten into an argument with his father and had tried to leave. He'd ended up falling down the stairs when his father had pushed him a little too hard. He had broken two ribs with that stunt. While his childhood wasn't something he could control, *this* relationship was something he could. Now, she knew that he was too weak to move past it all and grow up. He thought he was hiding it from her, but apparently not well enough.

"Reagan," Zac choked out.

"Hey. Hey." She rolled onto the tips of her toes, wrapping her arms around his shoulders. "It's okay. I know you don't want to talk about it, Zac. I *know*. But I just want you to know I'm here whenever you do."

"I don't want to talk about it," he said, more harshly than he intended.

He felt her flinch.

"That's okay. You don't have to," she said. "But if you do—"

"I don't."

Zac took a deep breath. And then another. Trying to calm his heart. He closed his eyes, unable to keep looking into her face of compassion and something else...

something deeper that he didn't want to look too closely at and examine.

"You don't fight fair, Ree." He swallowed.

"No, I don't. Not when it comes to someone this important to me."

He felt her mouth press gently against his.

"Reagan." He didn't kiss her back, too stunned to move.

"I'm right here, Zac," she told him against his mouth. "I'm all yours."

She kissed him again. He deepened the kiss. His hands cupped her ass. He enjoyed the feel of her cheeks in the palms of his hands. Let the feeling of having her in his arms consume him, pushing everything else out.

The gasp she made against his mouth was well worth it. He lifted her up onto the counter, pushing her knees apart and settling in between her thighs. She moaned as he kissed down her throat to the sensitive area of her neck.

"Zac."

"Mm." He pulled her flush against him, rocking their hips together. She moaned again.

She shook her head as if trying to clear her head. "We can't."

"Why not?"

"Because…" She seemed to lose her train of thought when he put his hands on her breasts and squeezed. He took her mouth again.

For a few more minutes, they made out. Until Reagan pulled back, gasping.

"Okay. Okay. No more." She took a couple of deep breaths. "Food first. Sex later."

"You sure about that?"

"Um…"

He smirked. She knocked away his hands, glaring.

"Yes, I am sure about that. Now, go and get the lettuce out of the fridge."

Before he could pull away though, she put her hands on either side of his face.

"Stay with me tonight."

"Ree, you know why—"

"Stay with me," she cut him off. "We'll take it one day at a time."

And like the previous night, he was unable to resist her. The smile on her face and the kiss she gave him was almost worth it. Almost.

Chapter Nineteen

Reagan juggled some files in one hand and a mug of cinnamon latte in the other as she made the trip back to her office. Walking down the hallway, she passed Mitchell's, her boss—or more correctly, her boss's boss—office. The entire wall was made of glass and allowed for anyone to see inside. This was supposed to promote openness, but that wasn't what made her pause. Trent Newman sat in the visitor's chair across from Mitchell's desk and Daniel, the condescending douchebag, was standing beside Mitchell. Trent Newman, her client. The client that she had to justify to Daniel that she knew what she was doing every other day, even though Alan, the Executive Managing Director, her and Daniel's boss, was fine with letting her take the lead. And they looked like they were arguing.

Oh, that did not look good.

"Reagan, could you—" Mari, one of her fellow junior agents, said, coming down the hallway towards her.

Reagan had no idea what Mari was about to say and she didn't care.

"Take this to my office please," she said to her, dumping her files into Mari's startled arms. She thrust the mug at her, forcing Mari to take it or spill coffee down her blouse.

"Thank you!" Reagan said, over her shoulder, hustling over to Mitchell's door on her four-inch heels. It was not easy.

Reagan took a deep breath. *Okay, Reagan, everything is going to be fine. Calm, cool and collected. You're going to ask them what they're doing and then you are going to listen to their rational answer.*

She knocked on the door.

"Come in," a voice answered.

Reagan opened the door and entered. Trent swiveled around to look at her. All three men watched as she came to Mitchell's desk, beside Trent's chair.

"Reagan." Mitchell greeted her with a blank expression.

"Mr. Mitchell, it's nice to see you again, sir," she said politely.

Pointedly ignoring Daniel, she turned her attention onto her client.

Trent Newman was a good-looking guy. With sandy blond hair and a killer smile, he looked like the poster child for surfers. He was young, only twenty-two years old, but he had a right arm that made him worth millions of dollars. And right now, he was fidgeting in his chair, looking extremely uncomfortable.

"Hey, Trent. It's good to see you." Reagan comforted him with a smile.

"Reagan," he said, in relief.

"Reagan," Mitchell called to her. "Is there a reason why you are here?"

She stared at him, dumbfounded. "I'm not sure why I wasn't asked to come in the first place."

"That's what I said!" Trent burst out.

"Have you not seen your emails? My assistant emailed this to you this morning." Mitchell crossed his arms on his desk.

No, she hadn't checked her emails. She had spent the morning helping a client not freak out at his photo shoot. It involved chamomile tea and a hot towel. Something she did not want to repeat, unless the person was buying her dinner first.

"I didn't see it, but shouldn't Alan be here?"

Mitchell looked to Daniel to answer. Reagan was already gritting her teeth even before he opened his mouth.

"I felt like Alan wasn't really addressing the concerns I had so I thought it'd be best I bring this issue to Mr. Mitchell's attention."

Of all the slimy, douchebag things—Reagan shook her head.

Trent's right leg bounced up and down. "They're telling me to sign the shoe deal, but I told them you said not to do it. That you'll find me something better."

"What?" Her mind whirled.

Why the hell would they do that? If Trent was a seasoned mediocre player with several other minor deals under his belt, it would be a fantastic idea, but as a rookie it was a dumb idea. If Trent was half the player he was, this deal wouldn't even be bad considering how global the shoe company was. But he was the most sought out baseball player of the decade. This deal would mean he was fucked out of a lot of money—especially if he played an amazing season, which in all likelihood he would—and locked into this deal for three years where anything could happen. That was crazy. Reagan had no idea what Daniel or even Mitchell was thinking.

"Because it's a good deal," Daniel said, smiling that smarmy smile of his that always rubbed her the wrong way.

Yeah, it was a good deal if you were an agent trying to stiff your client, like Daniel clearly was. And Reagan was all for telling him he could shove his opinions and his micro-aggressive behavior, but…she couldn't. Daniel still outranked her and she needed to stay cool, calm and collected.

She opened her mouth to vehemently deny that claim, when Mitchell spoke.

"Mr. Newman, will you leave us alone for a few minutes, please?"

As soon as Trent left, Reagan looked at Mitchell.

"Mitchell, I'm sorry, I don't know what Daniel has been telling you, but this isn't a good idea. Trent should be looking to squeeze every penny out of this deal, not to downsize. Besides, I'm currently working on getting him a deal with—"

"This is the best deal for him. We have no idea how well he will perform during his season or if he might get injured," Daniel dismissed with a wave of his hand.

"He's twenty-two years old with no record of getting injured, who's batting better than anyone else. He's at the height of his career," she said, in disbelief. "I think we should—"

Daniel pointed a slim manicured finger at her, over the desk.

"I don't need to explain my decisions to you. I have cleared all of my ideas with Mitchell and that is all you need to know."

If the boy interrupts me one more time, I'm going to... She clenched her teeth together. *They're not listening to me. And they're not going to.* Reagan took them in and realized that they weren't talking to her like she was in charge of Trent Newman's management or that she had any part in his career at all.

"What's going on here?" she asked Mitchell slowly.

"Nothing." Mitchell didn't move. His arms stayed crossed, those calm eyes focused on her. "We were talking to Trent about some ideas we had."

"Ideas that he doesn't like."

Daniel's eyes flickered with annoyance. "We all know that the clients don't always know what is in their best interest, which is why they have agents, thank god. Or they'd probably be flat broke."

"Sir—" Reagan began.

"It's nothing personal," Mitchell cut her off. "Trent Newman is a valuable client."

"I know that." She stepped forward. "I was the one who brought him in. And Alan gave me the okay to manage him."

"And you were rewarded for that," Mitchell reminded her.

Steven's party was her reward? And her consolation prize to soften the blow? She stared at him incredulously. But no way was she ready to give up that easily.

"I sent you and Alan a report detailing my plans for Trent's future. Have you seen—"

Mitchell nodded. "I have seen it and while it was adequate, the points I've made are still valid. You do not have the level of experience needed."

"And you're a junior agent," Daniel added from his little corner, playing with the end of his light blue tie.

"And junior agents are allowed to build up their own clientele," she shot back. "And Alan—"

"I'm sure Alan will come to see who the right person is for the job." Daniel smiled.

"*I'm* the right person for the job." She pointed to herself and then quickly put her hand back down to her side, resisting the urge to reach over the desk and strangle him.

He scoffed. "If you ever thought you were going to be allowed to manage Trent Newman then you are delusional."

"Daniel," Mitchell said mildly, turning his head to meet Daniel's gaze. "Please refrain from insulting people in my office."

Daniel fell quiet, looking away.

"But Daniel is correct, you are a junior agent, Reagan. I value your contribution to this agency, but there remains a hierarchy in place for a reason. While I value that Alan would put you in such an enviable position, I do think you cannot manage someone of Trent Newman's caliber. You do not have the expertise for it, but one day I assure you, you will. For now, however, Daniel will take the lead on Trent and I will allow you to help Daniel as he sees fit."

Reagan had no idea what to say to that. Shit, she knew what she really wanted to say. That what he had just told her was a chauvinistic piece of crap, seeing as how Daniel had signed Mason Dalton while he was a junior agent and Mason Dalton was one of the best American football players and continued to be amazing even though he had transferred to their LA branch. No, this was a power move orchestrated by Daniel. And because she didn't have a dick, she was being frozen out of the old boys' club. Or was it because of the color of her skin?

Daniel watched with a gloating smirk. Reagan swallowed her words. She would not give him the satisfaction of turning to Mitchell and saying, *"See, I told you. Hysterical females can't handle themselves the way that men can. She's nothing but an angry, black woman."* She pasted on a smile and focused on Mitchell.

"Thank you, sir. I'll be glad for any opportunity I can get," she said.

Inside though, Reagan had never wanted to punch something or someone more in her whole life.

Later that night, when Reagan opened her front door, Zac held up a single flower: a white rose.

"I hope you don't mind that I didn't get you a bouquet, but I thought you would…" His voice trailed off when he got a good look at her face.

"What's wrong?" he asked with concern.

"Nothing."

"Bullshit. Something's wrong."

Reagan turned on her heel and walked to her sofa. She flopped down into it and stuffed her head under the hundreds of throw cushions she had. Fuck, he was right, something was definitely wrong. He shut the door behind himself. Zac had spent the day wondering what kind of torture Reagan was going to put him through tonight. This morning when he had slid out of her bed, after another restless night, she had seemed fine. What the fuck had happened between then and now?

He crouched down beside her head.

"Reagan," he called softly.

"Go away, Zac," she said, her words muffled but still understandable.

"What about our date?"

"Fuck the date."

He almost laughed at that.

"Tell me what's wrong."

She lifted her head. Most of her curls covered her face, part of it frizzy, and her eyes were spitting mad.

"You want to know what's wrong: my boss is a dickhead, that's what's wrong."

She slammed her head into her cushions over and over again.

"Okay, stop," he said. "I really don't want to find out if you can cause yourself a concussion with cushions. And why do you need this many?"

When she ignored him and continued hitting herself, he grabbed her. Hands on her cheeks, he turned her head to face him.

"Tell me what's wrong, Ree," he said again.

"Remember me telling you about Trent Newman and how I signed him as a client?"

Zac nodded.

"Mitchell gave him to Daniel. He said it was because I didn't have enough 'experience' to be dealing with such a high-profile client. But we all know it's because I don't have the right skin tone or the right equipment between my legs."

Zac didn't know what he should say to that. This was not his area of expertise. He had his own agent, yes, and that agent happened to be a senior agent at his agency, but that told him next to nothing about the business. What he did know was how hard Reagan worked and how fucking amazing she was at her job. She was passionate about sports, but more she cared about people and getting the best for them. He'd watched her over the years devote so much of her time to going above and beyond, like helping Chris Morgan, the football player, with his interview with PSY TV. She'd spent hours listening to Morgan practice again and again, only stumbling into her dad's monthly dinner at midnight. Fuck, she was as hardworking as any of them.

"I know I haven't been doing this long, but he was *my* client," Reagan continued in a whisper.

"Do you think you can do this, Ree?" he asked her quietly.

"I'm—"

"Yes or no."

"Yes."

"Then, that's all that matters," he said.

She huffed. "Um, no, it isn't. I do answer to people, you know."

"Fuck 'em."

"That's real helpful!"

"You were the one who managed to convince Trent to sign with your agency, not them," he said, fiercely. "Trent trusts you, not them. He wants to work with you, not them. Everything I've said is true, isn't it?"

"Yes."

"So, prove to them that you can do this and that they can't do it without you."

Her big eyes showed her confusion. "And how do I do that?"

He grinned at her. "I can't do everything for you, Ree. You'll think of something."

Reagan groaned. Zac rubbed her cheek.

"Remember when Dean accidentally shaved off his

eyebrow during his beauty phase and he locked himself in his bedroom, saying he wouldn't come out because he wasn't beautiful anymore?"

"Yeah, but what the hell does that have to do with anything?"

"You sat with him for hours, arguing and pushing him until finally he let you draw on a replacement one so he could drag his ass to the airport and get back so he didn't get fired. You did that. And why?" He waved a hand at her and waited.

"Because I'm useful." She scrunched her face in confusion.

"Yeah, you are. The most caring person I know. You never give up, so why the hell would you give up now?"

Reagan nodded slowly. "I guess. I'll think about it."

"Sit up," Zac told her.

When she did as he asked, he pulled himself onto the sofa and reached for her. She sighed as she put her head in his lap.

"My boss is a dickhead," she mumbled again.

He smiled. "Do you still want to go out?"

"No. I just want to stay here." She buried her face deeper into his stomach.

"We can do that."

"Maybe eating some ice cream would help?"

He stroked her hair. "Do you have any ice cream?"

She shook her head.

"I'll buy some Rocky Road for you."

"You are the best."

"You're going to have to let me go if you want that ice cream." He smirked down at her.

She kept her face hidden but shook her head again.

"In a few minutes then."

"Careful with my hair. I don't want it to get knotted."

"I know how to handle your hair."

He kept on stroking her, feeling her body relax further until it seemed like she was asleep.

Half an hour later, Zac managed to coax Reagan into going outside with him. They bought ice cream and returned to the sofa. Now, a movie was blasting on the TV while they ate said ice cream. Mint flavor for him and Rocky Road for her.

As a car exploded on-screen, he felt Reagan turn to look at him.

"Why are we watching this goddamn awful film again?"

"You better watch yourself," he warned. "Don't you dare mock Vin Diesel."

"They never once stop for gas during this whole entire film and how do they not care that so many people died? I don't get it."

"I swear, Ree, keep talking smack about one of the greatest films of all time—"

"The greatest film of all time?" She laughed. "And what? What will you do to me, huh?"

A dare? Oh, Ree had no idea what she'd got herself into. He crept his hand under her skirt and she shivered in anticipation.

"Don't do it. Zac! I mean it. Please."

But it was too late. She'd insulted one of his favorite movies and now she had to pay the price. He tickled her sides and her stomach. She rolled onto her back, laughing, screaming, squirming. He trapped her beneath him, his thighs draped over hers.

"I warned you, again and again, Ree, not to make fun of my movies. And what did you do?"

"Stop! Stop!" she screeched. "I'm gonna piss myself."

He eased up, but he was laughing just as hard as her. "Say you're sorry."

"I'm sorry. I'm sorry."

Zac held himself above her, his hands on either side of her head, his arms flexing. Her hair was a mess of curls and there was a flush of color in her cheeks that had been previously absent.

He licked his lips. "You feeling better now?"

"The best. You?"

His eyebrows scrunched in confusion. *Why wouldn't I be?* Everything with work was going great, other than the impending decision of becoming captain or not, but he'd deal with that when he had to. For now, he wanted to focus entirely on her.

"You didn't sleep last night," she said, softly, gently. "Another nightmare?"

He tensed. "Don't—"

"Wait, Zac." She squeezed his arms, holding him to her. "Please, all I want is for you to talk about it. It's eating at you. I'm your friend, aren't I? You can talk to me about it."

For the last few hours it hadn't even crossed his mind. Fuck, why did Reagan have to bring this up when everything had been going perfectly fine?

"I can't, Ree." The words were pushed from his throat, low and hurt. "I just can't."

"Okay, okay."

She ran her fingers into his hair and pulled him down into her. At first, he considered pushing up and away, but he couldn't. He buried his face into her neck, melting into her, while she murmured soothing words to him. While she held him, he forgot that the nightmares were waiting for him. *I wish I could stay here forever.*

Chapter Twenty

Letty and Reagan stood side by side at the back entrance of the stadium. The charity hockey game had finished only a few moments ago and Reagan was still riding the high from the crowd's excitement. Her throat was slightly hoarse from all the screaming she had done. Watching Zac in his element was always a treat for the eyes. He was magnetic to watch. He was lightning fast, zooming around the ice rink on his skates, chasing after that puck. The other team's defense was no match for him or the other players. The game had ended three-zero.

"You were getting turned on watching him, weren't you?" Letty asked, amused.

She was leaning against the wall, one leg up. Wearing a leather jacket, a long pale pink figure-hugging sweater dress and knee-high boots, Letty looked like the epitome of a bad girl.

Reagan nodded, leaning against the opposite wall facing her. She was dressed the way she dressed at every sports game she went to: jersey, jeans and Converses. But the name on her back read THOMAS and not the one she truly wanted. She took a deep breath. *Things are going well*, she told herself. Things between her and

Zac had shifted, ever since she had given him the dream catcher and told him the simple truth that she was his; that she belonged to him. And when he'd helped her that night with her dickhead boss? She couldn't think about it without smiling like a person who should be locked up in an insane asylum.

"I don't blame you. Hockey players are mighty fine."

"Back off, bitch, he's mine."

Letty's throaty laugh echoed in the hallway. "Don't worry, I'm not going to go after your man. We all know he couldn't handle me."

"Who could?" she teased.

"Yeah," Letty said, wistfully. "Who could?"

They were in a more isolated part of the building. Technically, they weren't meant to be here at all. This section was exclusively for agents, players and sports personnel only. Lucky them that they made that short list.

"Tonight's the night, isn't it?" Letty asked.

Reagan nodded and kept nodding. Five days down into the second week of their relationship and they had one more date left.

"Nervous?"

Reagan shook her head and kept shaking.

Letty laughed. "Okay, you're freaking me out, girl. Stop."

"I can't stop. I think I'm broken. Tonight's the night, Letty. What if the last two weeks have been pointless and he doesn't want me? What if he'd rather be friends? What if—"

Her best friend pointed at her. "What if is for the weak and for the unimaginative. You, Reagan Thomas, are now a go-getter. So if you want answers, fucking demand them."

"You're right," Reagan said.

"Hells yeah, I'm right."

"Dial back the gloating. I was already halfway there." Reagan grinned. "I'll ask Zac tonight, before sex of course, point-blank: be with me. Or is that a little too 1950s homemaker woman? Should I try more of a rom-com thing and *Love and Basketball* his ass, but hockey edition?"

Letty stared at her. "You're overthinking this."

"Who, me? When have I ever overthought things?"

Suddenly, Letty straightened off the wall and pointed to the other end of the hallway.

"Heads up, they're coming and you need to relax."

Reagan followed her finger to see Aidan and Zac coming through the double doors. She wiped her hands nervously on the light blue jeans she was wearing as she watched them. They had both taken the time to shower with Zac's dirty blond hair wet and looking darker than usual. His sports bag was slung over his shoulder and he was staring down at his phone with a frown. He was wearing a dark suit, looking good enough to eat.

Zac looked up from his phone and his eyes met hers. His lips slowly curved until he was full-on smiling, dimples out. Her heart pounded and she felt his smile to the tips of her toes. *God, I want him.*

She stepped forward, wanting to be in his arms. The sound of a bag hitting the tiled floor was what broke her gaze. Startled, she shifted and noticed Aidan standing in front of her. *Oh god, oh god*, she thought in a panic. Had he seen the way she was looking at Zac? Or how she had been about to give him a hug?

While she was mentally hyperventilating, Aidan leaned down and kissed her on the cheek. *Okay, he's*

not looking at me any differently. Breathe, Reagan. He
didn't see anything or else he would have said something, right? *Right?*

"Hey, big brother," she said, faintly.

"Hey, Reagan." He lifted his chin towards Letty.
"Letty."

Letty pulled one hand out of her pocket and waved.

"Aidan. Nice block in the fourth quarter." She smiled.

"Thanks," he said, flatly, staring at her with an odd
expression.

Letty turned her smile onto Zac. "But you, Zachariah, were amazing."

"Thanks." Zac dropped his own bag onto the floor between his spread legs, crossing his arms. His eyes briefly
shifted away and met Reagan's. She lost her breath at the
look in them. Shit, she was going to get it later.

"You seemed like you were playing with more…pi-
zazz then normal. Something have you worked up?"
Letty asked, blinking up at him innocently.

What the fuck? Reagan shot her a sharp look that
Letty ignored. She was going to kill her best friend.
Kill her dead. And Aidan was frowning as he looked
between the two.

Zac let out a laugh, running a hand through his hair.
"Had to give you ladies a show. I wouldn't want you
guys to come and watch us lose."

Letty grinned back at him. "And we ladies very
much appreciate that."

"Reagan," Aidan cut through abruptly. "You need
a ride?"

Her brain short-circuited and she could not for the
life of her think of a plausible lie. She couldn't exactly
say, *"Sorry, Aidan, we chose not to come with our cars,*

because one, parking is a bitch and two, I made the plan for your best friend to take me to his place and fuck me silly. After, of course, I find out whether he wants to be with me for the rest of our lives."

So instead, she said, "Ah…"

"Actually, Reagan was planning to head to Nigel's Pizza," Letty said, smoothly.

Aidan tapped Zac's arm. "That's in your direction, isn't it?"

"Yeah." Zac nodded. "I can take her there and then drop her home later, if that's good with you, Ree?"

He watched her in a way that made her mouth water and her pussy tingle.

"Yeah," she breathed out.

It was so good with her.

"And I guess that means I'm riding with you," Letty said to Aidan.

"Why don't you ride with Reagan and Zac?"

Letty was shaking her head even before he finished his question.

"I live in the opposite direction, remember?"

"Oh yeah." Aidan sighed.

"Does that mean you're going to oh-so-kindly give me a ride?"

Aidan grunted.

"Thank you," she said, sweetly.

I really need to have a talk with Letty, Reagan thought to herself. Or pretty soon her brother was going to end up killing her best friend.

"Glad you came to see us play, little sis," Aidan said, as he hugged her.

"Me too," she said, returning his hug. "See you later."

They separated, both pairs heading to different parts

of the parking garage. As soon as Zac and Reagan turned
the corner and were out of sight, Zac's bag was on the
floor and Reagan's back was against the wall. She
moaned into his mouth, pulling him closer. He kissed
her, with one hand tangled in her hair and the other digging into her hip.

"You need to be more careful," Zac said, nipping
her bottom lip.

"I know." She groaned.

"Aidan almost noticed."

"I know…just shut up and kiss me." To her surprise,
he did. His hand drifted from her hair to her throat,
using pressure there to angle her head back and take
her mouth deeper, wetter. *Mm, so good.* He rubbed his
lips against hers for a few seconds more, before pulling
away. She panted as he reached for his bag and her hand.

"Let's get the fuck out of here."

She couldn't agree with him more.

They got buckled up in his car and within a few
minutes, they were out the parking lot and on the road.
Reagan watched him as he drove. He glanced at her,
smirking.

"You're staring."

"What can I say? You're amazingly good-looking."

He barked out a laugh. "I'm glad you came tonight."

His words warmed her, as much as the look in his
eyes did.

"Me too. You were amazing out there," she told him.

He looked away, back to the road. "You think so?"

"I know so," she said, softly.

He sighed, drumming his fingers on the top of the
steering wheel as they stopped at a traffic light. "I'm
just glad it was all worth it."

"Worth what?"

"All the sacrifice, especially from your dad. If it wasn't for him, I don't think I would be here today."

"And what? You did nothing to contribute to where you are today?" she said, on a disbelieving laugh.

"Nothing compared to what he did for me."

"Dad would be the first one to tell you that without all of your hard work, talent and sacrifices, nothing would have come from it. He might have given you the means, Zac, but *you* did this. Not him."

He said nothing. They pulled up in front of his apartment. She unbuckled her seat belt and was reaching for him, stopping him from getting out of the car. She touched his cheek. He gazed at her.

"Ree—"

"I think you underestimate just how amazing you are."

"Stop," he said through clenched teeth.

"You are amazing, Zachariah Quinn." She punctuated each word with a kiss to his mouth.

"Reagan." More desperate now to get her to stop. He cupped both of her cheeks in his palms. But she couldn't. She wasn't going to until he understood what she was saying to him.

"You are an incredible hockey player, but you are a wonderful person. One of my best friends." She choked on the last word.

He stroked her face.

"Stop," he said, gently. "I get it."

"Do you?"

"Yeah, you little vixen. So, you can stop now."

She grinned at him. "Or what?"

Zac kissed her, hard.

"Or I'm going to spank you again," he said, against her lips.

She shuddered and she knew he felt it when his eyes darkened.

"Yes please."

"Fuck, let's get inside now, before I fuck you in this car again. Can't even be bothered with my bag right now, I'll get it tomorrow."

It would not bother her in the least if they fucked in the car again, but she had a feeling once they started they would not be able to stop. And she did not want to give all the residents of Zac's apartment an unforgettable show of Zac's and Ree's orgasms. Also, she still needed to have that talk with him. She could do this. They'd spent close to every waking moment with each other for the last couple of days. Zac must feel the way she was feeling. She knew it.

Hand in hand, they walked into the lobby of the apartment. The security guard, Dave, who usually gave them a wave and smile, looked up from the monitors. Alarm crossed his face and he hurried towards them.

"Mr. Quinn, I've been trying to reach you all night."

"I saw the message. What is it?"

Dave took a deep breath. "Your father's here."

Zac went rigid. Reagan's eyes snapped to his.

"What?" she breathed.

"He arrived half an hour ago…and he refused to leave. He was disturbing many of the residents as they were trying to get in. I had to do something with him, so I left him outside your door. I thought since you own the whole floor, no one else would be able to hear him and you could have a private conversation." Dave swallowed.

Zac's expression was blank, a scary blank. He let go of her hand.

"Where's Kenny and Mark?" Zac asked Dave, his voice deep and crackling with something volatile.

"Out. I called them and they said they'll be here in ten minutes. That was five minutes ago."

"When they get here, bring them to my floor. Reagan, stay here," he snapped and then he was gone, running up the stairs.

Oh shit, this was not good. Not good at all. Zac's father was here. A father he hadn't seen in a decade. A father he hated, who messed up his childhood and ruined his mother. And now, Zac was about to confront this man. *Not good.* She had to stop him from doing something stupid.

"You heard him?" she asked Dave.

Dave nodded.

"Okay. Dave, tell them to hurry." Reagan ran after Zac.

Thank god for Converses. Zac lived on the eighth floor and by the fourth, she was huffing and puffing. *Why, oh why, didn't I take the elevator? I'm such a dumbass.* She finally reached the eighth floor, trying not to hack out a lung as she pushed open the door. A loud voice assaulted her ears immediately.

"YOU THINK YOU'RE BETTER THAN ME, DO YOU? DO YOU, YOU BASTARD? YOU'RE NOTHING! YOU HEAR ME, NOTHING!"

Silence. No reply from Zac. Reagan hurried down the hallway, almost afraid of what she was going to see. She turned the corner and skidded to a halt.

"DON'T IGNORE ME, YOU BASTARD! YOU GOOD FOR NOTHING, SON OF A BITCH!"

Zac stood with his back to her, arms to his side, frozen. A man was standing in front of him, yelling in his face. It had been five years since Reagan had seen Zac's father and he was almost unrecognizable. His abuse of alcohol had ravaged him. At fifty-five years old, the man was younger than her own father, but looked decades older. His once-brown hair was now entirely gray, except for the bald patches on his head. He was overweight, carrying most of that fat around his middle. His clothes were dirty, an unbuttoned checkered shirt, a T-shirt tucked into jeans that had seen better days. And his face was haggard, but his eyes were spitting mad and his mouth twisted in his usual hate-filled smirk. Even from here, Reagan could tell he was drunk out of his mind.

"Look at you," Sheriff Jeremy Quinn spat. "You were nothing as a child and you're still nothing now."

Reagan nearly jumped out of her skin when Zac spoke.

"Then, why are you here? It's clear that I mean nothing to you, so why are you at my house?"

He pushed a fat, red finger in Zac's face. "Because you owe me. And I came for what belongs to me. I think two million would do nicely for now."

Fuck no. He was owed nothing. Reagan opened her mouth to tell him that, but Zac beat her to it.

"No. You deserve nothing from me. Get the fuck out."

Sheriff Quinn's face twisted into something ugly. "YOU BASTARD! YOU OWE ME! YOU THINK YOU CAN SAY NO TO ME! DO YOU? I'LL SHOW YOU!"

Reagan watched in horror as he swung his fist. Zac

stepped back and the punch went wide. Sheriff Quinn stumbled and almost fell. He caught himself by grabbing onto the wall. The silence in the hallway was terrible. She couldn't move. Was paralyzed by some unknown fear.

Zac's father wiped the back of his mouth.

"I should have drowned you as a baby," he whispered. "I told her, I told that woman I didn't want you in my house and what did she do? She had you anyway. She should've never had you. You shouldn't be alive." He looked up at Zac, the hate palpable.

Zac didn't react. And they stood like that, until the door behind Reagan thudded open. Kenny, Mark and Dave ran into the hallway. They reached for Sheriff Quinn, who began screaming abuse again.

"GET OFF ME! I'LL SUE, YOU HEAR ME! THAT'S MY SON! HE'S MINE!"

His words rang through the hallway even after the security guards had dragged him out. His words haunting Zac and Reagan both.

Chapter Twenty-One

They stood there in silence. Reagan walked to Zac's side on shaky legs. His face was turned from her, his hands clenched at his side. Everything inside of her hurt from Jeremy Quinn's words and if she felt like that, she had no idea how Zac was feeling.

"Zac," she whispered.

"I don't want to talk about it," he said, harshly.

"Zac, your dad—"

He exploded. "Fuck, Reagan! I just said I don't want to talk about it!"

He pushed open the door to his apartment and strode inside, leaving her standing there in shock. She hesitated for a moment. *Should I go inside, or should I leave him to calm down? Give him some distance? No. I can't. He's in pain.* She couldn't just leave him in pain. She took a deep breath. *Put on your big girl panties, Reagan, and go help him.* She'd let it slide too many times before. Not anymore.

She followed Zac inside the apartment. He stood at the breakfast bar, hands on the counter, leaning forward with his head hung down. He looked up when she slammed the door shut. His face was strained, his jaw tight, as she came towards him.

"You need to leave," he told her.

She shook her head. "I'm not leaving you like this. I can't. Don't ask me to."

"Fuck! Fuck!" He banged his fist on the counter. She flinched. "What don't you get? I don't want you here!"

"I'm not leaving you!" she snapped, frustration leaking out.

"It has nothing to do with you, Reagan!"

"But it has everything to do with you!" She put her hands on her hips.

"No," he snapped back. "My fucked-up dad has absolutely nothing to do with me."

"He hurt you—" Reagan tried.

"I don't want to talk about him. He's gone. That's over with. Let's move the fuck on, already."

"If you're so over it, then why don't you want to talk about it?" she asked him desperately. God, why couldn't he see that he was hurting himself by keeping this all bottled inside? She wasn't naïve enough to believe that by talking to her, it would magically make decades of pain disappear, but it might help. It might give him an outlet for all the anger and pain eating away at him.

Zac ran his hands through his hair. "Look, I know you're trying to help, Reagan, but I don't need anything. I'm fine, okay. I'm fine."

"You're not fine, Zac. You think I can't see it, but I can't—"

"Stop."

"Your dad coming back here has torn open old wounds that you don't—"

"STOP!"

But she couldn't stop. She needed to get through to

him. Desperation drove her. She leaned on the counter towards him. His eyes were wary.

"I want to help. Let me in, Zac."

"There's nothing I need your help for," he whispered.

"Needing help doesn't mean you're weak."

"I know that," he said, harshly.

"I needed your help a couple of days ago, remember? With my dickhead boss. Why is it okay for us to share that part of our lives, but not this part? I want you, Zac! I want all of you!"

He laughed harshly. "I'm sorry I'm not like you, Reagan. Not all of us can spill out all our problems. You might want to, but I definitely don't. And I never will. You need to get whatever hero complex you have out of your system, because you're not going to save me. I'm not going to be your pet project or your boyfriend. That isn't what I want. Or does what I want not matter to you at all?"

She stumbled back. His expression didn't change as he watched her, not moving an inch. The distance between them felt more than just a few meters. There was more than just a breakfast bar separating them. Tears pricked her eyes. She let them fall.

"I'm literally begging you, but you don't care at all, do you?" Reagan whispered. "I'm so fucking stupid." She looked away, coming to a realization. Every moment that Zac had said "no" to her or showed her exactly what he thought of her ran through her mind. "All this time, I thought you just needed me to be patient and you would eventually see that I'm not going anywhere. That I love you. That I want to be with you. All this time, I thought it was fear that was holding you back."

* * *

She loves me.

Zac heard nothing but the roar of his own blood in his ears and those words. Fuck, she loved him. How was that even possible? He had no clue and he didn't know what to say to that.

"I don't know what you want me to say, Reagan," he admitted aloud.

She brushed away the tears trailing down her cheek, stepping further away from the breakfast bar.

"Nothing. This is not your fault. It's mine. I should have listened to you when you said you didn't want to be with me. It was my own stupid fault for ignoring you. For thinking that I knew more than you. That you would suddenly wake up and feel the way I feel about you. And… I shouldn't have pushed you, Zac. If you don't want to talk about it, I can't force you to."

Instead of her words calming him, it made him panic. He walked around the breakfast bar.

"Reagan—" he began, with no idea what he was going to say.

She shook her head, moving further away from him, towards the door.

"It's okay. I love you, Zachariah Quinn. I'm sorry I'm not what you need me to be."

He caught her by the arm. She jerked away from his grip.

"Don't go," he told her desperately. "Not like this."

"I can't stay. And tonight was going to be the end of our deal so it all had to end anyway."

"You promised, Reagan. You promised that we would still be friends after all this."

An expression washed over her face that he had never seen, but it was gone before he could decipher it.

"We are friends."

"I don't believe you."

"Please, Zac." Her voice broke on his name and his heart almost broke with it. "If you value me at all, please let me go. We can deal with our friendship another day, just…not now."

Fuck. What did he do? But she was literally trembling, arms wrapped around her body as if she was protecting herself from him. From *him*. Fuck. Slowly, Zac nodded. She left the apartment and him, leaving him wondering for the hundredth time since this all started: What the fuck had just happened?

Chapter Twenty-Two

Reagan was finding it hard to breathe. Partially because of the broken heart she was currently nursing, but mostly because of the pillow over her head. She was lying facedown in her bed, under her covers, where she had been almost every moment since coming home yesterday. She wasn't planning on moving anytime soon. She was in the ugliest pajamas that she could find in her closet and she hadn't bothered to fix her hair after her shower. She could feel the wet tendrils on the back of her neck. If it was up to her, she was going to spend the rest of her life under her pillows, in her bed. Doing nothing but eating cookies and pizza. Fuck her job, who needed it anyway?

So much had happened in only two weeks. In two weeks, she'd gone from thinking things between her and Zac would always be in this friends with almost benefits phase to dating to…this. She had been so hopeful about Zac's feelings for her only a couple of days ago and now…now, she knew the truth. Zac didn't feel the same way about her. How could he when he refused to let her in? She had given him plenty of opportunities, but still he only gave her a part of himself and never all of it. She couldn't do it. Not with him. She wanted all of him.

At least she knew now before…before what exactly? Before her feelings for him got too deep? Too late for that. Before things between them got messy? Yep, things between them were already messy and they had only gotten messier. The truth was always better though. Right?

No, it isn't, she thought hysterically. She would rather have lived in denial, thinking if given half a chance Zac would want to be with her. That he would see that loving her was worth all the risk and that she would never leave him.

Reagan felt the ever-persistent tears in her throat and burning in her eyes. She tried to beat it back since she didn't want to spend the rest of her life crying. She only heard the noise of her doorbell buzzing when she lifted her head for a second to rub her eyes. By the sound of it the person had buzzed more than once.

Reagan leapt out of bed. She skidded out of her bedroom on her fluffy socks, into the hallway to her door. She was definitely not presentable enough for guests, but she couldn't be bothered to fix herself up. Whoever was at her door was just going to have to deal.

"Coming! Coming!"

She didn't bother looking through the keyhole. She unlocked the door and threw it open.

"Dad," she said in shock.

Lincoln Thomas took her in, his eyes shifting to her socks, her cotton pants and oversized shirt to her face, where there were track marks from the pillow and probably smeared tears on her cheeks. Her dad didn't say anything about it. Another thing she had to think about today: her dad's avoidance of any uncomfortable conversations with her.

"Did we have plans today and I forgot?" she finally asked.

"Do I need to make an appointment to see my daughter?"

"No." She laughed softly.

She opened the door wider. "Um…come in."

Her father walked into her apartment. He had only been in her apartment maybe four times in the two years she had lived here. And one of those times had been the day she had moved in. It was kind of weird seeing him here. She had no idea if it was a good weird or a bad weird.

Reagan followed him into the living room. He made his way to the sofa and sat down. He placed his cane across his knee as he generally did. She sat down beside him, tentatively, still unsure what he was doing here.

"I was in the city for an errand and I thought it might be a good idea to drop in." He cleared his throat, not meeting her eyes. "I didn't think you would be at home during the day on a weekend."

Oh. He didn't expect her to be here. She thought maybe that explained things, but it didn't. It just made her more confused. Why would he have bothered to drive to her apartment if he didn't think she was going to be there? Her efficient, military father never did anything without a reason.

They fell into an uncomfortable silence. Usually, Reagan would have jumped in to fill the silence, but she felt so damn tired she couldn't think of any pleasant crap to talk about. Instead, she went with the truth.

"Is there something you want to talk to me about, Dad?"

He tapped his cane on his knee, a nervous gesture so out of character she stared at him. Oh god, there was something wrong with him.

"You're not dying, are you?" she asked, suddenly scared.

"No!" he huffed out. "Why do you children keep on asking me that? Are you trying to get rid of me? I'm as healthy as a horse."

She sighed in relief. "Oh, that's good."

"I've been seeing a therapist."

Reagan glanced at him. Her dad hardly ever talked about being in the military. He had retired before she was born, so she'd never really got to see that side of his life since he'd started his own furniture business. Except, he wasn't simply a carpenter. Lincoln Thomas still followed a strict regime, such as waking up early, cleaning, and keeping in shape, training with his guns and overall being the stoic and hardcore man that he was. She wouldn't even know how he had hurt his leg if it hadn't been for Aidan.

"You're seeing a therapist," she said, slowly, trying to wrap her mind around it.

"A friend recommended me to him after I told him I was having some issues."

Alarmed, she bit her lip. "Issues? What kind of issues?"

"I don't think—"

"Dad! Come on! You can't tell me that and not expect me to ask."

"It's nothing. I've been having some trouble sleeping. It's not something new, but it was easier to manage when you were all younger. Not as easy now."

She'd had no idea. Reagan wrapped her arms around her knees and drew her legs to her chest on the sofa.

"I'm so sorry, Dad. What can I do?"

He waved a hand. "The therapist is helping me manage and thankfully it's working."

"I'm glad," she said truthfully.

She didn't like the idea of her father being plagued by nightmares. Of not talking to her about it. God, why wouldn't the men in her life just talk to her? *How can I know what he's going through if he doesn't tell me?* She always thought if she was patient enough, *cared* enough, they'd come to her and trust her with their feelings. For him to consider getting help, let alone actually going to see a therapist of his own accord, showed how bad the nightmares must have been.

"But that's not why I came here. I came here because I had a talk in my sessions today about you."

"Me? Why?" Her head jerked back.

His cane tapped away on his knee. "Because we don't talk enough."

"Well, there's a reason for that." The words slipped out without her thinking about it.

Fuck. Shit. She should not have said that. *What's the point of keeping it all in anyway?* she thought tiredly. He was right, they definitely didn't talk enough and she was sick of feeling like it was all her fault when it wasn't.

The tapping stopped.

"What are you talking about?" he asked.

"You know." She sighed.

He shook his head. "I don't."

"Don't make me say it."

"Say what?"

"You know."

"Reagan, I have no idea what you are talking—"

"I killed Mom," she blurted out.

Another silence descended upon them, but there was nothing comfortable about this one. Her dad shook and it took her a moment to realize he was shaking with anger. Reagan tensed. He dropped his cane to the ground with a loud thud.

"You did not kill your mother," her father said harshly.

"Forget I said anything—"

"Reagan. You did not kill your mother."

"Dad—"

"You didn't kill her!"

"You don't need to lie," she snapped. "I know what happened."

"Do you? If you did, you would know that your mother made the choice to save you."

"Yes, but if I hadn't—"

"If you hadn't what? You were just a baby. It was not your fault that you went into distress and the doctor had to do a cesarean."

"It was my fault. She had the choice between whether to save herself or to save me. She should have saved herself. There was so much more she had to live for. You. The boys. All those lives for the possible life of one. She had no idea if I was going to live or who I would become."

"Not for a possible life. For you, Reagan. Please don't think like this. Don't dishonor your mother's sacrifice."

The words he used plunged her back to that night with Zac. *"Your mom wouldn't want you hating yourself, there are better ways to honor her."* What he said had meant everything to her. It had made her realize she needed to stop focusing so much on her dad's re-action and start focusing on making the most out of life to honor her mother's last wish that she lived in-stead of her.

"I don't want to dishonor Mom's sacrifice," she whis-pered. "But I see the way you look at me, Dad."

"How do I look at you?"

"Like you're looking through me. Or sometimes, it's like you can't even bear to look at me at all. Like now."

"Reagan." He turned and faced her.

She was the one who couldn't look at him now. She kept her face averted.

Her dad didn't touch her and she wondered what he was going to say—if he was even going to say anything. When he finally did speak, he spoke so low and the words sounded like they were being dragged out of him.

"You look like her so much."

Her eyes flickered up to his. For the first time in a long time, he met her gaze.

"Malcolm and Dean look like her a little. So does Aidan and Callum. But *you*, you look like her the most. Your hair, the way you smile, the way your eyes say ev-erything you are feeling, even the way you move. Some-times I don't notice it. Other times, I look at you…and it hits me right in the gut. And I can't breathe. Every time. It feels like I'm losing her all over again."

She swallowed. "I'm sorry. I know how painful it must be."

"No, baby girl. *I'm* sorry." He reached out and touched her hair. "For making you feel less than you are. For hurting you."

"I know. I know you don't mean to. You can't help how you feel."

"Doesn't mean it doesn't hurt any less." He smiled ruefully.

Yeah, it hurt and it hurts hearing it too.

"I loved your mother from the moment we met and I've never stopped since. And I probably never will, not until the day I die. But she's gone and you're here. I wouldn't wish it any other way. I'm not just glad for the sacrifice she made that day, I'm grateful because I have you. If she could see the woman that you've become, she would be so proud. Almost as proud as I am. I see so much of her in you, but don't think I don't see *you*, Reagan. I do. I see my bright and beautiful daughter."

Reagan couldn't stop the tears then. She buried her face in her hands and sobbed, her chest shuddering with the force of her crying. Her dad patted her awkwardly on the back and it was enough to make her laugh, because he had never done well with tears.

Slowly, she began to rein it in, wiping her face with the heel of her palm. Her dad pulled his hand back.

"I think it's time for me to leave."

She giggled. "What? You don't want me to cry on you some more?"

"I can't promise that I won't do it again," he said, quietly. "But I'm trying."

"Just knowing that you love me and are proud of me is enough, Dad." She smiled.

He smiled back at her as he stood up. She stood along with him. Together they went to her front door. He turned to her and opened his arms.

She threw herself at him. And just like when she was

younger, he lifted her up and cuddled her close. Reagan burrowed her head in his chest, breathing him in deep.

"Thank you, Daddy," she whispered.

"You're welcome, baby girl."

He gently lowered her to the ground and shifted back. Reagan took the hint and let go.

"I hope when you are ready you can tell me what put that sadness into your eyes."

"I…" Her throat clogged up. She swallowed painfully.

"Maybe soon." He tapped her chin once and walked away.

Reagan shut the door and rested her head against it.

The conversation with her dad left her feeling exhausted, but in a good way. Like finally something had healed between the two of them and they could finally move forward. Then, why did she still feel so hollow? She slowly lowered herself to the ground.

Wrapping her arms around her knees, Reagan cried. She cried about how deeply Zac had been hurt by the people in his life who should have protected him. She cried because he didn't love her the way she loved him. She cried because she had lied to him when she told him they would be able to go back to being friends. They were never going to be friends again, because things would never ever be the same between them. Mostly, Reagan cried though because it hurt so much and she knew it was a wound that was going to take a long time to heal. If ever.

Chapter Twenty-Three

Zac sat in his childhood kitchen, wondering what the fuck he was doing here. The house looked exactly the same. It was one of those typical suburban houses with the wraparound porch. Small, but comfortable. The kitchen, other than the living room, was probably the biggest room in the house. Nothing had changed in here, either. His mom's favorite purple curtains still hung over the back door leading to the garden. The tiled floors, stainless counters and old refrigerator were the same.

But something felt different. He ran his hands through his hair, before dropping his hands onto the dining table. Maybe it wasn't the house; maybe it was him. His stomach churned just being here. He had promised when he had left at eighteen years old, about to go to college, that he would never have to set foot in this house. After avoiding his mother's calls for the last two weeks, he'd finally answered. But he never did things halfway. Now here he was. Sitting in this kitchen.

His mom placed a cup of coffee in front of him. He looked up at her. She definitely didn't look the same. Amy Quinn had always been pretty. Even when she had black eyes and purple skin, but too many years of being knocked around and taking painkillers had washed away that natural prettiness. Now her plain summer dress hung off her, showing how skinny she was. Her hair had more gray in it than blonde and it hadn't been styled in years. She'd been seventeen years old when she had him, too young to know how to look after a child and too young to know it was a bad idea to marry a man nearly ten years her senior who couldn't control his anger. She looked older than forty-four years old, with deep grooves around her mouth and eyes. Her eyes were the same though. The same warm and nervous blue eyes, staring down at him.

He hadn't seen her in a few years, but when he came knocking she had greeted him like he had only been there yesterday. Another thing that had unsettled Zac.

"Do you need more milk?" she asked him, wringing her hands.

Zac shook his head. He took a sip, swallowing the bitter coffee. He didn't have the heart to tell her that he drank his coffee with sugar and with no milk. It was Sheriff Quinn who liked his coffee white and bitter.

His mom took a seat beside him, close enough that their knees touched. It made him want to run his hands through his hair again, but he kept them clenched around the cup.

"I'm so glad you're here, Zachariah." She reached for his hand but started to pull it away.

Without conscious thought, he extended his hand and she put hers into his. It was rough, with age spots and even more calluses than he had. Her little finger was crooked and would always stay crooked since she had broken it twice. Both times Sheriff Quinn's fault. Anger choked him.

"I've been watching you play on TV." She smiled. "You always were lightning fast, even as a child. I could barely keep up with you. Thank you for sending me those tickets. I will come and see you play as soon as I can get some time off."

"I didn't come here to talk to you about hockey," he said.

She gave him a bewildered look. "Did you want to talk about something else, Zachariah?"

He turned his head and looked at the woman who had tried to raise him. Layers upon layers of the past intersected with the present. He'd left this house to get away from it all and now he was back where he'd promised he'd never go. *I promised to never hurt Reagan either and look how badly I fucked that up.* But he realized the past wasn't a physical place, because he'd never truly escaped, had he? *I've been carrying it with me everywhere I go, every day thinking that...what? One day it'll just disappear if I wish for it hard enough?* He might not be that scared little boy anymore, dreaming of the day he could finally punch his father, but for him to heal, he had to stop running. And there was only one way to do that. To face it head on.

"Why are you still here, Mom?" Zac asked.

"What do you mean?" She laughed nervously. "This is my home."

"This place has no good memories."

His other hand clenched the cup tighter, his knuckles growing white. He tried to relax, but there were too many thoughts running through his mind for him to focus.

"Doesn't it?" She patted his hand. "I know you don't understand, but all my memories of you are here."

"Mom…" He trailed off.

His stomach continued to churn.

"This is the place you told me your dream of becoming a hockey player for the first time. This is the place where you lost your first tooth. Where I bandaged every scrape and bruise you got at practice that day. Where I made marble cake with you and you accidentally mixed up salt and sugar. Where you grew taller, stronger and bigger than I ever managed. I see all that every day and they are the best memories a mother could wish for. Hopefully one day, I will get even more memories of future generations here, crawling around, growing big and tall like you."

Zac stared at the wistful smile on her face. He didn't want to take away any happiness from her, but he couldn't hold it in. The anger he'd kept bottled down deep inside was rising up from his stomach into his throat, until he couldn't do it any longer.

"Do you know what I see when I look around?" He pointed with his chin at the kitchen counter. "I see the place where Sherriff Quinn slapped you so hard you fell back and banged your head into the counter. Knocked you out cold. Blood everywhere. It took hours for me to clean it up and still there are smudges on the wall. You wouldn't wake up for so long I wondered if you ever would. Five minutes went by and I had no idea if you were alive or dead. And I had no idea what to do since *he* forbade me from calling the ambulance. Instead, I sat with you, with a rag pressed against your head to try and stop the bleeding while I counted the seconds. Do you want to know how long it took you to wake up?"

Tears streamed down his mother's face as he spoke to her. Her breath hitched when he asked his question.

"480 seconds." He pressed on, driven by the anger. "Eight whole minutes. That's what I remember when I come to this house. And I have hundreds more of those moments seared into my mind. Of helping you with your bruises and cuts. Of seeing you unconscious, surrounded by nothing but blood. So much blood. Of having to listen to his fists pounding against your skin and your screams. I hear them at night sometimes. I remember all of that. The moments of being helpless, hungry, afraid and alone. *He* did that. He was always taller, bigger and stronger than me. You say that I grew up to be tall, big and strong, but I don't need that now. I needed to be that back when it meant something. When I could have fought him and made him stop destroying us. The irony is I can't even confront him now and make him face me, because he's not even that man anymore. He's just this sad, old drunk who can't even look after himself. I can't hit him. I can't scream at him for doing this to us, I can't let this all out because what happens when I do? What does that make me?"

He shook his head.

"I never knew what it was like to live in a world where your father didn't beat you and where your mother wasn't beaten every day. Not until the day I met Aidan and he took me home. For the first time and every time I went over, I realized that what was happening here at home wasn't normal. That my reality wasn't like the reality of most people. That it was fucked up."

Zac took a deep breath. "It fucked me up. It fucked me up *a lot*. Meeting Aidan and the Thomas family changed things for me in the best way possible, gave me a family I never even realized I craved, but it also made me realize that I was nothing like them. Love. Family.

These emotions come easy to them, but they're not easy to me. I don't even know if I want them…or if I even deserve them. *He* did that. He made me feel alone and less than a person, every single moment of the eighteen years I lived here. And the only reason I stayed for as long as I did was because of you."

He looked her in the eyes as he said these next words, trying to tell her exactly how he felt. He tightened his grip on her hand when she tried to struggle away.

"Because I was terrified of what he would do to you if I left. I love you, Mom, but whenever I think of you, I think of him and I don't want to think about him. I don't want to feel this helpless rage anymore. I don't want to keep carrying it around and letting it poison my life. I don't want to feel this guilt of not having helped you when I should have. I want to be able to think about loving someone without letting fear grip me and thinking of all the ways I could fuck it up or not being able to trust that love doesn't mean the person isn't going to leave me alone or destroy me."

His mom's bottom lip quivered.

"I never wanted you to feel alone," she said, quietly.

"I know."

"I wanted to raise you to be everything I wasn't. To give you all the things I never had growing up poor and alone."

Amy brought his hand to her cheek. She laid her head on top of it and began to weep.

"Everyone told me not to have you. That it was going to ruin my life, but from the moment I was pregnant to this day, I was sure that I wanted you. I never wanted anything more than I wanted you. But I never knew that it wasn't me who needed saving, it was you. Someone should have saved you from me. I did this."

"Mom," he whispered. "You didn't do this."

Tears slid down, in between his fingers, to drop onto his palm.

"I did. I hurt the only thing precious to me," she cried.

He didn't know how to stop this, how to stop the painful sobbing coming from his mother. So, he told her something he hadn't been planning on telling her.

"I met someone."

The tears didn't stop immediately and he wondered if she had heard him.

"Did you hear me, Mom? I met someone," he repeated.

Bloodshot eyes met his. "Oh."

"You don't sound very happy?"

She shook her head. "No, of course I'm happy for you. It's just that I thought…"

"What? What did you think?"

"I always thought you and Reagan would end up together." His mom rushed on. "I've seen the way she looks at you, the way you look at her—when you think no one is watching, that is. That girl has clearly carried a torch for you since she was a little girl. And the things that she has done for you over the years, like sneaking out with you in the middle of the night or standing up to your father are way beyond what a friend does for another friend."

Zac leaned back, stunned. She was right. Even before that day in Muckberry Field, Reagan had always been there for him. He barely had a single good memory without Reagan in it. During college, they had spent many days finding new coffee shops to feed her addiction. Now, as a professional athlete, with barely any time, they saw each other constantly or messaged each other. On the days he was feeling shitty about one thing or another, Reagan would pop out of nowhere and challenge him to a game and before he knew it, he was laughing and thinking about nothing but her. She also came to watch him play whenever she could and that wasn't just to see Aidan, because most of the time, they would end up going to a pizza joint just the two of them. It wasn't just her though.

He did the same thing. He constantly went out of his way for her. Like when she had been ill for a week last year, he had spent every day with her, feeding her soup and keeping her company watching TV. Her smile made his chest feel tight, so he did everything he could to make her smile, like take her to Comic-Con even though he hated events like that with a passion. And fuck, what about all the kissing they did? Zac ran a hand through his hair.

"I hate to break this to you, but I don't kiss my friends at night. I don't make out with them in my car or dry hump them on a sofa. And I definitely don't fuck them against the wall of some party." Reagan had said that to him. And she was right. They weren't friends. They had never been friends. He knew what friendship looked like. It's what he had with Aidan, with his hockey teammates and with the other Thomas siblings. They had always been more.

"I'm right here, Zac. I'm all yours." His. His little vixen. His Ree. She had always been his.

All these years, he had been too fucking blind to see it.

Zac looked at his mother and spontaneously leaned over and kissed her on the cheek.

"You are a very wise woman, Amy Quinn."

"That is what a certain son of mine keeps on saying." She grinned, shedding a couple of years off her face.

"I have to go," he said, standing up.

"I thought you might say that."

They walked out of the kitchen together. His mother paused while he continued towards the front door.

"Bye, Mom. I'll see you soon," he said, eager to get out of this place now that he had done everything he had set out to do, when his mother spoke.

"Are you going to come back?" she asked, nervously.

He turned around. "I don't want to lose you, Mom."

"And I don't want to lose you either."

"I never want to come back here, again. I can't. I can't look at this place and see the good that you do. I just can't," he admitted. "But I am willing to take you anywhere, at any place, for us to see each other."

"As long as it is not in this house, right?"

Zac nodded, relieved that she understood that much at least.

She didn't say anything for a moment. She was clearly thinking hard about something. He didn't want to rush her, but he needed to get back into the city. He had to do something before going to see Reagan. There were so many things they needed to talk about. He hoped she would listen.

"I'll sell it," his mother suddenly announced.

Fuck, that was not what he had meant at all. He stepped forward.

"Mom, you don't have to do this for me—" he began.

"You're right," she said. "This is the place where we

bled, where we dealt with more bruises and wounds than any person should ever have to. There might be good here, but for you, you will never see beyond the bad. As long as we stay here. I'm going to sell it. Get a new, fresh start. This is just a house after all."

He opened his mouth to say something, but she stopped him.

"For years, I didn't protect you. Let me protect you now, Zachariah. Let me be a good mom, for once in my life."

He wasn't expecting that, but he was grateful. The last tension he felt in his stomach eased away. He nodded slowly.

"Okay." She smiled. "Give me a hug before you go."

He wrapped his arms around her and squeezed.

"Thank you, Mom."

"I love you, Zachariah. You might be a little broken, but you are not alone. You have never been alone. Let other people in. Don't be afraid to love them back," his mother whispered in his ear.

"I'll try." He let go of her.

With one last smile, he stepped out of his childhood home.

Zac stood on the empty porch outside of his house and tipped his head back. He looked up at the bright sky. And he breathed. For the first time in twenty-seven years, he took a breath that wasn't filled with past regrets. He breathed easy.

Chapter Twenty-Four

A few days after Zac ripped out her heart, Reagan stood in Mr. Mitchell's office, shoulders back and eyes clear and direct. She didn't come to play; she came to get what's hers. She had dressed that morning with war on her mind. She was in her skinniest stilettos that were borderline work inappropriate, a black pencil skirt and a beautiful green blouse. Her curly hair was tamed and pulled back. She looked fierce if she did say so herself.

Alan, her boss, sat next to her, in a seat directly opposite the large desk from where Mitchell was currently staring at him intensely.

"What is this about, Alan?" Mitchell asked, not shifting his gaze, setting down his pen.

"This is about Trent Newman, sir," Reagan told him.

He sighed. "I know you're not happy with my decision, but I would hope you'd understand where I'm coming from. You, Alan, should know where I'm coming from."

Alan shook his head, his black hair streaked with silver barely moving from all the gel he used to keep it slicked back.

"No, I don't understand, Mitchell. Why would you allow Daniel to sway you into such a foolish decision?"

Mitchell's jaw twitched. *What, you can dish it out, but you can't take it?* Reagan smiled with a little more teeth than usual, but she was feeling particularly fierce. She'd worked her ass off for this company. *I'm not about to let them minimize who I am and what I've accomplished, no thank you.*

"This decision," Mitchell began, "was based on the fact that Daniel is a senior agent and Reagan is not. Trent is an important client and needs to feel like we are giving him as much support as possible."

"Trent chose to sign with Mitchells not because of Daniel, but because of me. He knows how important he is, because he can see how hard I'm working for his best interest. That's why the shoe deal is—"

"The deal is perfect—"

"Please, let me finish what I was going to say." She said it evenly, but firmly.

Mitchell leaned back and, for a moment, she wondered if he was going to throw her out of his office. Then, he nodded.

She let out a deep breath.

"Thank you. As I was saying, I understand I'm not a senior agent, but I do know what is best for my client and it's not that." She stepped forward and dropped the folder she'd been clutching onto the table. "It's this."

Mitchell flicked it open, casually. "And what's this?"

"A deal to become the face of Jude's tracksuits with a portion of the money going to children with disabilities and who want to play sports. Something Trent is really passionate about since his youngest sister has Down syndrome and is a netball player."

He finally looked at Reagan. *Good, now maybe he'll start to take me a bit more seriously.* As tempting as it was to scream about how his reasons were bullshit and that he just didn't want to let her into the good old boys' club, it was not the right tactic. She let out a deep breath, shaking off her anger at the situation, and focused on how she was going to work it to her advantage.

Reagan waited as her boss continued to leaf through the folder, reading the contracts intently. Her heart was beating fast and she had the urge to bite and lick away the ChapStick on her lips. But she was done second-guessing herself. She was damn good at her job and this was a good deal, amazing actually. If he didn't like it, then he could shove his perfectly ironed tie right up his—

"Everything looks good from what I can see," he said.

"Don't downplay it, Mitchell. You know it and I know it. She really is the best person for the job." Alan rolled his eyes.

"Fine, you're right, Alan. Reagan has clearly shown that she knows Trent very well and would be a good fit as an agent for him."

She blinked. Other than the fact that he was speaking about her, rather than *to* her, this was a win, right?

"You're saying you agree with me?" she asked, slowly.

He smiled. "Yes, Reagan. I'm saying I agree with you."

"Thank you, sir."

He nodded. *And look, he actually spoke directly to me!*

"Thank you, Reagan, you can go." Alan stood up, imposing as he was nearly a foot taller than her. "Mitchell and I need to discuss the appropriate reprimand for Daniel since he went above my head and could have potentially lost us millions."

She left the office, sniggering to herself. *I hope Alan roasts him over a fire and then chews his ass out.* Excitement coursed through her. *Oh god, I did it! I have to tell Zac that I finally—* She lost her smile. When she felt the familiar heat crawling up her throat and the burning at the back of her eyes, she swallowed. *No. No more tears.* She was done settling for less than she deserved. It was time to grow up and grow strong.

Chapter Twenty-Five

Reagan looked through the peephole, heart pounding as she saw the outline of a very familiar jaw. Why? Why? If he had come this time yesterday, she would have been in her work clothes, but now…she looked down at what she was wearing and groaned. It had *heartbroken* written all over it. Her short-sleeved comfy dress came up to her knees, holes in the hem and a bright blue stain over the left breast where her pen had accidentally leaked. And her hair was pulled back in a single ponytail, lifeless and unwashed. *I am a mess.*

The knock came again, the door shaking beneath her palms.

"Open the door, Ree," Zac ordered, his voice coming in loud and clear. "You can't avoid me forever."

I wasn't planning to, she thought in reply.

In the back of Reagan's mind, she knew that this was going to happen. That Zac would want to talk to her and convince her to still be friends. But when two days went by, then three, then four, she had been lulled into a false sense of security that maybe he would give her time. *I'm not ready*, she panicked. *I can't take it right now.*

But she had to. Taking a deep breath, she opened the door.

"I—"

Zac stepped forward and she took a giant step back, making sure not an inch of him touched her. He walked into her house, with long purposeful strides. She shut the door and quickly followed behind him.

"Zac!" she snapped. "Look, I'm not ready—"

He faced her in her living room. "If you think I'm going to leave and let you keep thinking whatever fucked-up things you are thinking, you're out of your mind."

"It's not fucked up."

He crossed his arms, his leather jacket creasing. "Yes, it is."

Reagan let out a sound of frustration, throwing up her hands. He made her so mad. But the mad was nothing compared to the hurt.

"I'll tell you what I'm thinking," Reagan said to him, looking him in the eye. "I'm thinking that our two weeks to explore a relationship between us is finished. And guess what? You were right. We don't work. We're better off as friends. Our friendship means more to me than losing you over sexual chemistry. We should forget about the last two weeks and go back to being friends. That's what I think."

The words physically hurt to say. They'd hurt the first time she had uttered them in front of the mirror in her bathroom and they hurt every time she'd practiced them in her head. At least her eyes were dry this time.

"Is that what you want? To be friends?"

"I…"

He took a step forward; she took a step back. But he kept on coming. Her back smacked into the wall.

"Stop," she told him, holding up a hand.

He ignored her. He reached for her hand and placed it over his chest, over his heart. Her own heart stuttered. Reagan was so confused right now. The way he was looking at her was so different than the way he usually did. His blue eyes were fixed on her. There were no barriers, no walls. He looked amazing, better than amazing in fact. The fatigue that had lingered in his eyes from the recurring nightmares was gone. He was clean-shaven, clear-eyed and seemed determined about something. He stepped deeper into her space, until she was surrounded by him. His jeans rubbing up against her bare legs. His chest against her chest. She couldn't breathe without breathing his scent. Or without feeling his breath against her lips. It made them ache. It made *her* ache.

"Zac," she whispered, looking up at him.

"You look confused, Ree."

"I am confused," she admitted. "I don't know what you want from me."

I've finally given him everything he's been asking for. She wasn't going to fight anymore. *So, why is he doing this?* Why was he tormenting her?

They said nothing for a moment. Zac finally sighed, lowering his forehead onto hers. Reagan closed her eyes, imagining for a moment that everything between them was fine and not a fucked-up mess.

"I'm sorry, Ree."

No, I don't want to hear this.

"Zac—"

"I need to say this," he murmured, before continuing. "You're not just Aidan's little sister to me. You're one of my best friends, one of the most important people in my life. And I hurt you. I hurt you when I threw you out of my apartment. I hurt you when I refused to let you in and when I ignored your feelings like they didn't matter. Fuck, Ree, I never meant to hurt you."

"I know you didn't."

"It doesn't make it any better that I did."

"No, it doesn't," she admitted. "But I get it, Zac."

"I don't think you do, Reagan. When I was living at home, I spent all my time dreaming of the day I could finally leave. When I finally left, I spent all my time determined to never go back and to only look forward. I pushed everything from my childhood into a small box in my mind and told myself I never needed to open it up again. And for a while that worked. I stopped thinking about it so damn much, the nightmares were almost nonexistent. Then it all started up again two weeks ago."

Two weeks ago, when she had made the stupid dating proposal.

"Something about us being together threw me back to a time I never wanted to remember—"

"I'm sorry," Reagan choked out. The nightmares. His fear. Everything was her fault. She had pushed and pushed.

He shook his head. "Let me finish, Ree. I've realized that even though I've mostly gotten over my childhood, I haven't gotten over how it made me feel. Worthless. Unworthy. You are so much better than me, Reagan Thomas. You are beautiful, caring, loving, an amazing friend. I don't deserve you."

She had no idea what to say to that, except for…

"How can you think that?"

"I come from a bitter old man and a weak woman. Together, they taught me that love is either nonexistent or not enough. I didn't think I knew what love was or even how to love."

"Zac," she began gently. "You've been showing me what love was since the first moment I met you. You know how to love."

She saw the pleasure her words caused him and felt it when he let go of her hand to wrap his arms around her. Oh god, to think he had been carrying this around all this time made her sick. How could she be so selfish? She had forgotten that above all else, Zac was her friend. And she'd been a shitty friend. Slowly, she put her hands under his leather jacket and around his waist.

"Yeah," he said into her hair. "I've been realizing a few things over the last couple of days. That I can't control where I came from, but I can control how I feel about it. I need to stop letting the past dictate my future."

She was sure he could feel how hard her heart was beating. *He's going to say it now. He's going to say how he just wants to be friends and nothing more.* Her mouth dried.

"I got you something." Zac shifted back and put his hand inside his jacket pocket.

Shit, she didn't want any more of Zac's "gifts." She tried to push him away.

"If it's flowers, I don't want it!"

He stopped her by tightening his grip on her waist. "It's not flowers. Look."

Okay, Reagan, just look, if you don't like it, you can pretend to... She stared down at the case in his hand.

"What is this?" she whispered.

"I really wanted to get you jewelry, but I remembered how much you were looking forward to this. A friend of mine works in the company and was able to give me an advanced copy. It's yours."

With shaky hands, she took it from him. It was the latest *Future Fantasy* game and it wasn't due in the shops for another month at least. She couldn't believe he got it for her. It was ridiculously the most romantic thing anyone had ever done for her—definitely better than the non-perfect perfect dates that had happened at the beginning.

"I don't know what to say," she admitted. What the hell did he mean by this? Even as she told herself not to, hope ignited inside of her. "I, um, thank you?"

"So grateful," he teased.

"I'm just glad it's not flowers."

He ran a hand through his hair, messing it up as per usual. "I should apologize for that, but I'm not going to lie. I loved seeing how irritated you got."

She slapped him on the chest. She couldn't stop the smile on her face, even if she tried. He stared at her. Self-conscious, the smile slipped off her face.

"What?" she asked.

He cupped her cheek, tracing her skin with his fingers. "I missed you, Reagan. You have no idea how much."

"Stop." *I'm going to cry.*

"I fucked up. I hurt you."

"It's okay."

Zac covered her mouth with his hand. His eyes were fierce and stern. "You need to learn to stop taking less than you deserve. You deserve it all. No more half measures, Reagan. All or nothing."

She breathed out. He was right. This whole two-week proposal was nothing more than half measures. Praying that he would come around and see what she had always seen. Fuck that. She needed to stop dipping her toes in and just cannonball in. It was all or nothing. She moved his hand gently from her mouth, his arm falling to his side.

This was it.

"I don't think we can be friends, Zac," Reagan told him.

There was dark amusement on his face. "Yeah, and why not?"

"Because I'm in love with you."

"Thank god," he growled.

And then Zac kissed her.

"I love you, Reagan Thomas. I've been in love with you since the moment we kissed when you were fifteen years old. I loved you when you made me help you move into your apartment. When you came to every game I played whether it was college hockey or the pros. When you looked at me with those fuck-me eyes like the vixen you are. When you were fighting dirty to get me to see you as more than my friend with benefits or my best friend's little sister. I loved you in every single one of those moments and I will love you in every moment from now."

Reagan stared at him. She stared for so long, Zac would have wondered if something was wrong, but he could see the effect of his words on her face.

"Say it again," she told him breathlessly.

Gladly. He planned to tell her every day for the rest of their lives.

"I love you," he whispered against her mouth.

He nibbled her bottom lip, before sucking on it. Her eyes dilated.

"Again."

"Love you, Vixen."

She buried her hands in his hair. "More. Give me more."

"I. Love. You." He punctuated every word with a hard kiss.

"I love you too," she sighed.

He wrapped his arms around and pulled her in close. She ran her nose over his shirt, breathing him in deep. Finally. Finally, that small ball of fear at the bottom of his gut was loosening. Zac wanted to stay holding Reagan forever, right next to her front door in her living room, but there was one main reason why he eased back. She stared up at him, blinking. He grinned. *Fuck, she's cute.*

"Now, let's get to the fun part."

Reagan was definitely ready for some fun.

"The fun part? What's that?"

He waggled his eyebrows. "Makeup sex."

He lifted her up the wall. Grinning, she wrapped her legs around his waist.

"I hope this makeup sex involves spanking."

She squealed when he tipped her body over his shoulder, fireman style. He slapped her ass as he walked them over to her bedroom. Her laughter filled the room as he dropped her onto her bed and dove on top of her. He stared down at her. No barriers.

"I love you," he said, kissing her softly.

She sighed. She didn't think she would ever get used to hearing him say that.

"Me too. I love you too." She deepened the kiss, helping him strip off his jacket.

"Do you know how much I've missed the taste of you?" he murmured as his mouth traced down her chest, to her stomach, then bit her belly button. "Touching you? Kissing you?"

"Probably as much as I've missed you."

He hovered over her pussy but found he didn't have the patience to tease her. He sucked her clit into his mouth. She moaned.

"I can't go slow," he admitted to her, as he pulled down her panties roughly. He needed to fuck her.

She grinned at him, reaching for his jeans. "Good. I don't want slow."

They undressed each other, until they were both naked, skin to skin, kissing. Reagan ripped open the condom he had thrown onto the bed and sheathed him. He fisted her hair and tilted her head back, licking and biting her throat. Her hands tightened around his cock and he bit down.

"Hold on," he murmured to her. He pulled her arms back and cuffed her wrists. Her fingers found purchase around the headboard. She held on. She had a feeling it was going to be a wild and dirty ride.

Zac gripped her knees and pulled her further apart. She watched him as he watched his cock enter her pussy. Despite his early words, he went slow. Achingly slow. She could feel every inch of him. It felt so good. Pleasure had her panting, wanting to move.

"Zac. Oh god." She lost her train of thought. He needed to move faster. To fuck her harder. But she was lost in the moment, unable to say anything beyond his name.

He still watched where they were joined, his face intense. He pulled out of her slowly and then thrust into her a little faster. She shuddered. He did it again. *Oh god.* He pushed her knees further up so her ass was slanted higher. When he thrust, he slid in deeper. Guttural groans were torn from both of them.

Zac leaned down towards her and pressed his lips to hers, his blue eyes now on her. It was so sexy, she couldn't help but wiggle under him.

"Don't move," he ordered.

"Then, you move!" she snapped back.

"Such a bossy vixen." He rubbed his nose against hers, an affectionate move that made her heart melt. And then he fucked her faster and she was focused on nothing but the all-consuming pleasure.

It only took a few more thrusts for her orgasm to crash over her. Her pussy tightened around him and he couldn't hold on any longer either. He came with a deep groan, collapsing on top of her. They both fought to breathe. Her arms came down and wrapped around him, holding him to her.

"You okay?" he murmured into her hair.

She nodded. "I love you."

He rolled onto his back and took her with him. He held her chin in his hand as he smiled at her.

"Love you too."

For the rest of the night, they took only short breaks, making love over and over again. Finally, they fell asleep exhausted sometime around 3:00 am. Reagan closed her eyes with a happy feeling in her heart and woke up to that happy feeling when she was met with bright blue eyes.

"Watching people sleep is creepy, you do know that, right?" she said, even as she snuggled in.

"I like watching you sleep."

She sighed. *Who am I to deny the man the pleasure of watching me sleep, then? But...*

"You can't not sleep, Zac," she told him, tentatively.

"I know," he said. "I'll...figure something out. Maybe speak to someone about it. You don't have to worry."

"Okay. What time is it?" she asked, changing the topic.

The curtains were closed in her bedroom, but there was some light. Zac turned his head.

"10:00 am." He paused. "You're not doing anything today, are you?"

Reagan was shaking her head, even before he finished the question. "Nope. I'm all yours today."

He bit her lip and growled, "You're always mine, Ree."

Yes, yes, I am.

"Okay. I need to use the toilet," he said as he loosened his arms from around her. She pulled back. "Be right back."

He kissed her softly.

She smiled at him. "'Kay."

He hopped over her and disappeared into the bathroom.

Reagan closed her eyes and let her mind drift. Until a random thought had her giggling softly. *I have to call Letty and let her know that Project Make Him Fall in Love with Me worked.* It actually fucking worked. *Or better, maybe I should—*

"Reagan!"

The front door slammed shut.

Reagan's head popped up. *No way*, she thought. That couldn't be...

A second later, her bedroom door was thrown open and Dean walked in, followed closely by Aidan, who was rolling his eyes.

"What did we say about knocking?" Aidan chastised.

Dean waved his hand. "It's fine. Hey, baby sis, what are you doing still in bed at this hour? Did you forget everyone was coming over?"

She opened her mouth and tried to say words, but all that came out was a jumbled mess. *Shit, shit, what do I do? What do I do?*

And then bad went to worse when she heard the toilet flush.

Aidan's eyes narrowed on her face. "Who's here, Reagan?"

"Um…"

"Do you have a boy over?" Dean grinned.

And worse went to colossally fucked up when the bathroom door opened and Zac walked out. In nothing but his boxers. At least he wasn't naked, right?

Chapter Twenty-Six

"This isn't what it looks like," Reagan said, desperately.

She held the covers to her chest as she got to her knees.

"You're naked, he's naked, are we missing some kind of new game that doesn't involve fucking?" Dean glared.

"Get dressed," Aidan said quietly.

"Aidan—" Zac started.

"Get fucking dressed," Aidan snarled. "And then we can talk."

"I can't believe it," Dean said, shaking his head.

They closed the door, leaving Zac and Reagan alone together.

"Fuck. Fuck," Zac cursed as he put on his jeans.

Okay, she thought, maybe this was going to be okay. Things were never as bad as you thought them to be, right? Shit, was she kidding? This was definitely bad.

She got out of bed and tried getting dressed as fast as possible. *Where the hell is my bra?* Oh, fuck it, she didn't need one anyway. Dressed, she looked at Zac. His hands were in his hair and he was staring at the door with a strained expression.

"I'm so sorry, Zac," Reagan whispered.

She completely forgot that the family was coming

over. *And I haven't even cooked anything,* a small part of her wailed. Or more like ordered something since she hated cooking. So stupid and careless to forget that brunch was happening and almost let them catch her with her pants down.

Zac turned to her, slowly dropping his hands.

He frowned. "What are you sorry about?"

"I know you didn't want to tell them. I know you never wanted to hurt Aidan or my dad or any of them and now they'll all know. And I have no idea what's going to happen, but I promise I won't let them get angry at you for this. It's not your fault. If they make us choose, I'll—"

He pressed his hands to her cheek and stopped her rambling. He tilted her face up to meet his.

"Stop. I'm not going anywhere, Ree," he told her. "I meant what I said last night. I love you. Did I want to tell your family that we were together by having them practically walk in on us? Fuck, no, but it happened. And I wasn't planning on keeping us a secret. Never again. If this wasn't going to happen today, it was going to happen sooner rather than later."

She stared up at him. She released a deep breath. She hadn't realized that was exactly what she needed to hear.

Zac ran his hand down her arm, until he reached her hand. Their fingers tangled.

"I'm here. I'm not going anywhere."

They walked out of the bedroom together.

Her step almost faltered when she saw all her family sitting in her living room, including her dad. They all stared. *I can do this. Oh shit, maybe. 50% sure.*

"Okay, if no one wants to say this first, then I will. This—" Dean pointed to the two of them "—is fucked up."

Reagan gasped.

"Watch yourself," Zac snapped.

"You're on thin ice, Zac, so you watch yourself." Dean bared his teeth. "And yes, I just made a hockey pun. I'm pissed, but I'm awesome too."

She really wanted to smack her older brother but resolved to smack him verbally instead.

"What you are is a small-minded dipshit. I don't know why you have a problem with this, because we're not doing anything wrong."

"You guys are like brother and sister."

"Eww, no." She wrinkled her nose.

"Fuck no," Zac said, just as vehemently. "I've never thought of Reagan as my sister and I'm damn sure she has never thought of me like that."

Dean made a gagging sound. "I just thought of something—was this the girl you asked me about a couple of weeks ago? The one you were banging and shouldn't be dating?"

Zac groaned as the room went on high alert.

"You were talking about my sister. Not cool, dude! Not cool!"

"Is that how long this has been going on for?" Malcolm asked, eyes narrowed on them. "Or have you been lying and going behind our backs for longer?"

She swallowed under her big brother's stare. "If you're asking about our physical relationship, then it's only been these last two weeks, but if you're asking how long I've felt like this, I would say since I was fifteen."

"Son of a bitch!"

Reagan closed her eyes at both Dean's and Malcolm's outbursts.

"Enough," her dad said quietly.

Everyone fell silent. Reagan opened her eyes.

"Sit down, Reagan. Zachariah."

The way he called him "Zachariah" and his tone of voice made Zac want to squirm. They sat down on the couch facing Reagan's father, still holding hands. Zac rubbed his thumb over her racing pulse at her wrist as if he could physically calm her down. He watched her, not her family—his family—because he meant what he'd said: *I'm not letting her go. She's mine, no matter what.*

"Dad—" Reagan began, but her voice died when Lincoln held up his hand.

"Reagan, you have been in love with Zachariah since you were fifteen years old," he announced suddenly. "And you, Zac, have been in love with her for just as long, even if you didn't see it."

Zac's eyes shot to Lincoln's.

"I may not be able to walk the way I used to, but I can still see," he said, mildly. "I told you, Zac. You are like a son to me and I never said those words in jest. I meant them. I love you and I trust you, so why wouldn't I trust you to love and honor my daughter?"

With his other hand, Zac disheveled his hair, ignoring the rock in his throat.

"You can't be serious, Dad!" Dean said, leaning forward.

"You want your sister to end up with a guy who you know nothing about or to continue dating random men? Is that what you want?" Dean instantly quietened at Lincoln's words. "That is what I thought."

"Dad, I'm really grateful you're taking this so well," she said, cautiously. "But FYI, you taught your girl to be able to take care of herself and I can."

"She definitely can."

"I can also date whoever the fuck I want. With as many people as I want."

Zac squeezed her hand hard enough that she looked at him. "I'm cool with that, babe. I hope you're cool with me doing the same thing."

His amusement grew when his comment sparked her indignation. Laughing, he kissed her.

"You're an asshole," she murmured against his mouth.

"I'm *your* asshole," he purred, forgetting for a moment who else was in the room.

That was until Dean yelled out, "Get a room!"

"We had a room!" Reagan retorted. "But you had to ruin it."

Dean sniggered.

"So, you're not mad, then?" Zac asked Lincoln, hesitantly.

"Oh, I'm mad." Lincoln tapped his cane. "I'm mad that you guys thought you had to hide your relationship from us and I take some of the blame for that."

"And we'll have to take some of the blame for that as well." Malcolm leaned forward.

"Malcolm," Aidan snapped, the first word he had spoken in the last few minutes.

"We didn't want you messing with Reagan, because we didn't want you using and hurting her. But that is an insult to you, Zac. I'm sorry."

Aidan looked at Malcom, anger etched on his face. "We have nothing to apologize for. Or have you forgotten that Zac is the one who broke *his* fucking promise to stay away from *our* sister?"

Zac tried not to flinch. "You're right. You have nothing to apologize for. I should be the one saying I'm sorry. I'm sorry, Aidan. I didn't deliberately set out to break my promise, but I did and I can't be sorry for that. Because I love Reagan. I've always loved Reagan."

For a second, Aidan said nothing and Zac was hoping he got through to his best friend. But Aidan shook his head as he stormed out of Reagan's apartment. Reagan stood up, but Zac tugged her down.

"I'll go. He isn't angry at you," he reassured her. "He's angry at me."

He nodded at the rest of the guys and went to find Aidan.

Zac found Aidan leaning against his car, head cocked back, staring at the sky. He came to stand next to him and said nothing.

"All this time," Aidan whispered, "and I had no clue. You never said a fucking word, Zac. We're meant to be best friends."

"I know," Zac said, shame burning inside him. "But it wasn't about you. It wasn't."

Aidan let out a sound of disgust at that.

"It was about me, Aidan," he continued. "I…didn't want to admit what I was feeling for Reagan and I was using that promise as an excuse not to let myself love her. You know what it was like growing up for me and for a long time, I thought I didn't deserve to have anyone love me. Why would I when I have no idea what it means to love someone?"

He felt Aidan's eyes on the side of his face, but he couldn't look at him.

"That's fucked up, Zac. You know how to love."

"Yeah. I'm starting to get that. I think I need to start seeing someone about this."

"You think, dumbass?"

Zac let out a startled laugh, Aidan joining him.

"You know," Aidan started when they stopped laughing, "I thought you were dating Letty."

Zac gave him a blank look. "What?"

"I could tell you were acting weird over the new girl you were dating, but I thought that it was because it was Reagan's best friend and not because it was her."

"Fuck no. Me and Letty don't like each other like that," Zac burst out.

"I know that *now*," Aidan said, impatiently. "But that day we played the charity game, you were being all cryptic and giving each other looks."

Zac shook his head. "She was just giving us shit, because she knew we were secretly dating. And even if me and Reagan weren't dating, and I *was* interested in Letty, it would never work. You know that, right?"

It was Aidan's turn to give him a blank look. Zac wanted to laugh, but he didn't think Aidan would appreciate it.

"Because Letty likes *you*. Why else do you think she fucks with you so much? She's trying to get your attention."

"No," Aidan said, vehemently.

"Yes." He laughed.

"Letty isn't the kind of girl to play games. If she liked me, she would have told me already."

"You know nothing about women, do you?" he said, in disbelief.

Aidan pushed him. "I know more than you, dumbass."

Zac grinned. "Keep telling yourself that."

Zac continuing to rib Aidan as they returned to the apartment. The relief he felt was immense when Aidan, with no prompting, walked over to Reagan and hugged her. He saw the echoes of his own emotions on Reagan's face.

"You good?" he asked her, when she was finally back in his arms.

"Perfect."

Yes, everything was perfect.

Epilogue

Six months later

"Good morning."

Zac opened his eyes slowly. A gorgeous pair of brown eyes stared down at him. Reagan was lying on top of him, elbows beside his head, breasts against his chest, legs tangled.

"Good morning," he murmured.

His eyes flickered to the alarm clock, another present from Callum, to his left and saw that it was 8:30 am.

"Why are you awake so early?"

It was Sunday and they had absolutely nothing scheduled for the day, other than a late brunch with her brothers and Letty and then a loose plan to catch a movie. He'd also have to swing by the rink and talk to the coach and run through some new plays. As the new captain of The Comets it was his job to make sure everything was running smoothly.

Zac ran his hand down her spine. Reagan shivered and his lips curled. She stroked his jaw, her mouth stretched in a wide smile.

"And why are you smiling?" he asked, his voice still rough from sleep.

"Because—" she leaned further into him, her excitement clear "—I have a question to ask you. What do you remember from last night?"

Confused, he tried to think back. "Nothing."

"You don't remember going to the toilet, or checking your emails?"

He shook his head.

"You don't remember waking up? Or going to the living room to watch the highlights of a game?"

"I don't remember any…"

His words trailed off. *I don't remember anything from last night.* His brain clicked on.

Reagan giggled, because she could see that he finally got it.

"You slept through the whole night, Zac." She wiggled against his erection.

"I did," he breathed out.

"That therapist is a miracle."

Lincoln, through his contacts, had recommended a discreet therapist for Zac to see and deal with his childhood issues. At first, Zac was overenthusiastic, expecting instant results, but when he got over his disappointment, he finally started focusing on the little details and not just the big picture. And not saying his therapist wasn't great, because he was, but…

"It's you."

"What?"

"Dr. Arnold isn't the miracle, you are, Ree. Without you, fuck, I have no idea where I would be."

She melted against him. "Zac."

"You're so brave, you astound me. Think of how much you've accomplished already. You're the senior agent for Trent Newman." He flipped her over, settling in between her legs. "Love you, Reagan."

"Love you right back." She grinned back at him. "Now feed me. I'm hungry."

* * * * *

Reviews are an invaluable tool when it comes to spreading the word about great reads. Please consider leaving an honest review for this or any of Carina Press's other titles that you've read on your favorite retailer or review site.

Can't wait for Letty and Aidan's story? Keep your eyes open for news about the next book in The Dirty Thomas Siblings series. To find out about more by Emma Salah or to be alerted to new releases, sign up for her monthly newsletter on her website: www.emmasalahwrites.com.

Acknowledgments

Writing has been a lifelong dream of mine, but, as it is true for all things in life, I didn't achieve this reward in a vacuum. Firstly, I'd like to thank my brother for giving me a laptop when mine crapped out—it was one of the best gifts I've ever received. He handed it to me with the explicit instruction of "write, you fool, write!" And look, I can finally prove to you I have been! To my lovely sisters for reading whatever the heck I put in front of them, especially with no warning of just how smexy my books could get. Sorry, I had to get my laughs in somewhere! I can't explain how grateful I am to my sister-in-law for coming into my life and letting me message her at all hours of the day to discuss scenes and characters. You opened your heart and your bookshelves to me and I love you for it! Of course, my friends have been endlessly supportive and wonderful, but special mention to Makia for all those nights we spent talking about writing and romance.

I appreciate Kate Marope, my wonderfully talented editor at Carina Press, who showed so much passion for my book I was blown away. She's been incredibly patient and just the best to work with! To everyone at

Carina Press and Harlequin, especially Kerri Buckley, Stephanie Doig and everyone who spent their time and effort to make *Dirty Tactics* into a reality. It has been an incredible experience.

About the Author

Born and raised in London, Emma Salah spent her childhood climbing mountains, killing dragons and sneaking Mills & Boon books into her bedroom as a teenager. While only one of those is true, she did go off to seek adventures after a degree in Literature, backpacking through Southeast Asia, living in Istanbul and enjoying her time in Japan. As a young black woman, she is interested in telling stories that don't always get heard. She writes playful, steamy stories about love with heroes and heroines with diverse backgrounds.

Dirty Tactics is her debut novel and hopefully there will be many more to come! You can check out her website for all of the latest news, subscribe to her monthly newsletter and get some really cool freebies at www.emmasalahwrites.com. You can also find her on Twitter (@EmmaSalahWrites) and Instagram (EmmaSalahWrites).